Straight Up Love

Straight Up Love

New York Times Bestselling Author
LEXI RYAN

Straight Up Love © 2018 by Lexi Ryan

All rights reserved. This copy is intended for the original purchaser of this book. No part of this book may be reproduced, scanned, or distributed in any printed or electronic form without prior written permission from the author except by reviewers, who may quote brief excerpts in connection with a review. Please do not participate in or encourage piracy of copyrighted materials in violation of the author's rights. Purchase only authorized editions.

This book is a work of fiction. Any resemblance to institutions or persons, living or dead, is used fictitiously or purely coincidental.

Cover and cover image © 2018 by Sara Eirew
Interior designed and formatted by

E.M. TIPPETTS BOOK DESIGNS

emtippettsbookdesigns.com

Other Books by
LEXI RYAN

The Boys of Jackson Harbor
The Wrong Kind of Love
Straight Up Love
Dirty, Reckless Love – coming August 2018
Wrapped in Love – coming November 2018
More to be announced!

The Blackhawk Boys
Spinning Out (Arrow's story)
Rushing In (Chris's story)
Going Under (Sebastian's story)
Falling Hard (Keegan's story)
In Too Deep (Mason's story)

LOVE UNBOUND: Four series, one small town, lots of happy endings

Splintered Hearts (A Love Unbound Series)
Unbreak Me (Maggie's story)
Stolen Wishes: A Wish I May Prequel Novella (Will and Cally's prequel)
Wish I May (Will and Cally's novel)
Or read them together in the omnibus edition, *Splintered*

Hearts: The New Hope Trilogy

Here and Now (A Love Unbound Series)
Lost in Me (Hanna's story begins)
Fall to You (Hanna's story continues)
All for This (Hanna's story concludes)
Or read them together in the omnibus edition, *Here and Now: The Complete Series*

Reckless and Real (A Love Unbound Series)
Something Wild (Liz and Sam's story begins)
Something Reckless (Liz and Sam's story continues)
Something Real (Liz and Sam's story concludes)
Or read them together in the omnibus edition, *Reckless and Real: The Complete Series*

Mended Hearts (A Love Unbound Series)
Playing with Fire (Nix's story)
Holding Her Close (Janelle and Cade's story)

OTHER TITLES

Hot Contemporary Romance
Text Appeal
Accidental Sex Goddess

Decadence Creek (Story and Sexy Romance)
Just One Night
Just the Way You Are

ABOUT
Straight Up LOVE

From *New York Times* bestselling author Lexi Ryan comes a sexy new standalone romance about a woman who'd do anything to have a baby and the man who'd do anything to have her…

For my thirtieth birthday, I'm giving myself the one thing I want most: a baby. Sure, this would be easier if I had a husband—or even a boyfriend—but I refuse to be thwarted by minor details.

When I drunkenly confess my plans to my friends, they convince me to ask Jake Jackson for help. Jake, the best friend who's been there for me through thick and thin. Jake, who also happens to be smart, funny, ridiculously good-looking, and the winner of all the genetic lotteries.

So when Jake takes me up on my request—with the stipulation that we get the job done the old-fashioned way—I'd be a fool to decline.

The only problem? I don't know if I can separate sex from all the things I feel for this amazing man. If I can't keep my heart under lock and key, I risk losing the relationship I need the most.

Jake has his own reasons for granting my baby wish. But when I discover his secrets, it could mean the end of us. I have to choose—run or stay and fight for love.

Fall for the boys of Jackson Harbor in Lexi Ryan's sexy new contemporary romance series. These books can all be read as standalones, but you'll enjoy reading them as a series!

THE BOYS OF JACKSON HARBOR
The Wrong Kind of Love – Available now
Straight Up Love – Available now
Dirty, Reckless Love – August, 2018
Wrapped in Love – November, 2018
More to be announced!

For Mandy, who wanted a baby and made a family

Chapter ONE

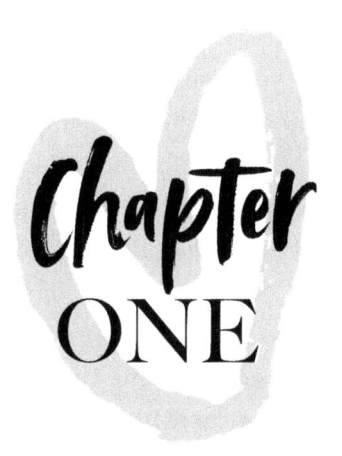

AVA

"It's a turkey baster." I frown at Teagan—my friend, holder of my latest secret, and bestower of the world's strangest birthday gift. Teagan laughs so hard she falls sideways in the booth. This is what I get for telling her my big plans. "You're a bitch."

All four of us—Teagan, Nicole, Veronica, and I—are crowded into a booth at Jackson Brews to celebrate my birthday, and I'm so damn happy I can't stop smiling because one, I love these women with the big, warm kind of mushy love that fills you from your gut out to your fingertips. Two, I've just turned thirty, and while that freaked me out yesterday, today I'm excited. Because today I have a plan.

And while giving me a turkey baster might make it seem like Teagan is mocking me, I know it's just her way of showing her support.

"I guess I should make an announcement." I put one hand on the table to steady myself. Tequila gets me every time.

"I want to hear your announcement, Ava. Spill," Nic says, tucking her light brown hair behind her ear. Even she indulged in a drink tonight—a rarity for the resident good girl in our group—and her cheeks are flushed a pretty pink.

"Since it's my birthday, I decided to get myself a present."

"You deserve it," Teagan says. She lifts her glass in salute. *How lucky am I to have such amazing friends?*

"What kind of present?" Veronica asks.

"A baby," I blurt, excitement turning my voice shrill. Veronica and Nic stare at me as if I just spoke in Latin, so I explain. "I decided I'm going to have one."

"Like, immaculate conception or . . ." Veronica says.

I squeeze the end of the turkey baster and glare at Veronica. "Okay, bitch. I'm fully aware of the missing piece of this puzzle, but I'm thirty years old, and that doesn't seem to be changing anytime soon. But I couldn't conceive the entire time I was married—"

"A blessing in disguise," Teagan says.

"—so I feel like I should start trying now," I say.

"Trying . . . to get pregnant?" Nic says.

"Yeah, 'cause who needs a dude to do that?" Veronica says.

I shake my head. Are my friends being intentionally obtuse? "Listen. I swear I'm not crazy." I scan our small group, feeling a bit like the ugly duckling in this bevy of swans. Next to the beautiful Nic is her identical twin, Veronica. Veronica is the very-pregnant, less-cheerful version of Nic. Across from Veronica is

Teagan, with dark hair, olive skin, and a pair of incredible God-given boobs I'd trade my left arm for.

My friend Ellie couldn't make it tonight—she and my brother, Colton, are fighting again—but she's just as gorgeous as the rest of them.

It's not that I think I'm *unattractive*, but without a good deal of eye makeup and some quality time with a curling iron, I'm closer to "plain" than "pretty." Add a bunch of baggage to my underwhelming appearance, and *ta-da!* A recipe for an eternity as a spinster.

"I've already been married and that didn't work," I explain. "As nice as it would be to find a guy to spend my life with, it's not necessary. But pregnancy and a baby? That's something I want to experience." A burst of adrenaline shoots through me, renewing my excitement. Or maybe that's the alcohol? It's hard to tell, but it doesn't matter. Honestly, since I hatched Operation Pregnancy plan yesterday, my only real question has been why I didn't think of it sooner.

I smack the table like a judge smacking a gavel when she's giving her final ruling. "I want a family, and I'm not getting any younger, so I'm making one myself."

"Good for you," Veronica says, raising her glass of water. She beams at me, her eyes shining, her smile wide. Maybe she's proud, or maybe she's just glad she's not going to be the only single mom in the group.

"I think that's great," Nic says. "Really, really damn brave, but great."

"So . . ." Teagan scans the room. "Do we get to just pick from the guys at the bar or what?"

I roll my eyes. Teagan knows my plan is artificial insemination—thus the turkey baster—but I guess I should have been more specific about *where* I plan to get the sperm. "I've already talked to some sperm banks. I'm looking through donors now, but here's the deal—what if these men are crazy? There's no checkbox for that on the questionnaire. How do you know you're not putting crazy-man semen up in your business? I want to love my child, not wonder if maybe his dad had some weird rubber-glove fetish."

Teagan nods. "This seems like a reasonable concern. Because genetics."

"I'm confused," Veronica says. "You're using the sperm bank, or you're not?"

I sigh. Okay, I'm really excited about my plan. And I'm determined. And I'm not going to change my mind. Only, I'm not sold on buying sperm. "I haven't decided. Obviously, that's the easiest way to get a baby in a position like mine, but . . ." I groan. "But ever since I got this crazy-guy thought in my head, none of the profiles are good enough. I'm nervous."

Teagan shrugs. "Why not just ask for some sperm from a friend? The turkey baster works the same way if the sperm is free, you know."

Free sperm from a friend? "That's a thing?"

"Sure," Teagan says. "My cousin did it. She was like you—wanted a baby, didn't want to wait—so she just asked her best friend for some sperm, and he filled a cup for her. Nine months later, *voila*! A baby of her own who she knows has no rubber-glove fetish gene."

"That would definitely be ideal." Honestly, a simple call to the sperm bank was awkward for me, and with my track record, I don't expect this to be a one-and-done kind of situation. "But how do you even decide who to ask?"

"Well," Veronica says, "not that I get to choose, since I already made my bad decision." She grimaces, and I feel a stab of pity for her. She effed up royally when she fooled around with her sister's ex-fiancé, but she eventually saw his true colors and has spent the last four months doing everything she can to get back in her twin's good graces while preparing herself to raise her baby on her own. There's a mischievous gleam in her eye when she says, "But if I were you, I'd definitely go after some Jackson genes."

"They do make some good-looking boys," Nic says. "And they're all brains, too."

There's no denying that the Jacksons are all in possession of sublime genetics. But *weird*. "I've been friends with the Jacksons all my life." They were literally the boys next door when I grew up. "Levi's probably the hottest," I say, referring to the youngest Jackson brother, "and he's easygoing and stuff, but I'm pretty sure that conversation would be awkward even with him." I lower my voice and look around to make sure no one is eavesdropping. "And I think he might secretly have a thing for my friend Ellie."

"And he'd want to actually fuck you," Veronica says. "No turkey baster."

Levi isn't the kind of guy who'd pass up an excuse to get a woman in bed, but I think these ladies underestimate the "sister" vibe I have going with all the Jacksons.

"Jake's your best friend, isn't he?" Teagan says. "What about him? I bet he'd do it for you."

I make a face. *Jake?* "It's kind of weird, isn't it?" I instinctively search the crowd, and my gaze lands on Jake behind the bar, his dark hair and the eyes the girls say are so dreamy. The broad shoulders they drool over, and the ink peeking out under the sleeves of his fitted shirt. Jake would do anything for me. Never mind the fact that he's a really good guy. Wouldn't it be a relief to know my kid came from that kind of genetic stock?

Teagan slides my glass closer to my hand. "Finish this and ask him to fill a cup for you."

There's a flutter in my stomach. Could it be this simple?

I don't want to think about it. When I think about things, I freeze. I just want to make this happen. "I guess it is my birthday. It can't hurt to ask, right?" I swallow hard. "Here goes nothing."

JAKE

Ava McKinley meets my gaze from her table at the back of Jackson Brews, and there's such an intensity in her eyes that my gut tightens. For a beat, I can imagine those dark eyes on me in a very different context. Maybe right here after last call, when she's seated on the polished walnut bar and watching me with hunger in her eyes. I'd step between her legs and untie the wrap dress that's been taunting me all night. I'd lower my head to her perfect breasts and tease her nipples with my tongue until she begged me for more.

Dream the fuck on, Jackson.

I can't fault myself for the fantasy, though. What man wouldn't imagine all that and more? Ava's easily the most gorgeous woman in this bar. Add in the fact that she has a wicked sense of humor and loves my cooking almost as much as she loves my beer, and it's no freaking wonder I can't keep my eyes off her.

Never mind that she's your best friend and one hundred percent off-limits.

She slides out of the booth with her glass in hand, leaving her group of friends behind as she marches straight toward me. The slight sway in her step reminds me she's been drinking. Nevertheless, I recognize a woman on a mission. Anticipation races down my spine before I can shake the feeling away or remind myself of the enormous divide between fantasy and reality.

Cindy nudges me. We're both working behind the bar tonight—me because it's Friday, and I like to keep an eye on the place on the busiest nights of the week, and Cindy because she's filling in for Ava, who I insisted take the night off for her birthday. "Are you in trouble or something?" she asks.

"I . . . don't think so?" Ava's been celebrating with her friends all night, and I'm glad to see it. She works too much, and having a group of girlfriends who won't let her sit at home and grade papers is the best thing that could have happened to her.

Tonight, for her thirtieth, she's really been letting loose. The table she's been sitting at with Nicole, Veronica, and Teagan is littered with now-empty glasses formerly full of Long Island iced tea and beer.

"Good luck," Cindy says, sneaking away just as Ava comes behind the bar to stand with me.

Ava stutters to a stop in front of me and puts her empty glass on the bar. Her proximity makes longing whip through my gut, sharp and impossible to ignore. She's always been beautiful, with dark hair, tight curves, and deep brown eyes that can put a man in his place without her ever having to speak a word, but lately, the old angst of wanting what I can't have has been hitting me hard. I blame my brother Ethan and his newfound happiness with his girlfriend, Nic.

"Hey there, birthday girl." Maybe it shouldn't be so easy to hide the fact that I'm half-hard right now, or that ten seconds ago I was fantasizing about getting her off on this bar. Then again, I've had *years* of practice.

She sways a little in her red Mary Janes and grips my wrist. Normally, any touch from Ava is something I tuck away to fantasize about later. This touch, however, is more a drunken attempt at balance than affection—not that she *ever* touches me sexually outside of my imagination.

"I'm gonna have a baby," she says, her voice a failed attempt at a whisper.

Goodbye, erection. "You're what?" I stare at her for a beat, trying to make sense of her words. I look to the crowd at the bar to see if anyone else heard this, but they're all too preoccupied with each other and their drinks to notice us. My gaze shifts to her group of friends, as if they might be able to explain what's happening here. She can't be pregnant. I didn't even know she was seeing anyone.

"It's okay," she says. "I can do it. I don't need a man. I can do this on my own. So . . ." The expression on her face makes me wonder if her last drink is on a short trip back out of her. She's not the only one feeling queasy. Her news is making me feel like there's an elephant playing hopscotch on my chest. "So, can you help me?"

I really have no idea what to say because I'm not sure what she's asking. Can I help her raise her child? Or will I work her hours at the bar around daycare? I frown and realize she's still holding something by her side. "Is that a turkey baster?"

"It was a birthday present. Aren't you listening? I'm gonna have a baby, and I want your help."

I still don't know what my help entails, but who am I kidding? It doesn't matter. If Ava needed my right arm, I'd look for the nearest hatchet. "Anything you need, Ava."

She fucking *beams* at me. "Oh! Seriously? I thought it might be too much to ask."

There's nothing she could ask me that would be too much. But this hitch in my gut at the idea of her having another man's baby? I can deal with that later. "You're drunk, aren't you?"

"So drunk."

"Right." Another thing to deal with later. Tomorrow, we'll have a conversation about drinking and pregnancy. An absurd conversation to have, considering she's the most responsible person I know, but we'll have it anyway. Maybe she just found out. Maybe liquid courage made her take a test in the women's restroom.

She giggles. "I can't believe this is happening."

That makes two of us. "Come on. Let's get you to bed."

She grips her turkey baster with both hands—I'll have to get the story on that tomorrow too—and dutifully follows me up the back stairs to the apartment over the bar.

As I shut the door behind us, I see my home with new eyes. I moved here in college while I was managing Jackson Brews and taking a full course load. It was convenient at the time, and then I never bothered to find anything else. It's never mattered. But if Ava's going to have a baby, is she really going to want to hang out here with the kid? While it's nice enough, the loft-style one-bedroom, one-bath isn't exactly childproof. As I imagine a kid falling through the rebar spindles and down the open staircase, I grimace. I'll definitely need to find something more suitable.

A baby. She's having a baby.

It's like the day she told me she was engaged to Harrison all over again. Except instead of making a fool of myself, this time I'm going to take it in stride. I'm going to deal with this like a *friend* should. Not like a lovesick idiot.

I head to my tiny kitchen and fill a glass of water for her, and when I turn around, she's right there. She scans my face with those big brown eyes. "I'm so lucky to have you in my life, Jake."

She's close. So close I could dip my head and kiss her, and long-denied desire makes my chest tight. "I'm not arguing." I hand her the glass of water. "Drink this."

She obeys, downing half the glass before handing it back to me. "Do you think I'll be a good mom?"

"The best." Swallowing, I take a step back to put some space between us. I half expect the ache in my chest to subside with some distance, but it doesn't. *She's having a baby.* "Come on. Bedtime."

She turns toward the couch, where she insists on sleeping when she crashes here, but I place my hands on her shoulders and turn her toward my bedroom.

"I need the couch tonight," I lie. "You're going to have to

sleep in my room."

"Oh, I'm sorry. Sure. I don't want to be in the way." She steps into my bedroom and unbuckles her Mary Janes. I pull back the covers, and she crawls into my bed, eyes already at half-mast. Will a baby put an end to girls' nights that lead her giggling and pink-cheeked at my place?

"Wait," she says as I pull the covers up over her. "Did we talk about the baby?"

I'm not sure she'll ever be able to talk about a baby without my gut knotting painfully. If anything, I've been cool and patient with Ava—just waiting for the day when she'd see me as something other than the goofy kid next door or the high school jock who'd jump into bed with any girl who was willing. I've been patient. Too patient. Because now she's having some other guy's baby. I'm already making plans to restructure my whole life to help in any way I can, but I've forgotten one essential piece to this puzzle. What happens when she tells the baby's father? Whoever he is, he'd be an idiot if he didn't find some way to make her his.

I swallow hard and tuck the blankets in around her. "We talked about it. We'll talk about it more in the morning, okay? And we'll talk about the drinking too."

"No more drinking. My body is a temple starting tomorrow." She closes her eyes and smiles. "You're such a good friend, Jake. The best."

"Yeah," I whisper. "I'd be the best kind of anything you'd let me."

Chapter TWO

AVA

When my phone wakes me up, I'm aware of a few things all at once.

One, whoever's on the other end of that call is a total asshole.

Two, I have a hangover to top all hangovers.

Three, I'm in Jake's apartment.

This isn't the first time I've slept over. While I don't drink to excess often, when I do, it's at Jackson Brews, because that's what you do when your best friend owns a bar. I drink downstairs, and when I'm ready to pass out and don't want to walk home, I borrow his couch.

But this time I'm not just in Jake's apartment—I'm *in his bed*. And that would be fine, because Jake's the kind of guy who'd rather take the couch and let his guest have the better night's sleep, but I've always insisted on sleeping in the living room.

But last night's coming together for me one piece at a time, and waking up in his bed seems . . . significant.

I told the girls about the baby and my decision to finally take my life into my own hands and start a family. I told them my reservations about sperm banks but how badly I wanted to carry a child. They told me to get Jake's sperm.

And . . . he said yes? Did he give it to me last night?

I sit up in bed, and my head pounds. Next to me, my phone buzzes to let me know I have a voicemail, and I press my palm to my forehead. Why is it that subsequent drinks seem like such a good idea when you're buzzed? Lots of things sound like good ideas when alcohol's involved. More liquor. Dancing on tables. *Asking friends for sperm.*

I spot the turkey baster in bed beside me and groan as I slink back down under the covers. Surely he didn't jack off into a cup and let me put that to use.

First of all, *awkward*. Second of all, what drunk me thought was a brilliant idea, sober me recognizes as a disaster. I'm not leaving Jackson Harbor, and neither is Jake. Even if he was willing to hand over his sperm, carrying his child would change things between us. Wouldn't it?

So why am I in his *bed*?

The sound of footsteps spurs me to open my eyes, and I see Jake leaning in the bedroom doorway.

"Good morning, birthday girl," he says.

"There's nothing good about this morning," I mutter. "I feel like death."

Jake's shirtless in a pair of jeans, the tattoos on his arms and chest on full display.

Intellectually, I can appreciate his body. It's not the sort of body you'd expect on a total nerd, especially not one who drinks as much beer as he does. But there's no gut in sight. He and his brothers spend too many hours together at the gym to let that happen. Also, they have freakish genetics that make them all ridiculously good-looking. Yes, intellectually, I can appreciate the body of the man in front of me.

But attraction isn't an intellectual thing. Attraction is an emotional thing. And emotionally, I think of Jake as my best friend. *That's it.* And that's been it for a long time now. So when a girlfriend of mine looks at him and purrs, or tells me how badly she wants to get in bed with him, I get *why*. I'm not blind to his appeal. I just don't get jealous. And that's good, since he'd laugh in my face if I did.

"Why did you let me drink so much?"

He folds his arms, and tension ticks in his jaw. "Because I didn't know you were pregnant, for one."

For the second time this morning, I sit up straight in bed, and for the second time this morning, the rapid movement makes me grab my skull.

"It's kind of bad to drink when you're pregnant," Jake says.

"You don't think I know that?"

"I'm not judging. I just would have thought—"

"I'm not pregnant." *Am I?* Did I use the turkey baster? God, I feel awful.

"Last night you told me you were going to have a baby."

"I am."

He scowls at me. "So which is it?"

I shake my head and immediately regret it. "Could I have

some Tylenol? And a cup of coffee, and some water, and, I don't know, maybe one of those knives for hara-kiri?"

He disappears, and when he returns, I'm lying down again, and he has everything but the knife. *Go figure.* He places it all on the bedside table by my head. "Are we going to talk about this?"

"I am so hungover and you're not making any sense, so no. I'll pass on the chat."

"*I'm* not making any sense?" He props his hands on his hips. "You told me you were pregnant."

"I didn't. I told you I was having a baby. There's a difference."

"How exactly?"

"I don't know. Something with verb tense, and conditions, and . . . don't make me talk grammar this early in the morning."

"It's ten o'clock, Ava."

I grab the Tylenol from the bedside table and use the cold bottle of water to swallow it down, grimacing when it hits my stomach. "I *want* to have a baby, Jake. And last night, I told you about it because . . ." The only thing that could make this conversation more awkward is if he were holding the cup of jizz in his hand while we discussed the possibility of him handing it over to me. I take a breath and spit it out. "I need some . . . help."

"With what?"

"Why are you making this so hard?" I throw a pillow at his chest. "Just go away. I'm tired and I feel like death, and last night was totally a mistake."

"I'm not trying to be thick-skulled here. I'm just a little slow to understand what you mean." He takes a deep breath and pastes on his most patient smile. "You want a baby. You're *not* pregnant."

"I'm not pregnant," I say softly. The words never hurt less.

Not at the beginning of my marriage, when my husband would pull me into his arms and promise we'd have better luck next time. Not in the middle, when the pink minus sign on those stupid sticks slowly formed a wall between us. And not even at the end of my marriage, when I was heartbroken by his betrayal and everyone told me I should be grateful we didn't have kids involved. They always hurt the same. *Not pregnant.*

Jake exhales, and his shoulders sag as he turns away from me. "Fuck. That's good news."

JAKE

"It's terrible news," Ava says, but the words come out in an uncharacteristic screech. "If I don't start a family now, do you realize my chances of conceiving go down every year after thirty? Do you understand how hard it's going to be for me to *get* pregnant?"

When I turn back around, she's crawling back down the bed and pulling the covers over her head. "Can we talk about this?" I ask.

"No," she says, her voice muffled.

I cross the room and pull the blanket off her head. I know she's hungover, but I can't just walk away from this conversation. I barely slept last night, freaking torn up about her pregnancy and all its implications, and now she's telling me she's not pregnant. She just wants to be, and she wants my *help.*

What the fuck does that mean?

"Talk." I fold my arms across my chest.

"I want a family, and I'm sick of waiting for Mr. Right to come along, so I'm going to do it on my own."

"And you want my help?" *Hell.* I'm trying really hard not to jump to conclusions here. Emphasis on *hard.*

"Yeah. I mean, *no.* I mean . . ." She takes a deep breath. "It sounded like a good idea last night."

Doing baby-making things with Ava sounds like a good idea to me every minute of every hour of every damn day, but I'm quite aware that doing that with me doesn't cross her mind nearly as often. Okay, or ever. "Last night, when you asked for my help, you meant you wanted me to get you pregnant?"

She scowls. "Are you being dense on purpose?"

"I promise I'm not." But if ever there was a conversation where I'm going to need things spelled out for me, this is it. "I just want to make sure I understand."

She presses her palm to her forehead. "I just wanted you to jack off in a cup and hand it to me. Not the weird way."

Right. Because *that* wouldn't be weird. "I'm sorry." I hold up a finger. "Give me a sec." I walk around the room, scanning the ceiling and the corners. I check behind the lamp and crack the closet to look in there.

"What are you doing, Jake?"

I spin on her. "I'm looking for the camera—the one you planted before you *Punk'd* me. Is that show even still a thing? Because I'm sure I'm being *Punk'd* right now." I crouch and look under the bed.

"You're not being *Punk'd*! Quit being an asshole!"

I stand, fold my arms, and set my jaw. "You're telling me that last night you wanted me to jack off in a cup and give the contents to you." My gaze lands on the turkey baster in bed beside her. Of course. It all makes sense now.

Christ. This is what my life has come to. This is what happens when you pine for your best friend for years instead of forcing yourself to move on. She wants your sperm. Not you. Just your swimmers. I feel like the kid who realizes he's been walking around school with a "kick me" sign on his back. "You can't be serious, Ava."

"No. I'm *not* serious now. I was drunk, and it seemed like a good idea then. Now, I'm sober and I *don't want your sperm.* It's a bad idea, and I know it's a bad idea. I'm sorry."

And then, fucking dammit, she starts crying. She uses her thumbs to wipe her tears away, but her chest shakes, and it's like taking an ice pick to the chest.

"Why can't I just be like everybody else?" she asks, her voice unsteady. "Why can't I find a nice guy who wants to knock me up? What's wrong with me that my only relationship that lasted longer than five minutes was a marriage that was clearly doomed to failure from the start?"

Dammit. "Ava . . ."

"What?" Rolling to her side, she grips the blankets in her fists and stares at me. "You know I suck at relationships. I really, really suck."

In my experience, it's not so much that Ava sucks at relationships. The problem is more that she doesn't really give them a chance. She meets a nice guy, and he's either a jerk—so she doesn't want to see him again because she married a jerk once and learned her lesson—or he's *too* interested, which makes her suspicious that he's a crazy person, because who would be interested in her? It's all sorts of fucked up, but that's just who she is—the most confident woman I know in every aspect of her life but romance.

She swings her legs to the side of the bed and cradles her face in her hands. "Oh, this is so stupid. I can't believe I even said anything to you."

"Well . . ." I clear my throat. "I guess I'm flattered?"

She peeks at me between her fingers. "You guess you're flattered? I asked to bear your offspring, and you *guess* you're flattered?" She groans.

I lower myself to sit on the bed beside her. "Are you serious about this baby thing?"

She drops her hands and nods. "I've thought about it for a long time, but I was hoping I'd find somebody. Like any other girl, I'd prefer to do it the old-fashioned way, but it's getting kind of late for that."

"You're only thirty, Ava. There's still time."

She drags her bottom lip between her teeth. "My mom had three miscarriages, months of infertility treatments, and finally me. She had to have the same treatments to have Colton. It's not going to be easy for me to conceive. I know it seems like I'm rushing into this, but I'm not. There aren't many things in my life that I'm sure of. I am *sure* I want to be a mom, and I'm not willing to wait and see if it 'works out.'"

Swallowing hard, I take her hand in mine and squeeze. "What are you gonna do?"

"I've talked to a fertility clinic about a sperm donor, but

last night, I was freaking out about my kid having a crazy man's genetics, so Teagan suggested I ask a friend. I could get the sperm free *and* know my child wasn't genetically inclined to develop a fetish for Barbie heads or something." She attempts to smile, but in her miserable state, it looks more like she's baring her teeth than feeling joyful. "I'll be fine, Jake."

"You're gonna raise a kid on your own, though? Do you know how hard that's going to be?"

"Yeah. I do. But I don't have any doubt in my mind that it'll be worth it. I would never regret a child."

If this were one of the novels Ava likes to read so much, I'd kiss her hard, climb over her on the bed, and tell her that I'd give her babies, and I'd be by her side. If this were one of those books, she'd secretly want me in return.

But I put myself out there for Ava once before and, in the process, found out exactly how she felt about me.

So here we are. Sitting side by side, both desperately wanting something the other can give, and unable to make it happen.

"Too bad we didn't make one of those pacts when we were kids," I say. When she screws up her face in question, I say, "You know, one of those *if we're not married by thirty, we'll marry each other* things."

She laughs and shakes her head. "It would be kind of like marrying my brother."

I press my hand to my chest. "Ouch."

"No offense."

"It's just emotional castration. No worries."

She rolls her eyes. "And anyway, don't you want to marry some hot young thing who can give you wild sex every night?"

"Yeah. Definitely." Wild sex with Ava sounds amazing to me. Too bad she's not talking about herself.

"I should get home. I have a thousand things to do before my shift tonight."

"Including research on artificial insemination?"

She nods, then studies my face. "Are you going to be okay with this? I know there are people who don't approve of a woman starting a family on her own, but—"

"Since when have I ever not been right by your side when you needed me? This won't be any different." Except it will. Because somehow, her decision to start a family on her own feels like the final nail in the coffin of Ava-and-Jake. Ever since her divorce, I've been holding on, waiting for her to see me differently, to give me a chance. But now . . .

I release her hand and stand. "Want me to make you some bacon and eggs? Salt is good for the hangover."

She lies back down instead of getting up like she said she was going to. "Yes, please."

I pinch her nose and head to the kitchen.

"Jake?" she calls when my feet hit the hallway.

I stop and turn, hope wobbling around in my chest like a newborn foal. "Yeah?"

"Would you put some cheese in my eggs?"

I take a deep breath, as if that might help me steady myself after this emotional rollercoaster of a morning. "Anything for you, Av."

Chapter Three

AVA

"Feel better?" Jake asks as I push away my plate.

"I do." Jake was right. My hangover was nothing a little salty breakfast couldn't fix, and by the time I was halfway through my food, I felt like a new woman. It helps that he's the best chef I've ever met. I lean back in my chair and put my hand on my full belly. "Thank you. That was so good."

He turns his wrist to look at his watch, and I realize in a sudden panic that it's Saturday. "Jake! Your mom and Shay are coming home from Grand Rapids today! You wanted to be there, didn't you?"

He shrugs. "It's no big deal. I texted Shay and told her I'd be late."

My shoulders sag. I'm the worst friend ever. "You stayed here and cooked the hungover girl breakfast while your family is rallying together around your sick mother."

"It's not like we're having a party," he says, amusement quirking his lips. "If I don't make it over today, I'll see them all at brunch tomorrow." His nonchalance doesn't fool me. Family is everything to Jake, and I know he'd have been at his childhood home already if he hadn't been tending to me.

"How's your mom doing?" I ask.

He stiffens. "She's tired, but that's to be expected. Yesterday was her last treatment in this round of chemo, so she'll get a break. The nausea was intense there at the end, and I've never seen her so exhausted . . ." He trails off, and I know he's not just thinking of his mom. He's thinking of his dad, who died of cancer five years ago.

The news of Kathleen's cancer was a blow to the whole family. She even tried keeping her diagnosis a secret and getting her treatments in Germany so her children wouldn't have to watch another parent die.

"When will you know if it worked?"

"Shay said they scheduled the PET scan for June. That'll show them the cell activity to see if the cancer is active or in remission. We're all optimistic."

Optimistic. But his smile is unsteady, and he avoids my gaze as he says it. That isn't the face of optimistic Jake. That's the face of a man who's bracing himself for the worst because he's been there before, and I ache for him. It's going to be a long couple of months while they wait for that test.

When he lost his father five years ago, I was caught up in planning a wedding and starting my life with Harrison, but I still saw enough to know they were the worst days of his life. The idea of losing Kathleen guts me—she's a second mother to me—but even worse is the idea of seeing Jake leveled by grief for a second time.

"I'll get out of your way," I say, clearing my plate. "You can still go visit."

"No, don't rush."

"You can see me anytime," I say, and when he flinches, I want to pull the words back. They imply that though I'll be around, his mom might not be. While that might be true, I don't want to be the one to remind Jake of it.

I step forward and wrap my arms around him, nestling my head into his chest and hugging him tightly.

"Whoa, what's this for?" he says.

I'm not the most physically affectionate of friends, but we all need a hug sometimes. "It'll be okay, Jake."

He strokes my hair and presses a kiss to the top of my head. "I know," he whispers.

He's so warm and solid. This week has been an emotional rollercoaster—first with my ex sending me an invitation for his new wife's baby shower and then a nasty week at work, all topped off with my thirtieth birthday, a date I wouldn't mind if it weren't a reminder of my ticking biological clock.

I close my eyes for a moment and realize that in my attempts to offer comfort to Jake, I've been comforted by *him*. That's probably the perfect metaphor for our relationship. He's always giving. I'm always taking. I hate that.

I release him, and when I step back, he searches my face. "Are *you* okay?" he asks.

"My problems aren't problems in the scheme of things."

He shakes his head. "Everyone's problems are problems. They might not be the same as mine, but they still matter. Seriously, are you okay?"

I shrug. "Considering our morning started with a conversation about your sperm and my childless womb, I've been better."

He grimaces. "Well, for what it's worth, at least you can still surprise me."

I don't want to think about that too much. What seemed like a good idea after too many drinks is so obviously ridiculous and reckless now that I'm sober. Thank the sweet Lord he didn't hand over the goods last night.

"Do you want your birthday present now?"

I frown at him. "You already gave me my present. Remember when I was stranded on 96 and you paid to have my car towed?"

"That's a shitty gift," he says, reaching into his back pocket.

I fold my arms. "Jake, we agreed."

"This one's for me too, okay? So it hardly counts." He hands me an envelope.

I take it reluctantly—because I may be on the winning side of this friendship, but at least I have the courtesy to feel guilty about it—and open it. The card has a man in a speedo on the front dancing with a margarita. I unfold the paper tucked in the card and gasp. "Jacob Jackson, you did *not*!"

He grins at me and arches a brow. "I can give them to someone else if you *really* don't want them."

I clutch the tickets to my chest. "Don't you dare! It's *Hamilton*! I wanted to go so badly!" I really didn't need to spend the money to go to the musical in Chicago, but I've been dying to see it, so I've practically had to sit on my hands to resist the splurge. I screech and do a little dance before throwing my arms around him in our second hug of the morning. "You are the best friend ever."

"I know," he says as I release him. "But those tickets aren't free. You have to take me as your plus one."

"Ellie won't like it, but she knows she has to share me."

He chuckles. "I hope the date works. I peeked at the calendar on your phone to make sure you didn't have anything scheduled."

"I'd cancel anything else for this anyway." I scan the print-off for the date and my breath leaves me in a rush when I see the venue. "Jake, these are for the *Hamilton* on *Broadway*."

"Is that a problem?"

"In *New York City*." I tear my eyes off the tickets to look at him.

"That's where Broadway is, last I checked."

I blink, mentally calculating how much I'll need for the plane ticket and hotel. Maybe I could save some money if I drive, and I don't need to stay anywhere fancy. I nod. "I'll make it work," I whisper, because *come on*. This is bucket-list stuff. "I work two jobs. I deserve this, right?"

"You absolutely do," Jake says. "But if you're worried about money, don't. Everything's covered."

"No." I shake my head furiously, as if the movement might knock some sense into him. "Jake, that's too much."

"It's nothing more than the tickets." He ticks off his reasons on his fingers. "We're using my free credit card miles for the flights, and Jackson Brews is going to pay for our hotel, since I'll need to do a little business while we're there."

"For real?"

"It's your birthday present. Just be happy and stop stressing about it."

I smack his chest even as my eyes fill with tears. There might be areas of my life that leave me wanting, but I scored big in the friendship category. "You can't spoil me like this every year."

"Can and will," he says. He turns to the sink, running the water hot.

"Hold up! You cooked breakfast. Let me get the dishes."

"Not a chance, birthday girl."

I swallow hard, but my throat is still thick with gratitude, my skin tingling with excitement. I don't know what I can do to return the favor for Jake, but I'm going to have to figure out something. "Call me later, okay? Let me know how Mom's doing."

"Sure thing." He loads dishes into the soapy water and winks at me.

I clutch the tickets to my chest again. Leave it to Jake to turn one of my toughest birthdays around by giving me the best gift I've ever received.

Chapter FOUR

JAKE

The gym is a ghost town Saturday afternoon, and I couldn't be happier. After the morning I had, the last thing I want is social hour while I'm trying to work off my frustration.

When Ava left, Shay texted to tell me not to come over. Mom was sleeping and said she'd see everyone at brunch tomorrow. I finished cleaning up breakfast, trying my damnedest not to think about Ava. Not the way she hugged me after I gave her the tickets. Not the way she looked lying in my bed. And definitely not the fact that she'd rather have me jack off into a cup than touch her.

I tried really damn hard not to think about any of that.

I failed.

Ava was *all* I could think about, and since that clusterfuck of emotions was making me more than a little stir crazy, I headed to the gym like I always do when I want to escape my feelings.

Despite thirty minutes of intervals on the treadmill and a grueling leg session, I'm still screwed up. Maybe you can't just sweat out a conversation like this morning's.

I'm setting up my bar for bench press when someone taps me on the shoulder. Pulling out my earbuds, I turn to see Ellie, Ava's other best friend.

"Ava has lost her mind."

"Hey, El. Good to see you today."

She rolls her eyes. "I need your help."

My mind flashes back to last night, to Ava in that sexy-as-fuck wrap dress and red heels, and her hand gripping my arm as she asked if I'd help her.

Ellie stares at me expectantly. "Please?"

I look around for Colton, since he and Ellie always come to the gym together, but he's nowhere to be seen. Judging by his condition when I kicked his drunk ass out of my bar last night, I'd guess he's still sleeping it off.

"Are you listening to me?" she says. "Ava wants to have *a baby.*"

"She told me." I shrug, as if I don't care. As if this news and the way it was delivered to me didn't rock my world in the most fucked-up way this morning. "What do you want me to do about it?"

If she suggests I hand over my sperm, I might lose my shit.

Ellie's eyes go wide, and she throws up her hands. "I want you to stop her! She has no idea how hard this is going to be. Raising a baby on her own? I watched my mom struggle for years. I want better than that for my best friend."

I slide a forty-five-pound plate onto one end of the barbell and grab another. "So tell *her* that."

"I have, but she won't listen to me. She's gone crazy since she got that invitation."

I slide the second plate on and look at Ellie. "What invitation?"

"The invitation to Harrison's wife's baby shower. What do you think started all this?"

Honestly, Ava's wanted to be a mom so long that I hadn't thought about what made her decide to act on it now. I've been too fixated on my bruised ego. But if she just found out that her ex-husband is going to have a baby, that would explain a lot. "Harrison's wife is expecting?"

"Yes, and now Ava's got it in her head that the only way she can have a baby is to do it alone. You know there's a good man out there who'd kill to be with her."

I can't argue with her there.

"She just needs to be patient," Ellie says, and there's so much intensity in her words that I think she's almost as screwed up about all this as I am. "Ava's amazing and fucking *hot*. Who wouldn't want to be with her?"

"I have no idea," I mutter.

"I don't want her to make a mistake."

I swallow hard. Ava was crushed when her husband left her, but it wasn't just losing Harrison that broke her heart. She thought she was losing her chance at having a family. It makes sense that him having a baby would fuck with her a little.

I drag a hand through my hair. "I can say something to her, Ellie, but it's not really my place."

"Come on," she says. "You and I both know she listens to you more than she listens to me. And anyway, at least you're single.

Everyone knows Colton and I are going to get engaged any day now, so it's hypocritical for me to say she shouldn't mind waiting when I don't have to."

What she's saying makes sense, but what does she expect me to say? *"Hey, Ava, you're being impulsive because your ex is having the baby you wanted. It's okay to be upset, but don't be in a rush to get knocked up. Wait until you're ready for* me *to do it."*

"You look tired," Ellie says.

"I slept on the couch last night. Ava was drunk and needed a place to crash," I say, leaving out the part about how I was up worrying because I thought Ava was pregnant. I cut my gaze to Ellie. "Which you would have known if you hadn't bailed on her birthday party."

She grimaces. "I didn't want to. Colton and I got in a fight, and I wasn't in the mood to party."

A fight with Ellie would explain why Colton was at the bar trashed and looking for trouble at last call. I went back down to retrieve Ava's purse after tucking her in, and there was Colton, swaying all over the place and eager for an excuse to take a swing at anyone. I was relieved he showed after I got Ava upstairs and not before. Ava seems to think the job of keeping her little brother out of trouble falls on her. "What were you two fighting about this time?"

"I don't want to talk about it."

Levi emerges from the locker room. "Hey, Jake." He lifts his chin in greeting, then his gaze shifts to Ellie and his eyes skim over her the way they always do. My little brother has it *bad* for his best friend's girl. My heart goes out to him. I know a little something about wanting a woman you can't have.

"Hey, Levi," Ellie says. "Thanks for bringing Colton home last night." She shakes her head and lowers her voice. "It won't happen again, okay?"

Levi nods, his posture stiffening. "What about you? You okay?" He scans her face, and I wonder what I'm missing.

"I'm fine. Just trying to convince Jake he needs to talk Ava out of having a baby."

Levi's eyebrows shoot up into his hairline. "I didn't know she was even seeing anyone."

"That's just it," Ellie says. "She's not. She has this idea she's going to go to a sperm bank and get herself pregnant."

Levi turns to me and locks his gaze on mine. "Really now?"

"I don't think she'll go through with it," Ellie says. "I'm *hoping* she's all talk. She doesn't realize what a tough road it's gonna be if she does this alone."

Sighing, I look away from Levi. I can't answer the question in his eyes—not here. Hell, not even in private. I shake my head and turn to Ellie. "You keep saying that, but she was raised by a single mom, so surely she has *some* idea."

Not that I love the sperm-bank plan. Honestly, I hate it even more than I hate the idea of personally providing her with unlimited semen for her turkey baster. I can't shake this feeling that if she goes through with her plan to impregnate herself, I might lose her again. And maybe for good this time.

"But it was different with her mom," Ellie says. "Her dad didn't leave until she was ten, so he was around all that time before. Then, even when he did leave, he saw them on the weekends and paid child support and alimony. Child support and alimony from a *lawyer*?" She shakes her head. "That's not the typical single-mom income. I stand by what I said. She has *no idea* how hard this will be."

Levi smirks at me. "Why don't *you* just offer to give her a baby?"

My breath leaves me in a rush, and I blink at my brother. I have no desire to embarrass myself by admitting to these two that Ava drunkenly asked for my sperm last night. First of all, it's none of their business. Second of all, I'm clinging to the shreds of my pride already.

"Ew," Ellie says, frowning at Levi. "Why would he do that? You're not helping."

Levi shrugs. "Seems like a simple solution to me."

"Ew?" I ask. "Seriously, Ell?"

"You're *friends*. Like Levi and me. It'd be weird." Behind her, Levi blanches, but she misses it because she's looking me over, a grin slowly tugging on one corner of her mouth. "But I'm sure there's nothing gross about sleeping with you, Jake."

"Moving on," Levi says.

"Will you *please* talk to her?" Ellie asks me again.

"I'll try."

She exhales heavily. "I'll take it. I need to get on the treadmill. I'm afraid I'm losing my appeal for Colton."

Levi grunts. "Then Colton's an idiot."

Ellie shrugs. "He'd never *say* that. He doesn't have a death wish. Anyway, I'll see you all later." She walks away, and Levi watches her go like the lovesick puppy he is.

"Don't do that to yourself," I say.

"Do what?" Levi asks, as if he has no idea what I mean. Look at us, both pros at pretending we aren't in love with the women we're not allowed to have.

I lie back on the bench and wrap my hands around the barbell. "Ellie thinks she and Colton are going to get engaged soon, so if you're going to tell her how you feel, do it now."

Don't be like me and wait until it's too late.

Levi tears his gaze off Ellie and looks at me. "Tell her what?"

I grunt and un-rack the barbell for my first set.

"What are you going to do about Ava?" he asks, coming to stand behind my head to give me a spot I don't need. "Does that fuck with you a little? Knowing she's going to start a family on her own?"

"Nope."

"Do you know you're a terrible liar?"

I focus on my breathing as I finish my set, exhaling as I push the bar up, inhaling as I bring it down. When I hit my tenth rep, I rack the bar, sit up, and look at my brother. "It fucks with me," I admit. "But it doesn't change a damn thing."

AVA

My front door groans as it opens and closes, and I hear someone walking through the foyer.

There are only two people in my life who let themselves into my house without knocking—Ellie Courdrey and Jake Jackson. After this morning's basketful of awkward with the baby thing, I'm grateful to hear the sharp tap of Ellie's heels instead of the softer thump of Jake's boots.

Ellie rounds into the kitchen, a wrapped gift in either hand. "Happy birthday to you," she sings, a grin on her face as she slides the presents onto the kitchen counter.

I push my papers to the side—work will wait—and walk over to hug my friend. "You didn't need to bring me anything."

She shakes her head. "I feel like an ass for missing last night. I'm so sorry."

"Do you want to talk about it?" I was already at Jackson Brews with the girls when I got Ellie's text saying she wouldn't make it.

She looks away. "No. I don't." When she looks back to me, her smile is wobbly. I'm grateful that my brother brought Ellie into my life—I barely knew her before she started dating Colton—but I wish he'd grow up a little. Half the time I want to tell her to break up with him because she deserves better.

"I know my brother isn't perfect," I say, studying my friend. "You don't have to pretend around me."

"I'm no saint either, but we're fine. I promise." She nudges the stack of gifts on the counter. "Open these."

More presents. There's no topping Jake's gift, but I'm all warm and fuzzy about being spoiled by another awesome friend. "You really didn't have to."

"But I wanted to."

Grinning, I unwrap the first gift, pulling off the paper and opening the box. Inside, there's a black teddy made of the softest lace I've ever felt. "This is gorgeous." I try to keep the *what the fuck* from my voice. The gift *is* gorgeous, and if I had someone to wear it for, I'd be really excited to show it off. But I don't, and it's not exactly the kind of thing you wear to binge-watch Netflix by yourself. Never mind the fact that if all goes according to plan, this won't fit me in a few months.

"I know what you're thinking," she says. "You're thinking you don't have a man, so you don't need this, but I fixed that. Open the next gift."

"If you got me an inflatable boyfriend, I swear I'm never speaking to you again."

She chuckles. "I thought about it, but I think we can do better than that."

I pick up the next gift. The box is light as air, and when I pull the lid off the box, I realize why. There's nothing inside but a slip of paper. I unfold it and stare in disbelief. "Ellie, you didn't."

She beams at me. "I did."

I'd like to think I'm keeping the cringe off my face, but I'm terrible at hiding my emotions, so more than likely she knows how I feel about her gift. It's a voucher for Straight Up Casual, a local dating company that hooks up area singles for casual, low-pressure blind dates that have only one requirement: you start your date with a shot of hard liquor to "loosen up." I always thought the idea was absurd, but since the service introduced Ellie to Colton, I've kept that opinion to myself.

"I love that you want to take your life in your own hands," she says. "I get it. You're thirty now, and you're afraid it's too late for love, but I promise you it's not. Don't rush to the sperm bank yet."

I study the piece of paper, even though it has no new information to offer. "I have different priorities than you do, Ell." Ellie's young. She and Colton might get married sometime soon, but Ellie isn't like me. At twenty-five, babies are likely the furthest thing from her mind. When I was twenty-five, I was engaged. A year later, Harrison and I were newlyweds trying to get pregnant.

Trying and failing.

"Your priority isn't having a baby," she says.

"Actually, it is." Did she miss my whole explanation yesterday morning about how a child is the one thing I'm *sure* I want from my life? In retrospect, I went about this all wrong. Instead of announcing my plan to my friends, I should have kept the news to myself until the pregnancy test was positive. I don't even know if I *can* get pregnant.

"No. It's not a baby that you want. It's a family." She bites her bottom lip. "You can make a family in lots of ways, but I don't want to see you struggle the way my mom did. It's *hard* doing it on your own."

My mom was single most of my childhood too, but I know what Ellie means. My dad might not have lived at home, but he was still around, and I know our financial situation would have been completely different without him. When I was a kid, Mom was a secretary at a construction company. She didn't finish her Ph.D. or get her first tenure-track position until I was a junior in high school.

"It can't hurt to give Straight Up Casual a shot—even if it's not love, it could be fun. I bought you ten matches."

My jaw drops. "*Ten*? Jesus, Ellie, I don't think there are ten single guys in this town I'd be willing to date."

"And *that* attitude is exactly why you're still single."

"Okay, for argument's sake, let's pretend there are ten guys right here in Jackson Harbor I'd be interested in. I suck at dating," I say. Ellie knows this. She's *seen* the disaster that has been my love life since my divorce.

"That's why I hired Straight Up Casual to help. They have a way of finding people their matches, and you deserve oodles of fun dates, and if they're all duds, I'll personally squirt the spooge up your hoo-ha. You have my word."

I make a face. "Thanks for the offer, but I think I'll pass."

She laughs. "You know what I mean. I'll support you in any way you need."

"Thank you," I say softly.

"So the dates?"

"I'll think about it." I want to mean it, but I'm already thinking of calling the company and asking about transferring the dates to someone else. Teagan might be interested. She's always complaining about how hard it is to find decent single guys in Jackson Harbor, but I don't think she's given up on love like I have.

"Yay!" Ellie stretches her arms overhead in victory. "Now, let's go to Ooh La La! so I can buy you a piece of birthday cake."

Chapter FIVE

AVA

Everyone knows that the best place to go for coffee in Jackson Harbor is also the best place to satisfy your sweet tooth. Ooh La La! is a coffee shop and confectionary just a block down from Jackson Brews, and also the place Ellie and I became best friends. Two years ago, after she and Colton started dating, she insisted we meet for coffee. At the time, I was in the early stages of my divorce, and I quickly discovered that I needed a girlfriend I could share my heartache with—it didn't feel right dumping everything on Jake. It turned out Ellie was a great listener, and our friendship blossomed.

The offerings here are so delicious that I have to restrict my visits to once a week. Not only would daily gourmet coffee and a pastry blow my waistline, I simply don't have room in my budget for such habits, but I figure I can make an exception for my birthday.

"Happy birthday," Star calls from behind the counter. She owns this place and is responsible for the delicious offerings behind the glass. From handmade chocolates to melt-in-your-mouth croissants to the perfect cup of coffee, Star knows how to make the good stuff. "Did you have fun last night?"

I nod. "Maybe a little too much fun." I rub my forehead. My headache's mostly gone now, but the reminder that I overindulged still lingers in the background.

"Nothing a little caffeine and sugar can't cure." Star grins, tucking a lock of her curly red hair behind her ear.

Ellie walks up to the glass case and scans the contents. "What kind of cupcakes do you have today? My birthday girl needs a treat."

Star puts her finger to her lips. "Not much up here but the double-chocolate fudge."

Ellie gasps. "How dare you speak of anything *double-chocolate* as *not much*."

"It's not special enough," Star says. "I'm working on samples for a bride who's coming in tomorrow, so I might have some options back there. Lance, get their drinks while I'm gone. It's on the house for Ava's birthday."

The lanky teenager nods glumly, as if she just informed him that our drinks were coming out of his paycheck. That's Lance, though. I know him from my drama club, and he's one of those kids who takes the Eeyore approach to life—always looking for the gray, cloudy lining to any situation.

"What do you want to drink?" Ellie asks. "I think we should get something really indulgent. Like something with full-fat milk and sugary syrup."

"What do you recommend, Lance?" I ask.

He shrugs. "I don't like coffee."

Ellie rolls her eyes. "How about two of the turtle sundae lattes?"

Lance nods. "Happy birthday, Miss McKinley," he says, then turns to make our drinks.

Ellie and I flash a grin at each other. Lance might not mean to, but he makes us giggle.

"Let's sit over there," Ellie says, pointing to a booth on the other side of the café.

I head in that direction but stop when I see Myla Quincy, one of the other English teachers from my school.

"Go on," I tell Ellie. "I'll be there in a minute."

Myla's sitting in front of a stack of papers, a large, steaming cup of black coffee at her side. "Beautiful day for grading, huh?" I say, because grading is the plight of every English teacher's life.

She looks up from the paper and blinks at me. Myla is the coach of our cheer team and is usually a walking cheerleader stereotype—peppy and full of energy. Today, she looks exhausted. "Gotta enjoy it while it lasts, am I right?"

I frown. "What's that supposed to mean?"

She shakes her head. "I'm just nervous ever since I heard about the layoffs this morning. I have this ache in my gut that won't go away."

"What layoffs?"

She bites her bottom lip and studies me. "Didn't you hear? The Windsor Prep board voted on a new budget. They're going to get rid of the middle school program and lay off a quarter of the faculty."

Suddenly, I have no appetite for cupcakes and coffee. In fact, my stomach was in better shape with a fresh hangover than it is trying to digest this news. "Are you sure?"

"I guess the actual number is more rumor than official at this point, but the layoffs are coming." She rubs her eyes, and I realize she doesn't look tired. She looks like she's been *crying*. "I'm a wreck. I just bought a house."

I don't blame her for being worried. She's the newest teacher in the English department and teaches primarily the middle school students, meaning she'll probably be the first to go. "I'm sorry, Myla." I reach out and squeeze her wrist. "I know it's hard, but try not to worry until we know more, okay?"

Her eyes fill with tears, and she nods. "I know. Don't borrow trouble, right?"

"Right. We don't know what's going to happen yet." I try to smile, but I'm not feeling it, and I'm afraid my worry is obvious on my face.

"Thanks, Ava." She takes a deep breath. "I'd better get back to this grading."

"We'll talk more on Monday," I promise as I head to the booth to meet Ellie.

"What was that about?" Ellie asks as I slide in.

"Windsor Prep is going to do a big round of layoffs." I rub my temples. "The middle school program never grew like they thought it would, and apparently the board voted to get rid of it."

"Well, shit," Ellie says. "And the cheerleader chick has her head on the chopping block?"

I draw in a ragged breath. "I don't know. Maybe. I hope

not." Honestly, the only colleague I'd *like* to see go is my asshole principal.

"What about you? You teach in the high school part, so you're okay, right?"

"Maybe. I don't know how they'll handle it."

"I'm so sorry, Ava."

I shake my head. "Don't apologize. We don't know anything yet." But until the layoffs are done, I know my plans are postponed. Having a child on my own will be tough, but embarking on this mission without a steady job would be nothing short of careless. A weight settles onto me, crushing the joy I've been carrying since I decided to launch Operation Pregnancy.

JAKE

By the time Saturday night rolls around, I'm kicking myself for agreeing to talk to Ava about her baby plans. There are a lot of conversations I'd prefer to never have. A conversation with Ava about having someone else's baby tops the list—tied with a conversation with my mom about her sex life. In other words, if I didn't think this was *really fucking important*, there's no way I'd indulge in such emotional masochism.

I leave my apartment and take the stairs down to Jackson Brews. Ava's scheduled to close tonight. Maybe this isn't the best place to have such a delicate conversation, but I'm ready to rip off the Band-Aid. At least here we can talk over a beer instead of in the awkward silence of her house.

"Jake!" Ava spots me as I push out of the kitchen. "What are you doing here?"

I shrug. "I live here."

She rolls her eyes. "You know what I mean. You're not on the schedule for tonight."

"Nothing else to do." That's not true. I scheduled myself off because I had a date with a peppy pharmaceutical rep who calls me up when she's passing through town. I canceled after Ava left my apartment this morning. Call me crazy, but after discussing the possibility of making a baby with Ava, I wasn't up to a date with another woman.

I wander behind the bar to scope the scene. There's a decent crowd tonight for off-season, with most of the barstools and half the tables occupied, but behind the bar there's no sign it's been busy. Ava keeps everything clean when she's back here. I never have to get on her about scrubbing the coolers or flushing the keg lines. She takes pride in her work, as if Jackson Brews was her own.

Ava's worked at Jackson Brews on weekends and the occasional evening since her husband left her two years ago. She started for the extra money, but I like to think she stays on because she likes her nights behind the bar with me. God knows the nights we work together are my favorite.

The truth is, despite Ellie's concern that the life of a single mom would be too hard for Ava, I know without a doubt that Ava would embrace the challenge. And I know she was right when she told me she wouldn't regret a child. My only concern boils down to the timing. Is this something she'd want to do if

Harrison's wife weren't pregnant?

"I just wanted to check on things," I say, unwilling to admit I came down here just to talk about her plans. "I thought I'd see how everyone's liking my new white stout."

Her eyes go wide. "Oh my God! I didn't even know you tapped it." She grabs a sampler glass and fills it halfway. "Do you mind?" she asks as she brings it to her lips.

"Of course not."

She drinks half of the sample in one long swallow and closes her eyes. "Jesus, that's good."

Reason #2603 I'm in love with Ava McKinley: she *gets* good beer.

My family's business is beer. Dad risked everything to start the family brewery. After years of brewing his own concoctions in the garage, he sold his share of his father's construction company and founded Jackson Brews. My oldest brother, Brayden, is the face of the business now. He's responsible for marketing and our distribution deals, as well as the ins and outs of turning our microbrewery into the sizable craft beer empire Dad dreamed it could be. I run the other face of the business—the Jackson Brews Brewpub—and am responsible for eighty percent of the new recipes with the Jackson Brews label. I love to toy with beer almost as much as I love to toy with food, so the job suits me, even if it isn't anywhere near what I imagined I'd be doing with my computer science degree.

"You really like it?" I ask when she opens her eyes again.

"It's smooth, but the flavor's more interesting than the stuff we had from Grand Rapids. Seriously, you wouldn't know it wasn't a dark stout if you weren't looking at it. Crazy!"

"Crazy good or just crazy different?"

"Crazy good," she says.

Satisfied, I grin and reach around her for a snifter glass to pour my own. This stuff packs a punch at almost thirteen percent ABV—nothing as crazy as a shot of liquor, but strong enough that it should help me through this conversation. "How was your day?"

"Good."

There's a hesitation in her voice that makes me frown. "What? What happened?"

She searches my face, then shakes her head. "Nothing. Ellie came over and spoiled me with gifts, then we went to Ooh La La! and consumed irresponsible quantities of sugar and caffeine."

"That's what birthdays are for, right?"

"Right." She drags her bottom lip between her teeth—an old habit that's always put knots in my gut. "I ran into Myla Quincy while I was there."

"She's one of the other English teachers, right?"

She beams. "I'm always impressed that you can keep my coworkers straight."

"It's not like there are hundreds of you." Some days I feel like I should thank her ex-husband for being such a prick. He makes me look like a fucking prince by comparison—not that my princely status ever got me real far with Ava.

"Myla told me the school's doing layoffs. She was pretty shaken up, worried she'd be out of a job, and honestly, I was at first too."

"Who can blame you?" I ask. "But you feel better now?"

She grimaces then nods. "Yeah—I mean, better about my

own situation, at least. Myla might be screwed, though. I called Francine—the art teacher. She's been there for twenty-five years and said they've always gone by seniority when they've had to do layoffs in the past. Nothing's set in stone, of course, but since I'm the English teacher who's been there the longest, it was good to hear."

I release a breath. It would be criminal to lay off Ava. Not only is she an amazing teacher, I've watched her take troubled kids and help them funnel all of their energy into theater until they shared her passion. "When will you know for sure?"

She shrugs and swirls her beer in the sample glass. "I don't know. There are only six weeks left in the school year. I honestly wouldn't be surprised if they waited until the beginning of summer to make the cuts."

"But you're feeling okay?" I ask. "Not too worried?"

"Not too worried, but I'll be sad to see anyone go."

I nod. "I get that."

"But my head was whirling from that news when I did something crazy." She shakes her head. "It was impulsive, really, and I'm kind of freaking out now."

I frown. *Shit.* Am I too late? Did she go to the sperm bank already? Don't they have a waiting period or something?

Instead of revealing that I'm panicking inside, I try to keep it light. "Let me guess. You asked Mr. Mooney for some of his sperm."

She scowls at the mention of her chauvinist principal and slugs me lightly in the chest. "You're an ass."

"Guilty as charged." I laugh and take a pull of my porter. "But seriously, what'd you do?"

She takes a breath, then finishes the rest of her sample. "I blame Ellie," she says. "She refused to leave my house until I did it. She almost made me late for work."

"If you don't start getting specific, I'm just going to fill in the blank with dirty things."

Grinning, she rolls her eyes. "Stop it. I mean Straight Up Casual. I'm officially enrolled, and I even scheduled two dates. My first is next Saturday."

My breath leaves me in a rush, and I fucking pray she doesn't notice. I've watched Ava date for years and I've never liked it, but I've handled it. Hell, I even danced at her wedding. But somehow now, with the full understanding of her endgame, the old kick in the nuts packs a little more punch. "You're supposed to close next Saturday."

"I've asked Cindy if she'll swap shifts with me, and she's cool with it if you are." That cute little line appears between her brows as she frowns. "You *are* okay with me taking a Saturday night off, aren't you?"

"Sure." I'm not just okay with it—I've encouraged her to do it more often. She works too damn much. Between school and theater and Jackson Brews, she barely does anything *but* work. But for a Straight Up Casual date? For Ava?

I've used Straight Up Casual a few times in the past—though I'd rather eat crow than admit that to her right now, or ever—and in my experience, it's a hookup service used by people looking for a hot night in bed, not a lifetime of love. What else would you expect from a blind date that starts with a shot of straight liquor? "Yesterday it was sperm, and today it's drunken blind dates." I shake my head. "You're full of surprises, Av."

Her eyes go wide before she turns her gaze away from me completely. She busies herself putting a rack of clean pint glasses on the shelf. "What's that supposed to mean?"

Fuck. Now my hurt feelings are turning me into an asshole. What's wrong with me, anyway? I decided years ago that I was okay with accepting Ava's friendship and never again asking for more. I'm not a glutton for punishment. But now that she's talking about starting a family, suddenly I can't cope? I shake my head. "I'm being a dick. Ignore me."

"You kind of are." A regular at the end of the bar raises his empty glass, and Ava pours a fresh beer and runs the tab for another before coming back to stand by me. "Seriously, if you think I'm hyped about using a dating service to find a man, you don't know me at all."

I know you better than anyone. "So why are you doing it?"

"I promised Ellie I'd try."

Ellie is taking Ava's baby-making plans even harder than I am, so of course she'd want Ava to date around instead of getting knocked up. "But Straight Up Casual? Really?"

"That's how Ellie and my brother met," she says.

I'm not sure I'd use Ellie and Colton as the metric by which to measure a successful relationship, but I keep my mouth shut and force myself to shrug. "Well, I hope they match you with someone good."

She bites her bottom lip and wrinkles her nose. "Is it terrible that I'm not super optimistic?"

"More realistic than terrible." I take a breath, remembering why I came down here. "Listen, can we talk for a minute?"

She refills her sample glass and nods. "Sure."

The bar is quiet, and Cindy is working the floor, so she can handle it without Ava. I nod to the kitchen. "In private?"

She arches a brow. "Is everything okay? Is it your mom?"

"Mom's fine. It's not that." I push open the swinging door to the kitchen and follow her through it. "I wanted to talk about this morning . . . what we discussed."

She does a slow turn, scanning the empty kitchen before turning back to me and saying in a low, conspiratorial whisper, "You mean about the *sperm*?"

I set my jaw. "Yeah. That."

Her lips twitch. "Is it a bad word now? Or is pregnancy a taboo conversation?"

I shove my hands in my pocket. "Neither, but it's your private business, and I didn't think you wanted every barfly to know it."

She swats my chest lightly, and I want to grab her hand and hold it there. I'd tell her to pay attention to my heartbeat and feel it accelerate from her touch. I want all the things I've spent years aching for and denied myself.

And just like I have for years, I push those feelings aside and prioritize our friendship.

"You didn't tell me Harrison's wife is pregnant."

"I didn't know you cared."

"I do when it's making you do crazy things like try to get knocked up."

Her gaze drops to the floor. "That's not why."

"Isn't it?" I shove my hands in my pockets. I wish I could tilt her chin up so she was forced to meet my eyes, but we don't touch like that, and if I touched her face right now, I know I'd want to slide my hand into her hair and lower my mouth to hers.

I've kissed Ava once. Only once. What would I give for another go at that kiss?

"I've wanted a baby for years. The invitation to Harrison's baby shower just . . . I'm not young anymore."

"You're going to be an amazing mom someday. But suddenly you're going to desperate measures to make it happen? And how does letting Ellie send you on blind dates fit into this?"

"Oh my God!" Her jaw drops, and her eyes go wide. "Is that what you think the dates are for? Jesus, Jake. I'm not some crazy woman who's going to poke holes in condoms and sleep with every guy I can get in bed."

I wince. "Christ, I didn't mean—"

"I promised Ellie I'd go on a few dates before I launched Operation Pregnancy. She's convinced I can find Mr. Right, but if I can't—and we both know I won't be able to—she's going to support my plan."

I fold my arms across my chest. "What happens if you meet someone you like? Do you tell him about your ticking clock and your baby-making plans?"

She props her hands on her hips and glares at me. She's wearing a red Jackson Brews T-shirt and a pair of jeans that fit her like a glove. Somehow, she looks just as sexy in this as she did in the black dress she wore last night.

"I might be shitty at dating," she says, "but I'm not *that* stupid. If I find someone I like . . ." Her glare falls away, and she drops her gaze to the floor. "It's been so long that I have trouble imagining that happening, but if I did, I'd put my plans on the backburner for a while."

"How many dates did you agree to?"

"Ellie bought me ten."

My jaw drops. "Wow. That's . . ."

"A lot. Tell me about it. But I figure I'll get through most of them before school's out, and then this summer I can launch Operation Pregnancy. I'm not going to get pregnant if I don't have a job. By summer I'll know for sure that I'm safe from the layoffs, so a little delay will be perfect."

Why the hell did Ellie need me to talk to Ava? She's already got it under control. By the time Ava gets through ten dates, the shock of Harrison's new baby and the blow of turning thirty will have worn off. It's a genius plan, really: make Ava go on dates and remind her just what she'll be missing out on by doing this alone.

A genius plan that might just make me lose my mind.

Chapter Six

JAKE

Sundays are for Jackson family brunch. Every Sunday we all prioritize brunch because we know it's a chance to remember that no matter how good or bad the week before may have been to us, at the end of it all, we have each other, and family is what matters most.

With rare exception, we gather at Brayden's house—or what is *now* Brayden's. This was the house we all grew up in, but Brayden moved in here after Mom moved out to help Ethan with Lilly. Nobody was ready to sell the place, and having Brayden here makes sense, even if the house is way bigger than what a workaholic bachelor needs.

Every time I walk in the door, I'm wrapped in the warmth of sweet nostalgia. I had a good childhood. The best. And even though Brayden has remodeled a bit and replaced some of Mom's old furniture with more contemporary pieces, I'm always taken back by the house's smell—the pine cleaner Mom favors and Brayden uses to this day, the lavender from the front garden wafting in through the open windows.

Today, though, I walk in the door, and nostalgia is met with a rush of love when I see Dad out of the corner of my eye. For a beat, right before I turn, before I can even take a breath, I think my father is really there. Just for a second, I can anticipate the warmth of his smile and the feel of his hand as he gives the back of my neck a reassuring squeeze.

Even as I turn, I realize it's Brayden, not Dad, who's standing in the living room. My eldest brother is as tall as Dad was, and has the same dark hair and broad shoulders, but while he resembles my father, he could never pass for him. It's just my mind playing tricks on me. Again.

This happens every once in a while. I think I see my father and forget that's not possible, that he's been gone for years. The moments pass as quickly as they come, but the ache in my chest isn't as easy to shake off.

"You look like you've seen a ghost," Brayden says.

I exhale heavily. "I saw you out of the corner of my eye, and you looked like Dad."

He doesn't mock me; instead, he nods in understanding. My brothers and I jab at each other about anything and everything else, but never about this. Never about the grief of losing our father, or the heartache of watching our mother take her turn fighting the same battle. "I did that the other day with Ethan," he says. "I was at the bar and I saw him from behind. I was two steps in his direction ready to say hi to Dad before I remembered that wasn't possible."

"I thought it'd be better by now," I say.

Brayden nods. "It is a little bit. Used to happen to me more often, but it's less common these days."

"Yeah, me too."

"Now it's usually only when I'm feeling particularly anxious about something and have been thinking about how much I wish I could bounce an idea off him." He studies me. "Which would explain why you did it just now."

I frown. "What's that supposed to mean?"

"I heard you had an interesting night Friday." I don't know what he means, and when I don't respond, he adds, "With Ava."

"Who told you that?" I swear, you can't stand sideways to take a piss in this town without everyone running their mouths about it.

Brayden nods toward the kitchen. "Our brothers are in there getting a real kick out of your luck." He smacks me between the shoulder blades, just like Dad used to do. "You might finally get your wish with Ava after all."

I don't know what they all think they know, but I do know I'm not in the mood to have my brothers laugh at my expense.

I push past Brayden and into the kitchen, which is packed with my siblings, Ethan's girlfriend, Nic, and my niece. Sure enough, Carter and Levi laugh when they see me. Even Ethan smirks.

"Big night for you Friday, huh, *Daddy*?" Levi asks on a chuckle. "You could have told me the whole story when I saw you at the gym yesterday."

"They're being jerks," Nic growls at my side. She's as sweet as she is beautiful, and when I turn to her, she's worrying her bottom lip between her teeth as if this is all somehow her fault.

"What the fuck are they talking about?"

"I told Ethan that Ava was going to ask you for . . . you know, your sperm. I thought that was what she was doing when she left us Friday, and then you two disappeared up into your apartment." She shoots a scowl in Ethan's direction. "I promise I wouldn't have said anything if I knew he was going to tell your brothers."

Ethan bites back a smile. "How was I supposed to keep that to myself? We should all be celebrating. Jake and Ava, finally together."

My gut clenches. "Except we're not together."

The smiles fall off my brothers' faces. I feel like a fool. I know that my feelings for my best friend aren't a secret among my family members, but my brothers have always done me the courtesy of not speaking of it unless absolutely necessary. Having them in here talking about my relationship—or lack thereof—with Ava makes me feel exposed, and I fucking hate it. "Not even a little."

"What were you doing up there?" Nic asks softly.

"She told me she was having a baby." I speak quietly so only Nic can hear, but everyone else is loudly speculating about the future of "Jayva," as Shay calls Ava and me. I'm already weary of this conversation and not in the mood to explain myself to everyone. "When she said she wanted my help, I thought she was saying that she was pregnant and wanted me to help her as a new mom—not with making her into one."

Nic shoots Ethan another dirty look. "It's not what you guys think," she snaps. "Now stop."

"Jake's a big boy," Levi says. "He doesn't need you protecting him, Nic." He grabs a spoon and piles hash brown casserole on his plate.

Shay sits quietly in the corner, sipping her coffee and watching me, making her and Brayden the only two of my five siblings not laughing at me. I make a mental note to get them both extra-nice gifts next Christmas.

We fill our plates and head to the dining room. I can't help but watch Nic with Lilly, my six-year-old niece. They're all smiles when they're together, and as much as I'm sure that Ethan and Nic were meant to be together, the real soul mates here are Nic and Lilly.

Longing unravels old dreams from where they're coiled in my chest. I can't deny I had a bit of a crush on Nic when she first came to town. She's gorgeous and fits into our family as if she's always been a part of it. I think each of the Jackson boys had a thing for her, though Levi was the most vocal about it until Ethan put a stop to it. But it's not any specific feelings for Nic that have this tugging in my chest. I want what they have.

I'm gonna have to beat Ethan's ass if he doesn't put a ring on that finger soon, but I'm pretty sure I won't have to. Ethan's smart enough to know what he's got. He almost lost her once. He won't let that happen again.

I pull out a chair at the table, and Shay takes the seat beside me. She's actually eating today, which is a rare sight, though her plate of wheat toast and scrambled eggs has nothing on the thousand-plus-calorie breakfasts my brothers and I are about to inhale. Ever since Shay lost the weight she put on in undergrad, she's been very careful about her diet.

"Where's Mom?" I ask, looking around. The table is crowded with us six Jackson siblings, Nic, and my niece, but crowded around it as we are, the sight of Mom's unoccupied chair makes it feel empty. I spoke with her on the phone last night when I called to congratulate her on finishing the last of this round of treatments, but I was looking forward to seeing her today.

"She's napping upstairs," Brayden says. "She's having a rough day."

Shit. Poor Mom.

"Poor Nana," Lilly says, her small face pulling into a frown. "She feels pukey."

"Why didn't she stay home?" I ask.

"You know Mom," Shay says. "Doesn't want to miss Sunday brunch, even if she can't stomach the smell of it."

I nod. I do know, and there's a sharp pang in my chest at the thought of her having to miss every Sunday brunch if this cancer gets the better of her. I fucking hate feeling this helpless. I want to fix it. To find a way to fight it for her so she doesn't have to.

"Sorry I wasn't there Friday," Shay says quietly. "Maybe I could have shut Teagan up before she told drunk Ava to ask for your sperm."

"So I have Teagan to thank for this?"

Shay pushes her eggs around her plate. "That's what Nic said."

I shrug. "It's not a big deal. She woke up sober and knew it was a bad idea."

She nods. "But is it a bad idea?"

I arch a brow. "Letting her have *my* kid *without* me? Yeah, sounds like a pretty fucked-up plan."

"Hmm." She scoops some eggs onto her fork and studies

them. "Last I checked, Ava doesn't do much of anything without you, Jake." She chews and swallows her bite before turning her attention to Lilly, who's chattering on about something that happened in school last week.

I'm too distracted by my own thoughts to listen. I know Ava well enough to know that if she's made up her mind about starting a family on her own, she's going to do it. Ellie's dates might slow her down, but unless Ava actually meets someone she can fall for, this summer will begin Operation Pregnancy, as she calls it.

Either she falls in love with someone else or has a baby on her own.

I don't know which option freaks me out more. But it's out of my hands. I just need to remember to keep our friendship the priority. Ava knows how I feel about her. I put it all out there almost five years ago. I'm just lucky I didn't lose her then.

JAKE
Five years ago . . .

I rap on the door to Ava's apartment three times and hold my breath as I wait for the sound of her steps coming toward the door. I'm going to do it. I'm going to tell my best friend how I feel about her.

The weather is a match for my mood—dark gray clouds, hard wind, and a storm that lights up the sky and rumbles through town.

I've been trying to find my courage for six months, but after my brother told me that her boyfriend Harrison had her in tears again last night, I'm determined to say something. I'm sick of Harrison taking her for granted and making her feel like shit every time something better comes up and he cancels their plans. I'm sick of him finding ways to push me out of her life. And I'm sick of pretending that I don't die a little inside every day I have to watch her fall madly in love with someone else.

I'm going to do this, and I'm going to do it now.

When the door swings open and she smiles at me, I shove my hands into my pockets.

"Jake! What are you doing here?" she asks as she steps back to let me in.

As soon as I'm in the door, I relax. This is one of my favorite places to be. Ava has made the apartment her own. She has artificial flowers in vases on her counter, stacks of books on her shelves, and cozy furniture with throw pillows and fuzzy blankets. It's different than the apartments of other people our age, and to me it feels like home. But maybe that's just because she lives here.

"Is everything okay?" She grins even as she asks.

Last night's tears are gone, replaced with a good mood that radiates off her. She's back to cheerful Ava in an oversized sweatshirt and a pair of soft jeans. Her dark hair is down but mussed in the back, and there's a romance novel laid open on the arm of the couch. I must have interrupted her while she was reading.

Everything in my chest is coiled into one tight ball. I'm

terrified, a fucking coward. Ava's been my best friend since we were ten, and I'm an idiot because, until she started dating Harrison, I never realized my feelings for her extended beyond friendship. She came home from her first date with him all rosy-cheeked and giddy. *"I think he could be the one, Jake."*

Jealousy hit me so hard and fast that I felt like I'd been knocked over.

I tried denying my feelings. Tried waiting them out. Tried dating every beautiful woman within a fifty-mile radius of Jackson Harbor. Nothing worked. Every day, I accepted more and more that my feelings for Ava weren't going anywhere. And every day she fell harder for the asshole junior lawyer her father set her up with.

"Can we talk?" I ask in a croak.

"Of course." She shuts the door. "I actually needed to talk to you too. I'm glad you came over."

"Can I go first?" I have to get this off my chest before I turn into the chicken shit I've been for months.

"Sure." She shrugs and attempts another smile, but now concern is etched into the lines between her brows. My nerves must be obvious. Her brown eyes go soft when they look at me—reminding me that Ava and I have been together in our own way far longer than she and Harrison. The thought gives me the last bit of courage I need.

I open my mouth to speak, but the speech I mentally recited in the car has fled. I don't want to fumble over the words I need to say. I don't want to risk her misunderstanding for even a second what I'm here to tell her.

Between one heartbeat and the next, I change my plan. I step toward her, and before she can react, I cup her face in my hands and lower my mouth to hers. I breathe in her scent of flowers. I memorize the heat of the skin at the back of her neck. I take the kiss I've imagined for longer than I can remember.

She gasps under me. Her whole body stiffens then relaxes, and for a beat—the sweetest fucking beat in the history of time—she kisses me back. Her hands fist into my shirt, and her lips part. *Fuck yes.*

The moment is gone as quickly as it came. She releases my shirt and pushes me away. "Jake, stop. What are you doing?"

I search her eyes and see panic and confusion there. "I'm in love with you," I say. Now, with the taste of her on my lips, the words are easier to find. "I'm in love with you, and I want to be with you."

She swallows and shakes her head. Her brow creases and her lips part and close again and again, as if she's speaking but has been muted. "I'm with Harrison," she finally manages.

"He made you cry last night." My whole body stiffens. She should be with someone who makes her smile and laugh. Not someone who makes her feel insecure and sad.

"What? Who told you that?"

"Levi saw you two out at Jordan's Inn. You deserve better than someone who hurts you, Ava. Let me be the better that you deserve."

She shakes her head again. "Harrison didn't hurt me. I wasn't sad. I was happy." She waits, as if giving me a moment to make sense of that. "He asked me to *marry him.*"

For a beat, I think she's lying, concocting an outrageous story to explain away the behavior of a man who's never been worthy of her.

But then I see the truth on her face and I feel like I disappear. I hear the cars on the street outside the apartment, the stereo playing in the apartment next door. I hold my breath—daring to hope she declined his proposal—but I already know. Even before she pulls up the too-long sleeve of her sweatshirt to show me her sparkling diamond, I already know she said yes.

I stare at the ring. "Are you sure this is what you want?"

"Yes. I *love* Harrison." She folds her arms over her chest. "Jake?"

I tear my gaze off the ring to meet her eyes.

"I care about you very much. You're my best friend, and I don't want to lose you."

The words are an icepick to my heart. I don't want to lose her either. But I think I already have. "Don't do it. Don't marry him. I can't do this anymore if you marry him."

"Do what?" She tilts her head to the side and studies me. "What are you saying?"

"Ava, I want more. I tried to let this be enough, but . . . I can't anymore."

"Why are you doing this?" She shakes her head, and a lock of hair falls across one eye. I want to sweep it away. I want to pull her into my chest and beg her to listen to my heart. "You're not . . ." She lifts her chin and studies the ceiling for a beat before leveling me with her hard gaze. "I know you hate Harrison, but this is too far."

I step back—one step, then another—the sweet taste of her mouth still on my lips. "You don't feel this at all?"

"I'm sorry. You're my best friend."

Those words hurt. *Fuck.* "I need to go." My gaze snags on her ring again.

She's really going to marry him.

And maybe if he were a more obvious asshole, a loser, or a cheat, I'd stand a chance at talking her out of it. But he's a young lawyer, fresh out of law school, her father adores him, and he does something for her that I've never done.

I'm just Jake. The boy who grew up next door and put a snake in her bedroom when she was eight years old, the one she raced down the sledding hill with at ten, and mud-wrestled with at thirteen.

"We're still good, right?" Panic curls the edges of her words.

"Why would I be good if you're marrying him?"

"Because you're my friend? Because you want me to be happy?"

"I'm in love with you."

"No, you're not," she snaps. "We love each other because we've been friends forever. You're not *in love* with me. I'm not even your type."

"Don't tell me how I feel." Rage flares in my gut. I need her to hear me. To fucking *believe* me.

"You like busty blond girls who know the difference between Gucci and Versace."

I can only shake my head. *Busty blond girls.* It's true. I've gravitated toward women who are Ava's polar opposite. If she gave it any thought at all, she'd know it's because I was trying to get over her. Dating anyone too much like Ava made me compare them, whether I wanted to or not, and any woman I compared to Ava came up short.

"Don't let my engagement freak you out," she whispers. "Nothing has to change between us."

"Don't *settle* for someone who's not worthy of you just because you're scared your father will never love you." I regret the words as soon as I say them, and more when she flinches as if I've slapped her, but I can't take them back. And maybe that's a good thing. Maybe she needs to know what I see when I look at her and Harrison.

"I want you to leave," she says softly.

"Bye, Ava." I reach around her to open the door and storm out into the rain, my body numb, my heart somewhere back in her apartment, shattered under her feet.

Chapter SEVEN

AVA
Present day...

Dad asked me to come by his office on Monday, so even though I usually hang with my theater students in the drama classroom during my lunch hour, I let them know I wouldn't be around today and walked the two blocks from the high school to Dad's office.

If I had my way, I probably wouldn't ever come here. Harrison works for my father, and whereas one time walking in these doors made me feel like a proud daughter and wife, now it just makes me feel like a failure. Another good reason why a girl shouldn't weigh her worth by the man she's with. I believed I was valuable because Harrison wanted me, and when Harrison left me, I had to grapple for the remaining shreds of my identity. It made me question everything—my relationships, my talents, even my job. I had to fight to rebuild my self-confidence.

Today, when I walk through the doors of McKinley, Morton, and Zimmerman, it's just as it has been the last two years: a reminder of where I fell short. Harrison's still here, his last name, Zimmerman, added to the door just a few months ago when he became partner, but I'm no longer in Harrison's life. Not only was I not good enough for Harrison, turns out I'm not good enough for my father either.

I head past reception and down the hall to Dad's office and am greeted by the sight of my stepmom at her desk. Unfortunately, Dad is that much of a cliché. He left my mother for his secretary.

Jill beams at me. "Hey, birthday girl! I'm sorry we didn't get together this weekend." She stands and walks around the desk to hug me. "Your dad had those tickets to the Cubs game and was dead set on going. I know he was sorry to miss your special day, though."

I give her a quick squeeze, and when I release her, I return her smile and wonder if she believes the crap she's shoveling. My father probably didn't think twice about missing my birthday. "Jill, don't worry about it. I was busy all weekend."

Her shoulders sag in relief. "You are the sweetest girl. So understanding and always putting others before yourself."

My stepmother doesn't fit her end of the cliché. While I have no trouble thinking of my father as an asshole, I can't think of Jill as a bitch or a floozy or any other match that would suit him. Maybe I wanted to believe the worst of Jill when Dad first left, but I was too young and too enamored by her beauty and sense of style to question if her kindness was genuine. Luckily, it was.

"Your daddy's expecting you," she says. "Can you stay? Maybe I could cancel his one o'clock and we could sneak out and take you to lunch?"

I shake my head. "I've gotta get back for fourth period."

"Another time, then." She smiles and leads the way to Dad's office door, then knocks softly on the frame before cracking it. "Nelson, Ava's here to see you." She opens it the rest of the way and waves me in.

"Hi, Dad," I say as I head toward him.

"Ava!" He stands, pushing himself up on the desk. My father must have some Dorian Gray thing going on, because I swear he hasn't aged a day since I was a kid. At fifty-nine, he still has a full head of dark hair and the body of an athlete. Since I know he values his appearance, I'm glad he's aged so well, but his good fortune means I've had to endure years of hearing my girlfriends talk about how they're hot for my dad. *That* I could do without. "Did you have a happy birthday?"

He walks around the desk and wraps me in a hug, and I'm ten years old again—a little girl who believed her father left because she wasn't good enough, and who cherished the moments he gave her any reason to believe she might be. I may wish I didn't want his approval, but I still seek it out.

"It was a great birthday, Dad." Pulling out of his arms, I look up at him and smile. "Did you and Jill have a nice trip to Chicago?"

"We did, and luckily for you, I ran into my old law school buddy while we were there. I don't know if you remember meeting Vern and Martha Stone."

I shake my head. "I'm sorry. The names don't ring a bell, but maybe I'd recognize them if I saw them."

"Well, I met Vern in law school and they're dear friends, and now probably the best thing that ever happened to you."

I frown. "How do you figure?"

He rubs his hands together, as if he's hatching a great plan. "I heard about the layoffs, Ava, but lucky for you, Vern's wife is an administrator for a school system down in Florida. I'd just read the news about the cuts that morning and found it rather serendipitous running into him. I gave him a heads-up that you'd be looking and reminded him that he owes me a few favors." He chuckles like this is the funniest joke, but I don't feel amused in the slightest.

My father assumes I'll be one of the teachers let go. *Way to have faith in me, Pops.*

"We don't know yet how many people are going to be laid off," I say, trying to sound more patient than I feel. "I don't have any reason to assume I'll be one of them."

Dad gives me a tight smile. "Let's not be foolish by failing to cover our bases." He arches a brow. "If we have an opportunity in Florida, then we're going to make sure we nurture that opportunity in case we need it."

"Yeah, but even if I do lose my job, I'm not even sure I'd want to—"

"Always so defiant." His tight smile turns into a wrinkled expression of disapproval. "Perhaps you need to take a moment to reflect on the best words to say right now."

If I were a flower, that sentence would have me withered and brown. Once again, I'm ten—the chastised child who isn't showing the proper gratitude to her father for including her at Sunday dinner with his new family. I'm seventeen and living with my father's perfect family and falling short with every other step.

I'm twenty-eight and being lectured about why I should be more sympathetic toward my cheating husband.

I swallow hard and shake my head. I hate that my response disappointed him almost as much as I hate that I care. "I appreciate you looking out for me, Dad."

His posture softens. "You'll want to prepare yourself for their call. Martha was very enthusiastic when I told her how much experience you've had at the local children's theater."

Prepare myself for their call? That seems premature—and, I pray, unnecessary. But there's only one appropriate response for my father. "I'll prepare. Thanks for the lead, Dad."

"You're welcome. Now, can Jill and I take you to lunch?"

I shake my head. "I have to get back." After all these years, he still doesn't understand that I can't just take a long lunch break on a whim. Then again, my father doesn't make much of an effort to understand anyone's world but his own.

He leans down and presses a kiss to my cheek. "Happy birthday, then. Jill will walk you out." He walks around his desk and presses the button by his phone to signal to Jill that we're done.

She dutifully appears at the door, and my father's attention is fixated on the computer screen in front of him, as if I'm already gone. "Have a good day, Dad," I say as I exit the office with Jill.

I'm perfectly capable of finding my way out of the building without Jill leading me, but she always walks me anyway. I wonder if she's just being polite or if she knows how uncomfortable I am here, always afraid I'm going to run into Harrison in the hallway.

When we reach the front and push through the gleaming glass doors, the sun is shining, and the air is warm.

"It feels like summer is coming," she says, tilting her face to the sky.

I smile. "I can't wait." Most people assume that summer means a three-month vacation for all school teachers, but I've never used it as such. Because of my position with the local children's theater, I work as many hours during the summer as I do during the school year, helping with theater camps and directing our biggest production of the year. Local youth, aged five to eighteen, work on it all summer and perform right before they return to school. It's my favorite time of the year. I spend my days hanging out with kids who are passionate about theater, my nights working extra shifts at Jackson Brews, and I even take the occasional weekend with the Jacksons at their family cabin.

"Guess what?" Jill says, pulling me from my thoughts. "Molly is coming home in a couple weeks."

Oh, my stepsister. Ellie and I call Molly "Mother Teresa" because she's always doing something to make the world a better place—an awesome quality in theory, but when it belongs to the person you're always measured against, it's a little hard to swallow. "That's great. How's she doing?"

"She's good, but you can ask her yourself. She said she needed to talk to us about something important, so I think she has big news."

"That's great!" I force a smile.

Molly moved away for college—she went to a fancy liberal arts school where a year's tuition costs more than my house. She left and only came home as the rare exception. Unlike me. I stayed as close to Jackson Harbor for college as I could. I had no interest in putting roots down in a new place. But when Molly started her degree four years after me, she was always getting this new internship or that new fellowship. I have no doubt that her big news is more of the same.

"Will you be able to join us for dinner when she's in town?"

The truth is more that missing such a dinner wouldn't be worth my father's wrath. I might not want to go, but I know I will. Dare I share my big news when Molly shares hers? Mother Teresa is probably opening an orphanage in Calcutta while I, the underachieving daughter who might be out of a job, am contemplating an investment in sperm. "I wouldn't miss it."

When I get back to school, students are trickling into my classroom for fourth period. Drama is my favorite period of the day, and the group I have this year is full of enthusiasm.

"Good afternoon," I say after the bell rings. I grab the stack of papers from my desk and start passing them out. "As promised, I brought in the applications for the children's theater summer program. I really encourage you to look at the opportunity and talk it over with your parents. If you think you'd like to help me, get your application in by the end of next week. I always have more volunteers for the youth leader positions than I have positions available, so don't put it off."

Lance raises his hand from the back row as I distribute the last of the stack. "Miss McKinley?"

"Yes, Lance?"

"Was Miss Quincy serious when she said they were going to let a bunch of teachers go?"

There's a collective inhale, and I draw in a sharp breath of my own. When Myla and I talked at the coffee shop on Saturday, she probably didn't think about Lance listening from behind the counter. The layoffs aren't exactly a secret, but no one wants to upset students either. "We don't know anything for sure yet," I say with what I hope is a comforting smile.

In the front row, Sydney waves her paper. "If you're not the one running the summer program, I don't want to do it."

I shake my head. "The children's theater isn't connected with Windsor Prep. I promise you I'll be running the program regardless of what happens here."

"So you might get laid off," Lance says.

"What if you have to move somewhere for a new job?" Corrine asks.

"What about next year's musical?" Sydney asks. "There's no one else at this school who gives a shit about the drama kids."

"Sydney, *language*."

Sydney's cheeks flare pink. "Sorry, but it's true."

I take a deep breath. "Please don't worry until we have more information. I don't want to promise anything. Obviously, it's not my decision to make. I'll know when I know."

"But you'll tell us when you do?" Corrine asks in a small voice.

These kids act so tough and grown-up. Most of the time it's easy to forget that they're still just that—*kids*. But I see the vulnerability in the eyes of the fifteen students waiting for me to answer. They need the reassurance that I'll be here next year because I'm a symbol of what they've come to love—bringing words to life on stage. I want to tell them I'm not worried and explain that I've been here longer than both of the other teachers in my department. But I bite my tongue just in case I'm wrong to be so confident.

"I'll tell you when I know," I promise. I point to the summer theater applications and grin. "But I'm doing children's theater this summer no matter what, and so should you."

Chapter EIGHT

JAKE

Jackson Brews is packed. After a few teases in March, another seemingly endless Michigan winter has finally released us from her clutches, and the balmy temps and sunshine have chased everyone out of their homes and to the streets of downtown Jackson Harbor. It's one of those nights when patrons have to squeeze through a mass of bodies to get to the bar. Soon enough, school will be out and the tourists will return, and nights like this will be the norm at Jackson Brews. I'm grateful for the tourists and all they do for our community, but seeing the place packed with locals fills me with pride.

Jackson Brews was just a hole-in-the-wall brewpub when I took over. Dad didn't set out to open a bar; he wanted to brew beer. He was good at it, and before he got sick, he was distributing all over town and into Grand Rapids. The Jackson Brews brewpub was here, but it wasn't anything special. Customers could stop by and get one of Dad's brews, and maybe a deli sandwich and some fries. It was functional, but not a destination.

I was in college when Dad was diagnosed with cancer, and when the treatments were making him too sick to work, we all stepped up. Brayden had already been working at Dad's side on deals to expand distribution. It made sense for him to take over that side of things, but everyone knew he wasn't the right choice to manage the bar. Carter had just gotten on at the Jackson Harbor Fire Department, and Ethan was in med school. Shay and Levi were both too young, so that left me: a twenty-one-year-old kid who wanted his family's bar to be the best fucking bar in town. It didn't happen as fast I wanted it to, but it happened, and I can't help but be proud. I think Dad would be too if he could see it.

The bell rings as the front door opens. I instinctively glance in that direction but freeze when I see Ava, dressed to kill and looking right at me. Anticipation jackknifes down my spine before I can check myself.

She's dressed for her date, you idiot.

She squeezes her way through the crowd and steps behind the bar to stand by my side. I inhale deeply and close my eyes for a beat as I process her floral perfume—a junkie taking a hit. When I open my eyes again, she's surveying the crowd with a shake of her head. "I think I need to cancel my date and help you. Jesus. Where'd they all come from?"

I shrug. "Gorgeous day. I think it's the first sunny day over forty we've had this spring."

"Do you have the back patio open?"

"Yep, and it's standing room only out there too." I wave to a regular then step away to pour his beer and start his tab. I fill a few more drinks and send an order back to the kitchen before turning back to Ava.

Her face is scrunched up with worry. "You need me."

"*You* are trying to get out of your date." When she dodges eye contact, I dip my head to catch her gaze. "Cindy and I have this covered."

"Are you sure?"

"Absolutely." Not that I want her to go on this date, but I'm not going to be the guy who stands in her way either.

"I'm so nervous. I suck at first dates, and the pressure is on, you know what I mean? I've pretty much given up on finding someone." She tugs at the hem of her dress. "But I didn't dream about growing up and finding the perfect *sperm* to have a baby with. I dreamed of the perfect guy. What am I supposed to say? 'Hey, nice to meet you. I'm Ava, and I'm hoping we're a great match so we can fall in love, get married, and have babies ASAP.'"

I swallow hard and put my best-friend hat back on. "Maybe don't lead with that."

She shakes her head. "But I'm a thirty-year-old divorcée who can't even put on her own makeup. I had to have Ellie help me."

Her eye makeup is darker than she usually wears it, and she's swapped out her typical light pink gloss for a pink that's so dark it's almost red. It's all a step up from what Ava would do on her own, but not over the top. "She did a nice job."

"I feel like I should be working the corner somewhere."

"Relax. You look amazing." I'm not exaggerating. She's wearing a little black dress—emphasis on *little*—with her favorite red heels. I haven't seen this dress before. If I had, I'm positive I'd remember, so I'm guessing it's Ellie's. It shows her off. The neckline exposes more cleavage than she usually does, and the hemline exposes more leg. No red-blooded heterosexual male is going to be able to resist her, even if she uses "I want a baby" as her opening line.

"I feel like a washed-up old lady who's trying too hard."

"Well, you *look* like a wet dream."

She frowns and studies me. "You mean it?"

Fuck yes, I do. I'd like to pull her into the kitchen, press her against the walk-in cooler, and show her just how much I mean it.

But I'm supposed to be prioritizing our friendship. I fold my arms. "Fishing for compliments tonight?"

"Maybe." Her lips twitch. I'm having a lot of trouble keeping my gaze off those lips, but it'd be best for everyone involved if I did.

She fidgets with the hem of her dress again. "Is Levi around?"

I shake my head. "Why?"

She shrugs. "Just wanted to see him before my date. You know, for the confidence boost. He knows how to give compliments and make a girl *believe* them."

Grunting, I press a hand to my chest. "I'm hurt. Are you calling me a liar?"

"No, I'm calling you my best friend. You're the one who's going to have to feed me Oreos and chocolate martinis if I end tonight feeling ugly and not good enough. You have a vested interest in bolstering my confidence."

"I'm pretty sure you're still calling me a liar. But that's cool.

I've been called worse."

She laughs, and her dark hair brushes her bare shoulders as she shakes her head. "Hey, guess who's coming to town?"

"Who?"

"Mother Teresa."

I frown. It's been so long since I heard that nickname, and it takes me a minute to understand she's referring to her stepsister. When that realization hits, my stomach sinks. "Wow. Molly? Seriously? When? Is she coming back for good?"

Smooth. Real smooth.

I take a deep breath and ignore the sick gnawing I get in my gut any time Molly's name comes up in conversation.

Ava doesn't seem to notice my awkward rush of questions. She rolls her eyes. "I doubt it. She never stays more than a day or two. Apparently, she has some big news to share with everyone."

Thanks to her father's obvious favoritism, Ava has always been incredibly jealous of her younger stepsister. Ava was ten when her dad left her mom. He immediately moved in with Jill, and Jill's beautiful blond daughter became the center of his world.

When Ava first told me about it, I figured she was just being a jealous kid, but then I saw it for myself over the years. I can't blame her for the innate sense of competition she feels toward Molly.

The only thing Harrison ever did right when it came to Ava was to make it clear that he wanted *her* and not Molly. Her father initially tried to set Harrison up with Molly on one of Molly's brief visits to town. The story, as Ava's father tells it, was that Harrison said he didn't feel right taking Molly out when he couldn't stop thinking about Ava. That sentiment alone was enough to win

Ava's heart.

"What do you think her news is?" I ask.

"God only knows. I mean, if I had to guess, I'd say something like an all-expenses-paid trip to Haiti to launch a not-for-profit that uses rehabilitated circus elephants to improve local literacy rates while providing the impoverished access to clean water." She chuckles softly, and I grin. Her ridiculous exaggeration of Molly's volunteer work is a good approximation of how Ava's father represents it to the world. "Whatever her news is, can you imagine me following it with my plans to buy myself some sperm? Dad would flip and use Molly as an example of all the ways I've screwed up my life."

I grimace, imagining the scene. "Are you really going to tell your dad your plans?"

"I think my news can wait. In fact, the more I think about it, the more I think it might be wise to not tell anyone else and pretend I got knocked up by accident. Even my friends don't seem to understand why someone would make the choice to be a single mom, and I don't need them to. If they're more comfortable believing I was irresponsible and accidentally ended up pregnant than with the truth—that I desperately schemed and plotted for a baby—then so be it."

"So be it," I say, forcing a smile. Christ, she's serious about this, and I can't believe I'm thinking it, but I'm grateful for Ellie and her Straight Up Casual idea. Ava needs a chance to mull this over for a couple of months.

She looks at her phone. "I should probably go."

On a date. To find Mr. Right. To interview a potential father of her children.

This blows.

I sweep my eyes over her again—because she needs the confidence boost and because I fucking *want* to—and shake my head slowly. "I hope the asshole you're matched with appreciates the value of your company."

She wraps her fingers around my biceps and squeezes. "Thanks, Jake. I needed that."

"Message me when you're home safe."

"Sure thing." Then she heads out of my bar.

After the front door swings closed behind her, I push out into the dining area and stand at the window. The sidewalks are lined with people enjoying the perfect weather, but I spot Ava instantly. Her hips shift side to side as she heads down the block to Howell's. I breathe through the tightening knots in my stomach and start counting down the seconds until I get that text.

Chapter Nine

AVA

Only Ellie would think that blind dates that begin with shots of alcohol would be the best way to find myself a future baby-daddy. But even if I think she's out of her mind, I'm determined to make the best of this, and that means I need to follow the rules.

Step One: show up.

Step Two: drain my shot like a good girl.

I twist my purse strap in my hand as I walk up to the bar. *Time to pick my poison.*

The bartender scans a paper in front of her, taps it, then grins at me. "I see you're here for Straight Up Casual. Good for you, Ava."

"How have you been?" I recognize her from high school—she was a year or two ahead of me, and nice enough, but I can't remember her name. *Small-town problems.*

She waves a hand. "Living a dream. What can I get you?"

"Patrón?" Tequila's always been a bit of a happy drink for me, and a little mood booster can't hurt, given how nervous I am about my first date in . . . Well, let's not put a number on it. I'll just have to limit myself. Tequila is really good at making me think I should have *more* tequila, and the last thing I need is to get drunk tonight.

"Bold choice." She pours a shot and hands it to me across the bar. I shoot it back fast, and she laughs. "Should I make that a double?"

I grimace. *Shit, that burns.* "No, one shot is more than enough for me."

"Anything else while you wait for your date?"

My date. Oh, hell. I'm so bad at this. Maybe I should have made it a double. "How about a margarita?"

"Rocks and salt?"

I nod and watch, mute with nerves, as she shakes it up.

"Over there," she says when she slides my drink across the bar. She points to a small round table in the back corner. There's a small *Straight Up Casual* sign on it—because this wouldn't be embarrassing enough if everyone didn't know what I was doing here. "You're a little early, but I'll send your date your way when he gets here."

"Thanks." I start to walk away.

"Ava," she says, and I stop. "Relax. You look fucking hot."

"Thank you." Whether I want them to or not, her words boost my confidence and make me walk a little taller on my way to the table.

I put down my drink and slide onto my chair, crossing my

legs at the knee. I grab my phone from my purse, then think better of it and slide it back in. I don't want to look aloof when my date arrives.

Across the bar, Mr. Mooney, the Windsor Prep principal, is walking toward my table. Shit. My gaze lands on the Straight Up Casual sign in front of me and I wilt. *Great.*

I take a long pull from my drink. Because now it's necessary.

"Miss McKinley?" he says, stopping at my table. "I believe you're my date."

I cough on my drink and spray my boss with margarita. "Shit! I mean, *shoot*! I mean . . ." Standing, I grab napkins from the table and awkwardly shove them in my boss's direction. "I'm so sorry. You took me by surprise."

He gives me a slow, amused shake of his head as he dabs at his shirt with the napkins. I can honestly say this is the first time since I met him that I've felt anything but small when he directed his smile at me. "Relax, Ava. I'm surprised by this too."

Mr. Mooney is a handsome man. He's tall, with a runner's build, and is always dressed impeccably. Tonight, he has on a dark blue button-up shirt that's tucked into his jeans and is unbuttoned at the top, and his blue eyes seem softer than usual.

"Sit down, please." He sets his beer on the table.

I stare at him dumbly. Sit? Does that mean we're going to do this? As I was spitting margarita all over him, I assumed we'd have a little laugh and part ways. *Because he's my boss.*

He waves to my chair and pulls out his own, dragging it over a bit so it's positioned closer to mine before he sits.

I stiffen at his proximity. The music is loud in here, and this will make it easier for us to have a conversation, but he's just a little too close to my personal bubble.

Don't be ridiculous, Ava. Ellie's always telling me that my bubble is bigger than most. I just need to relax.

"Ava, Ava." He grins at me. "What are the chances?"

I exhale heavily. Given the size of Jackson Harbor, I suppose I was likely to know anyone I was set up with. Regardless, Straight Up Casual is going to get an earful from me about this. Somewhere on their form they should include your job so people don't find themselves "matched" with their employer. And on the same note, is *Mr. Mooney* truly the best match they could find for me? This does not inspire confidence.

"So you're in the dating scene too, huh?" I ask, desperate to diffuse the DEFCON-one levels of awkward I'm feeling. I reach for my margarita. The moment my fingers touch the glass, I make myself release it. I'm already feeling a little fuzzy around the edges, and if I'm officially on an accidental date with my boss, I think I'd like to keep the fuzzy edges in check.

Color rises in his cheeks, and he clears his throat. "I'm only here because my sister . . ."

I nod. "In my case, it was my best friend. A birthday present, believe it or not."

He laughs softly. "Well, happy birthday. I hope she gets you something better next year."

It occurs to me that maybe I've always been too hard on him. After all, I usually see him at work, where he's operating under a lot of pressure, but tonight, his rough edges seem softer, his demeanor warmer—despite the fact that I just sprayed him with tequila and sweet-and-sour mix.

"Good for you," I say. "I imagine your job has to be pretty

stressful right now." I drag my bottom lip between my teeth and wish I hadn't brought it up.

"With the layoffs?"

I nod. "Yeah. Everyone's worried, but I'm sure it's stressful for you too."

"Are you?" he asks. His gaze dips down to my cleavage. *Why did I let Ellie talk me into this dress?* "Worried about the layoffs, I mean?"

I shrug. "I'm trying to prepare for anything, but obviously it's hard not to worry a little when the future is uncertain."

"May I tell you something in confidence?" His gaze dips again, this time lingering.

Okay, his eyes on my tits are making me feel super slimy. "Of course."

"You don't have anything to worry about. You've been there longer than anyone else in your department."

"Seriously?" I let out a long breath, and relief washes like a cool shower over me. "That's good to hear."

"We've gotta look out for each other, right?" He thumbs the condensation off his glass. "Two single people just trying to get by."

There's that vague sense of sliminess again. "Um, right." I force a smile, lecturing myself to be kind to him. What can a smile hurt?

He scoots his chair a couple of inches closer to mine and leans in. I rest my gaze on my margarita. Looking at him when he's this close makes this feel like the date it was supposed to be. "I can't say I was disappointed when I realized you were my date," he says.

I snap my gaze to his just as he puts his hand on my knee.

Holy fucking shit. Mr. Mooney is touching my bare knee. Alarm bells go off in my head. "Mr. Mooney?"

He squeezes lightly. "Call me Mark. This is a date, right?" He winks at me, and his hand inches a little higher.

I shift in my seat, trying to pull away from his touch in the most casual way possible. I don't want to make a scene or make him uncomfortable, but his hand on my leg is definitely *not* okay with me.

He doesn't take the hint. Instead, he shifts too, following me, slipping his fingers beneath the hem of my skirt. "What do you say we get out of here? Get what we both came for?"

I shake my head. "No thanks," I whisper. I hate how weak I sound. I'm not the kind of girl who's afraid to shut a guy down when he's making unwanted advances, but this is my *boss*. "I don't think that would be appropriate." I shoot up from my chair, and it squeaks as it flies back behind me and clatters to its side. "I think I should go."

He stands too, and color blooms in his cheeks. "Please, wait."

I grab my purse and hold tight, as if it's a life preserver in this disaster of an evening.

"I'm sorry, Ava. I hope you can forgive me for reading this situation all wrong."

Swallowing hard, I shake my head. "Let's forget this happened, okay?"

"I hope this won't make things at work awkward. I value you as an employee."

Just breathe, Ava. It was a big misunderstanding. "It's fine."

He nods, but something in his expression tells me he knows *fine* is my favorite lie.

Chapter Ten

JAKE

I show up at Ava's house Sunday morning with a box of fresh donuts and two giant cups of fresh coffee from Ooh La La! I knock on the door before using my key to let myself in, practically holding my breath. *Please be here. Please tell me you came home last night, and the date was a complete bust.*

"Ava?" I call softly as I walk into the house. It's dark, but I head to the kitchen, expecting to see her sitting at the table with a book and a cup of coffee. The kitchen's dark too. "Ava?" I call again, a little louder this time.

I hate the idea of her going home with someone. It's ridiculous. She's young and beautiful and deserves a healthy sex life. But the idea eats at me. *And she never texted.*

Still holding our coffees in each hand and the box of donuts under my arm, I decide to check her bedroom.

Soft morning light filters in through her sheer blue curtains. She's twisted in her sheets, one bare arm thrown over her head, her hair splayed out on her pillow. The gnawing jealousy of imagining her spending her night with someone else—waking up with someone else—fades and is replaced by a gut-deep ache of lust. Her pink lips are parted slightly, her cheeks flushed.

What would I give to be the man who got to wake up to that face? To start my day by brushing my knuckles over her cheek before lowering my mouth to hers?

I swallow thickly and try to make my feet move, but they don't. I just want to keep looking at her.

Ava wants a baby more than anything. Being a mom has always been important to her, and ever since she told me her plan, I've caught myself plotting ways I could make that happen.

I could grant her the favor she drunkenly asked of me. Jack off into a cup, watch her belly grow with my baby, watch her raise my child. On the one hand, it would feel good to give her what Harrison couldn't, but on the other hand, I know without a doubt I couldn't handle the outcome. I'd insert myself into her life so completely that she'd resent me. If Ellie's worried that a kid will make it hard for Ava to find love, imagine if the kid's dad refuses to get lost. I can't stop thinking about her proposal, but I also know it's not an option.

I've always wanted to give Ava everything, but for once I'm thinking of offering her what she wants. But on *my* terms. Would she go for it? Or would she panic and shut me out?

I walk into the room, slide the coffees on the bedside table, and put the donut box next to them. "Good morning, sleepyhead." I lower myself to sit on the bed.

Her eyes flutter open and she looks at the clock then at me. "Good morning." Her voice is husky from sleep and tugs at my gut. "What are you doing here?"

I open my mouth to answer, and she stretches—both arms over her head, her back arched, her breasts thrust forward—and I forget her question.

She blinks at me. "Is everything okay?"

Right. Words. Use your words, Jake. "I just wanted to check on you. You never texted me last night, and I wanted to make sure you weren't tied up in some creep's basement this morning."

"Oh, shit." She pushes herself up in bed and the sheets fall, exposing her thin tank top and the outline of her perfect breasts beneath it.

Her eyes are up there. But I don't know that I can be trusted to keep my eyes where they should be, so I turn my attention to her coffee, handing her a cup.

"You're a prince. I'm sorry I didn't text. Last night was so weird that I just wanted to get home and wash it all off." She shudders delicately.

"What happened?" My guard goes up immediately. "Are you okay?"

"Yeah, I'm fine. It's just . . . my date was my *boss.*"

"Mr. Mooney?"

"Yeah."

"Gross."

"It gets worse," she says. "He made a move on me."

"Do I want to know what Mr. Mooney's idea of a *move* is?"

"He tried to put his hand up my skirt."

I jump to standing. "He did what?" I'm already reaching into my pocket for my keys, ready to head out the door.

"Jake, calm down."

Brayden and Mark Mooney graduated high school together. Mark was the recipient of the one fight I've ever heard of Brayden getting into. Brayden was the poster child of a good kid, but he let loose on Mark. I remember sullen-faced Brayden sitting at the kitchen table with a shiner, waiting for Dad to get home and learn of his two-day suspension. Mark had been harassing this girl for weeks, Brayden told Dad, and when the girl told the school counselors how uncomfortable it made her, they told her Mark was a boy with a crush and his attention was harmless. But that day, when Mark grabbed her ass in the hallway, Brayden had been there, and he'd decided someone needed to teach Mark the consequences of touching a woman who doesn't want to be touched.

"Mooney is slime," I growl.

Ava shakes her head. "Nothing happened."

"And nothing's going to happen. Somebody needs to remind him—"

"Jake." She grabs my wrist. Like always, the feel of Ava's skin on mine calms me. She only holds for a beat before releasing me, and like always, I find the contact too brief. "He apologized, and we parted on good terms. Don't make a bigger deal about this than it is."

"Fuck." I drag a hand through my hair and study her face. "Are you sure?"

"He didn't steal my virtue," she says around a smile. "Just my Saturday night."

"He shouldn't have touched you."

"Agreed, but when I made it clear I wasn't interested, he *apologized*."

I force my shoulders down and my fists to release. "I never would have imagined Mooney using Straight Up Casual. Don't they screen their clients or something?"

"Don't be mean." She wrinkles her nose. "I mean, objectively he's a catch. He's got a good job. He's good-looking."

"Mooney? You think *Mooney* is good-looking?"

She takes a long gulp of her coffee and shrugs. "Intellectually, I can see that he has the characteristics of an attractive man, yes. I'm not saying *I'm* attracted to him." She does an up-and-down motion, waving toward my body. "It's like you. I can look at you and know you're attractive, but that doesn't mean I want to jump into bed with you."

I ignore that kick in the nuts and arch a brow. "Now you're lumping me in with Mooney?"

She rolls her eyes. "You're much better looking than him and way more fun to be around. Does that help? Does your fragile male ego feel a little appeased now?"

Not really.

"Whatever, whether he's a stud or a dud doesn't matter," she says. "I don't understand guys who think they need to push themselves on women. Does that ever work out? Are there women who like that?"

I take a deep breath. "I wouldn't know, because I'm nothing like Mooney." I try to deliver my answer casually, but the words feel like they're being pushed out through two grinding stones.

She sighs and holds her coffee to her chest, right between her breasts. "Anyway, it's over. Now if we could never speak of it again, I'll be golden."

"You need to tell the administration," I say, and *Christ,* I still want to hit something. "What he did was inappropriate on so many levels."

"It's not his fault that Straight Up Casual set us up. It's a blind-date service."

"The setup isn't his fault, but he has control of his own hands. Don't let this go."

She chews on her bottom lip. "I think making an issue of it will cause me more trouble than it's worth. Anyway, he told me last night that my job's safe, so I'd hate to do anything to change his mind."

Relaxing at that bit of good news, I lower myself back down to the side of her bed and reach for the box on her bedside table. "I bought you donuts."

She grins and leans toward me. "Are you trying to win brownie points with me or something?"

I shrug. "Maybe."

"What was on Star's menu this morning?" She takes the box from me and opens it. "Did you know she was going to have the chocolate peanut butter this morning? These are my kryptonite, Jake. You practically have to be at the door at six a.m. to get them."

"Lilly's going to try out for *Charlotte's Web,*" I say, as if that has anything to do with me standing at Star's door before she turned on her *open* sign. I'd happily do backflips to feed Ava her favorite foods.

"That's great news!" She lifts a chocolate-frosted donut from the box and takes a bite. She closes her eyes and lets out a long, low moan that makes blood rush to my dick.

Shit. Ava in bed, moaning. I don't know if bringing her breakfast in here was the dumbest idea ever or a stroke of genius.

Star works voodoo with her food. It's all delicious, but once a week she makes donuts that make all other donuts seem boring. This one, Ava's favorite, has chocolate ganache frosting and peanut butter cream filling inside a flaky dough that's closer to croissant than yeast donut. The only thing that's more enjoyable than having one myself is watching Ava eat one.

Her tongue darts out to catch the spot of peanut butter on her lip. She only gets half of it, and I swallow hard to keep my hands at my sides.

"She'll shine on stage."

It takes me a minute to remember what we're talking about. *Lilly. My niece. Children's theater. My excuse for bringing Ava donuts in bed.*

"Is Ethan okay with it?"

I nod, trying and failing to keep my gaze off her mouth. "She wanted to know if you'd listen to her audition before the big day."

She smacks my arm. "Of course I will! You didn't have to bribe me for that."

"You have . . ." *Oh, hell.* Reaching forward, I wipe the spot of peanut butter cream from her lip, and she stills, her eyes meeting mine.

I've spent a lot of the last seven years wondering how it could be possible to feel something so intensely for a woman who doesn't feel anything beyond friendship for me, but every once in a while, like this moment, with my thumb on her lip and her eyes on mine, I know that Ava has to feel something. She just doesn't want to admit it to herself.

If it weren't for moments like these, maybe I would have made myself move on long ago. Then again, I didn't move on when she married someone else, so the chances of me successfully letting her go when she's single are slim to none.

I pull my hand away before the heat in her gaze can morph into anxiety over what she's feeling.

She turns her eyes down to the donut in her hand.

"Lilly wants to join the swim team too," I say, brushing past the moment as if it wasn't even there. "She's six years old, and I think her social calendar is busier than mine."

Ava grins. "She's an amazing kid."

I nod. "Some days I think she's handling Mom's cancer better than the rest of us."

Ava looks up at me through her dark lashes, her expression soft. "She might be. Kids can be more resilient than adults."

"She certainly is," I whisper, thinking of my niece when she was three and holding her dad's hand as he watched them lower his wife's casket into the ground. "She hasn't had it easy." I hear footsteps in the hall and turn to the door.

"What the hell, Jake?" Colton asks. "Would you mind getting the fuck out of my sister's bed?"

"Colton," Ava says with her teacher voice—equal parts patience and authority. "Jake brought me breakfast."

"He shouldn't be in your bedroom, and certainly not in your bed." His chest is all puffed, his dark eyes full of fury. Someone's in a mood and looking for a fight.

He's probably right, and not because anything inappropriate is happening but because it puts ideas in my head. But if it puts ideas in her head too, this slow death by lust might be worth it.

"Good morning, Colt." I stand. "You want a donut? They're from Ooh La La!"

Some of his bluster falls away.

"Chocolate peanut butter," Ava says, hoisting the box in the air like an offering.

"Seriously? You think you can manipulate me with donuts?" Colton asks, but he's already stepping forward and reaching into the box.

Ava snatches it away before he can grab one. "There are too many people in my room. Everybody out."

Colton snatches the donut box from her hand. "I'll take these."

She points a finger at him. "You can have *one,* but if you eat more than one of my donuts, I'm coming after you!"

Her little brother grins. "Yes, ma'am." He turns and leaves the bedroom.

I watch him go. "You sure I'm safe out there?" I ask, waving toward the door, and not at all worried about Colton. "It might be smarter to stay in here with you. I'm afraid he might beat me up to protect your virtue."

Chapter ELEVEN

AVA

"Why's everyone so worried about my virtue all of a sudden?" I ask Jake. "You both need to calm down. I'm a grown woman." Seriously, I'm not sure what Colton's problem is this morning. He's always been protective of me, but he knows Jake's just a friend.

That said, I am suddenly all too aware of my thin tank top and Jake's proximity. Funny how just last night I was thinking about how I like to maintain a bigger personal bubble than most people, but the need for that extra space never seems to apply to Jake.

Then again, after the way my insides seemed to shimmy and melt when he touched my lip, maybe it should. *Shit. What was that?*

Nothing. It was nothing but the response of a body that

hasn't had much physical contact lately.

"Get out," I tell Jake. "I need to get dressed and brush my teeth."

"Need any help?"

I arch a brow. "Help brushing my teeth?"

"Help getting dressed. Or . . . *un*dressed." He gives me that devilish grin that makes most girls drop their panties. It could totally work on me too if I hadn't worked so hard to build up an immunity.

I grab a pillow and launch it at his chest. "Get out. Colton's out there, and if he heard you saying that he'd punch you."

His gaze drops from my eyes to my chest. "Might be worth it."

"Out."

Chuckling, he tosses the pillow back on the mattress and leaves my room.

I crawl out of bed and take a big gulp of my coffee, grateful for Jake's thoughtfulness. Then I go into the bathroom and shudder at my appearance. I took a long, hot shower when I got home last night and then slept on my wet hair. This morning, it's a mess of tangled waves. And even though I washed my face in the shower, I didn't bother getting all my eye makeup off, and now the remnants are smudged around my eyes.

Sighing, I grab a makeup remover cloth and take care of it. Then I brush my teeth, pull my hair into a sloppy bun on top of my head, and dress in a pair of black leggings and my favorite *Hamilton* hoodie.

When I go back out to the kitchen, Colton and Jake are already there, shooting the shit, and someone's made a fresh pot of coffee.

"It was awesome," Colton says. "I was flying through the air and then the bottom of my bike, just"—he makes a cutting motion with his hand—"gone. It drops, but I'm still up there, handlebars in my hands and nothing underneath me. My team was freaking out on the sidelines, and I was *flying*."

They must be talking about the last motocross race when Colton nearly killed himself. Not the first or the last time, just the most recent. Thank God I wasn't there to see that. I don't think I could have handled it.

"You're lucky you didn't break a leg," Jake says.

I nod in agreement. "Or your neck." Colton needs more voices of reason in his life. Levi just eggs him on.

Colton shrugs. "I'm fine. The crowd loves that shit anyway. It was great." He turns to me. "You look better."

"Thanks, I guess?"

He smirks. "Jill left me a message about dinner at Dad's place in a couple weeks. Molly's coming back to town?"

I nod. I kind of forgot, and I'm not thrilled about the reminder. I wonder what Molly would do if her boss tried to put his hand up her skirt. I can't imagine her confronted with such a situation, but if she were, I have the feeling she'd handle it with grace. And she probably wouldn't do something like Straight Up Casual to begin with. "Apparently she has some sort of big news."

"Maybe she's moving home," Colton says.

Jake stops his coffee halfway to his mouth. "You think?"

I frown at him before looking back at my brother. "I can't imagine she'd want to. She's been here a grand total of five days in as many years."

"That's true." Colton studies the contents of his mug.

I stifle a growl. Just the mention of Mother Teresa and all the men in the room go somber. I'm four years older than her, but I have younger friends who told me the guys in high school all wanted a piece of her. I always knew Colton had a thing for our stepsister, but I hate to imagine Jake just as lust-stricken. "Are you going to make it to dinner?" I ask my brother.

"Can't," he says. "Have a thing."

"A thing? Sounds super important. I'm sure Dad will understand."

Colton shrugs. "Since when do I give a fuck what Dad thinks?"

That's true. Colton can't stand our father, and when Mom moved to Florida, he went with her rather than living with Dad. For me, it made sense to stay. I was a junior in high school, so I only had a year and a half till I finished school, and I figured I'd rather be the odd man out with Dad's new family than leave all my friends. In retrospect, I think Colton made the wiser decision, but at the time I wondered if part of his motivation was his fear that moving in with Molly made him more like a brother to her, rather than a potential . . . What? What did Colton want with Molly? To screw around, or more? Before Ellie, Colton wasn't serious about anyone, but I always wondered if Molly was the exception. Maybe even the reason.

I turn to Jake and catch him staring at the stack of ungraded compositions on my kitchen table. He looks a little stricken as he grabs his keys from his pocket. "I need to head to Brayden's for brunch. Do you want to come with?"

I put my hand on my stomach, already full of Star's incredibly rich donut. "I think I'm all set."

He shakes his head and smiles. "You don't have to eat. You can just hang out with us. I know how much you like Shay's coffee."

"That's tempting, but I have a bunch I need to get done around here." Papers to grade, laundry to fold, weeds to pull. Since I work two jobs and volunteer as the director of Jackson Harbor Children's Theater, I have to be stingy with my time off.

"I'll see you later, then," Jake says, heading to the door.

"Give Mom my best," I say.

"Will do," he calls back.

I wander across the kitchen to see whose paper Jake was looking at, and my heart does a stutter step. Not composition papers. *Potential sperm donors.*

Colton looks over my shoulder and chuckles behind me. "Jake doesn't seem to be handling the news of your potential pregnancy very well."

Any awkwardness from Jake was less about a potential pregnancy and more about me asking for his sperm, but since Colton would flip out if I shared my embarrassing drunken request, I think I'll keep that to myself. Maybe I shouldn't be allowed to drink.

I look at my brother, narrowing my eyes. How'd he find out, anyway? "Ellie told you about that?"

He nods and studies my face. "Would've rather heard it from my sister."

"Well, it's only a possibility. Let's not get ahead of ourselves." I shrug. "How's your season shaping up?" I ask, intentionally changing the subject.

Sometimes I think my brother chose his career in motocross just to spite our father. Then again, everything about racing appeals to Colton. The travel. The constant thrills. The life-threatening levels of danger. *The women . . .*

"Season's good," he says. "There are some new guys trying to make a splash, but we'll see if they last."

"And how are you and Ellie?"

"We're fantastic."

I grin. "That's why she keeps hearing wedding bells."

Donut halfway to his mouth, he freezes. "Did she tell you that?"

Folding my arms, I frown. "Not in so many words, but she talks about you two getting married like it's inevitable. I think we all assume it is."

He cuts his gaze from mine and studies the big calendar I have taped to my fridge. The silence grows heavy between us. I sip my coffee, waiting him out.

"I love her. I'd just hate to ruin it by rushing into something."

"You've been together for more than two years. Is that really rushing?"

"If we're meant to be together, what's the harm in taking our time? Where exactly is it that we're trying to get to?"

I sigh. I know Ellie doesn't feel the same way, but the last thing I want to do is guilt my brother into a proposal he's not ready for. "Just make sure you're telling her how you feel."

When he turns back to me, there's more anguish in his eyes than I would have expected. Sometimes I forget my kid brother isn't a kid anymore, and he has problems of his own. "I'm not like you, Av. I'm not happy with the status quo. I want *more*."

I'm not sure he intended to insult me, but it stings. "Who said I'm happy with the status quo?"

He arches a brow and points to the papers on the table. "So you're going to go through with the sperm-donor plan?"

"It's complicated. I think so. Maybe in a couple of months, but . . ."

He folds his arms and studies me, and for a split second I see my father in his stern expression. All the McKinley men look so much alike. "Do you remember when we were kids and Mom sold the camper and put the addition on the house?"

I smile, remembering. I was twelve, and Colton was seven. Mom had gotten the camper in the divorce, but Colt and I hated camping, so we never used it. We convinced her she should sell it and use the money to buy something for herself—an elaborate vacation, a new wardrobe—*anything*, as long as it was for her. She decided to put an addition on the back of the house with the master bedroom and *en suite* she'd always dreamed of, and we had so much fun helping her with all the design decisions. "I still can't believe we talked her into that."

"Do you remember how excited you were to move into her old bedroom?"

Frowning, I shake my head. "You moved into her old bedroom, not me."

"I did, but only because you decided you didn't want to. You were so excited about having all that space and the big windows, but the closer it got to moving day, the more anxious you became. None of your worries made any sense, but you refused to move."

"Oh, yeah." I vaguely remember that now. Mom had said the old master could be mine because I was the oldest, but I decided Colton should have it. I don't remember why I made my decision, only that afterward I was jealous of Colton. He had space for three friends to roll out sleeping bags during slumber parties, whereas my friends and I had to spend our sleepovers in the living room.

"You were so scared that you'd miss your old room that you refused to take the bigger bedroom even though you wanted it."

"It worked out okay." I punch him on the shoulder. "And I don't remember you complaining."

"And then when you got the fellowship to get an MFA in drama in New York City . . .? You worked so hard on that application, and when they offered it, you declined."

"I'd started dating Harrison. It didn't make sense to leave. And anyway, I avoided a lot of student loan debt by passing on that program."

He steps forward and taps the stack of potential sperm donors. "And now you want a baby, but you've put the brakes on that too."

My cheeks heat because I'm still embarrassed about my plans, and it's weird to have this conversation with my brother. "Is my wild-and-free brother actually trying to talk me *into* having a baby?" I ask.

"Maybe." He folds his arms. "When Ellie told me she'd successfully stalled your plans, I was pissed. You need to be reminded to *go after* life, not to be cautious. Your whole life has been cautious."

"She just doesn't want me jumping into anything."

"I know you, sis. You don't like change. It scares you to death. So I know it's a big deal for you to have even gone this far.

Don't stop short of your dreams because you're afraid of change. Change can be *good*."

"This decision isn't just about me. I have the child to consider, and Ellie's right. It'll be so hard to do it on my own."

"The timing will never be perfect." He narrows his eyes and shakes his head. "You gotta take risks if you want to be happy."

"Coming from the boy who spends his whole life taking risks and never feeling content, I'm not sure that's great advice." I bite my lip. "No offense, Colt."

"Nah. I get it. We're different. Maybe you need to be a little more like me, and I need to be a little more like you. But you're prepared for this. You have a job—two, really, and three if you count that summer thing you do with the kids. And that's not even accounting for all the rainy-day savings you've worked so hard for and refuse to touch." He taps my nose affectionately, just like he used to when we were kids. "Everything will work out if you just let it."

"I never would have guessed you'd be so in favor of me doing this." I expected him to be more like Ellie—terrified I'd be wasting what was left of my youth. But as shocking as it is, it also feels good. I like having my brother on my side.

"I know you. I know what matters to you. Focus less on making the safest decision and more on making one that's true to you."

"Damn." I prop my hands on my hips. "When did you get so wise?"

He grins. "I gotta jet. Let me know how dinner goes, and tell Molly I said hey."

"Will do."

He leaves, and I turn to look at the calendar on my fridge. My hectic schedule is all there—theater rehearsals, drama club meetings, and shifts at Jackson Brews. I love this life. I'm truly, truly grateful for everything that fills it. So grateful that I've spent years feeling guilty every time I wanted a little less *busy* and a little more *meaning*.

A baby. A family of my own.

Maybe Colton's right. Maybe I should be a little less afraid of change and a little more willing to grab on to the life I want.

Chapter Twelve

AVA

"I'm torn between the six-foot-tall physicist and the five-foot-eight therapist," I tell Jake behind the bar on Friday. "I want my child to be smart but also empathetic, so it's a tough decision."

He folds his arms, and his dark T-shirt pulls across the bunching muscles in his shoulders. "You're seriously choosing the father of your future child based on his height and profession alone?"

I shrug. "There's some additional information too, but all other things being equal, the details are definitely limited."

"So once you decide, then what happens?"

"Well, I'm going against the advice of the doctor at the clinic and taking the cheap route, which means self-insemination."

"Turkey baster?"

I roll my eyes. "Not exactly." *But close.*

"Why does the doctor advise against that?"

"The clinic offers all this fertility help, and he thinks that's what I need. I want to be careful with my money, though, so I'd rather do it on my own. At least at first. Maybe I'll get lucky."

"Fertility help?"

"You know, they'll figure out when I'm ovulating and do the insertion at the best time. They can even give me some meds to make me ovulate, but all that costs money, so I want to try it this way first. Truth be told, I'm probably a prime candidate for the additional help, but I want to believe that my inability to get pregnant with Harrison was a fluke and doesn't point to serious fertility issues."

Jake winks at a girl across the counter and fills her beer before turning back to me. "Explain this to me. What makes the doctor think you need additional help?"

"I don't have regular periods, so it's hard for me to know when I'm fertile. I could buy those ovulation detectors, but really those are best used around the time you think you *might* be ovulating. Since I have no clue, it's a giant waste of money."

Wincing, he pulls a tap and pours himself a beer. I'm pretty sure the only time we've talked about this without Jake reaching for a drink was the morning at his apartment, and I'm starting to think he might have done so then too if it hadn't been before noon. He looks horrified—like, truly horrified to be having this conversation—so I snap my mouth shut. I've been thinking about this so much that it poured out of me. I can't tell Ellie because I know she's not a fan of my plan anyway. But Jake's a dude. He doesn't want to hear about irregular periods and ovulation testers.

"I'm sorry," I moan. "You were just being polite, and I responded with total diarrhea of the mouth. I'm becoming one of those women who overshares everything. I'm just trying to plan it all out before I get started, but I can't plan like other women, and that's frustrating."

"Yeah." He clears his throat and stares into his beer. "It's too bad you can't just have a guy you sleep with regularly, so you don't have to worry about conserving the precious sperm for fertile moments."

I grunt. "If I had a guy I slept with regularly, I wouldn't be in this position, would I?"

He takes a long drink from his beer and wipes his mouth with the back of his hand. "I guess not."

"Am I being an entitled brat? I just want a baby. I've worked really hard to set my life up so I'd be in a good position for a family. I have summers off, and I've worked two jobs so I could pay off my little house and have a good nest egg. I don't drive a fancy car or go on elaborate vacations. I make good decisions because—" I snap my mouth shut and shake my head. "I am. I'm being an entitled brat. I think that just because I want something, I should have it and I should have it now. But it's gonna be fine."

Jake rubs the back of his neck and stares at me. "Fuck," he mutters. Then he grabs my arm and pulls me through the swinging door into the kitchen. "On your birthday, were you serious when you asked me to help you?"

"I mean, drunk serious, but yeah." I make a face. Did I ever properly apologize for putting him in that position? *I am the worst.* "Jake, I'm sorry about that. No one should ever ask something that big from a friend."

He taps his fingers to his lips and studies me. "You know you're never going to get knocked up on your own if you're this stressed about it."

I wince. Harrison used to say that.

"Stop putting so much pressure on making this happen."

"You try to control everything. It's no wonder your body won't accept a baby."

"Can't you meditate or something?"

I lift my chin. "You might be right, but that's not a very nice thing to say."

"Shit. I mean . . ." Reaching out, he tucks my hair behind my ear, then he puts a hand on the wall on either side of my head and leans in. And I mean he *leans in.* His heat is close, his eyes are on me, and his forehead is nearly touching mine.

A shower of flurries goes through my belly and up my arms, and long-ignored lust for my best friend wakes up and stretches her arms.

Down, girl. This is Jake. Not some hot stud preparing to take you home.

"Let me help you," he says. "I want to help you."

I drop my gaze to his mouth. It's so close to mine and making me feel things I'm not allowed to feel. "Are you offering me unlimited sperm until I'm knocked up?" I'm trying to be funny and force a laugh, but laughter fails me when he's this close and my heart is hammering.

His Adam's apple bobs as he swallows. "I guess you could put it that way."

"How would that even work? Would you just hand over a fresh cup of the goods every couple of days?" My second attempt at a giggle sounds maniacal, but my body is a flurry of excitement—because, yes, I have my reservations about doing this with a friend, but that doesn't change that he's offering me my dream. I want to wrap my arms around him and squeeze him hard. Instead, I study him and unsuccessfully try to read his thoughts. More than once in the last week, I've looked at potential sperm donors and thought about that awkward morning at Jake's apartment. He never said *no,* did he? He had misunderstood my request, and then I shut it down as a bad idea before he could answer. "You'd really do this for me, Jake?"

"You're my best friend. I'd do anything for you."

My chest is warm. "I'm not sure I deserve that."

"But I'm not jacking off into a cup."

I frown. "Now I'm confused."

His smile is soft, and his eyes sweep over my face. "I'll help you have a baby, but we're gonna do it the old-fashioned way so you can relax about it." He shakes his head. "None of this 'am I ovulating, am I not' nonsense. Just you and me and old-fashioned baby-making until you have a little one growing in your belly."

I blink at him. I think I know what he's getting at, but considering the subject matter, I think it's best if I get some confirmation. "I'm sorry. What exactly do you mean by *old-fashioned* baby-making?"

He straightens, putting some space between us. My heartbeat steadies, and I can breathe easier . . . yet I miss his heat.

"You know," he says, "when a boy likes a girl a whole lot, sometimes they do this thing where they kiss, and then they give each other a special—"

I smack his arm. "Shut up!"

"You do know how to do it the old-fashioned way, right?" His face splits into a grin, but his voice is soft. "I mean, it hasn't just been you and that turkey baster your whole life, has it?"

I can't believe I'm smiling. He's talking about us *sleeping together,* and I'm *smiling.* And . . . kind of hot. What's wrong with me? Do I have a fever? Am I delirious? Is this even real? "You're an asshole."

"I'm an asshole who's making you an offer. Take it or leave it." Then he turns around and walks out of the kitchen, and I'm left standing here trying to wrap my mind around what just happened.

JAKE

"This is the dumbest fucking thing you've ever done," Levi says. He folds his arms and leans back against the bar. The place is closed. Barstools have been flipped, and the floors have been mopped. Outside, the streetlights gleam.

I meet my little brother's eyes and shrug. "I'm not denying that."

"So what happens when she gets pregnant and carries on with her plan to be a single mom? Then you have a kid out there."

And at least she's part of my life. "Lots of kids are raised by parents who aren't together. But if I have my way, that won't be what we're dealing with here. You don't understand, Levi. I decided a long time ago that I wanted Ava in my life one way or another. That's why I kept my mouth shut when she married that asshole."

Levi grimaces. "This is different. This changes everything for you. Have you thought about that?"

"I can either watch her have some other man's baby, or I can watch her have mine." I shrug. Honestly, once that became the crossroads in my mind, my decision was clear. Offering to give Ava a baby is the biggest gamble of my life. But is it really a gamble, given the alternative?

When I saw that stack of papers on Ava's table with details of potential sperm donors, my mind was made up.

"Somebody's gonna get hurt," Levi says. "Seriously hurt. And I'm afraid it's gonna be you."

"At least I'll know that I tried."

AVA

"He said *what*?" Teagan says.

"He said he'd do it, but only if we did it the old-fashioned way, because that's the only way I'm going to be able to relax enough to get pregnant."

Teagan snorts. "Well, *that's* a line I've never heard before."

I slap her on the arm. "Come on. This is Jake we're talking about. It's not like this is all some elaborate scheme to get in my pants."

"But isn't it? I mean, he's single, and not a manwhore hopping into every available chick's bed—because trust me, I've tried—so you *know* he jacks off from time to time. What harm would it do to hand over the goods? But instead, he's all"—she lowers her voice to a low rumble—"*It's better if we do it this way, sweet Ava. We're more likely to succeed if I'm actually doing the dirty with you.* I bet he'll have an excuse for going down on you, too."

My cheeks flame *so hot* at that image. I've been trying to ignore the bits and pieces of me that are interested in Jake's proposal for non-maternal reasons. "Shut up," I growl.

Teagan winks at me. It's girls' night, and we're sitting in our booth at the back of Jackson Brews. I told Teagan I'd fill her in on my personal drama before the others arrived, but the truth is, I need someone to give me guidance. Since I already know how Ellie feels about my baby-making plans, I wanted to hear Teagan's take. I'm so afraid I'm going to make a bad decision that I'm paralyzed. "You think it's a bad idea," I say.

Teagan's eyes go wide, and her grin stretches across her face. "Are you kidding me? I think it's a *great* idea. I have been in favor of you fucking Jake since . . . I don't know, since I knew there was an Ava-and-Jake. You two are amazing together. There should be a name for you. *Avake. Jayva.*"

I grimace. Back in high school, Jake's sister called us *Jayva*, and Jake hated it, which always made me think he hated the idea of anyone thinking we were a couple, so I hated it. "Please don't use those words ever again."

She chuckles. "Okay, okay, but you know what I mean."

"I know we're *friends*. I know this is complicated."

"Right, right, and nobody wants to ruin a friendship for a couple of hot nights, but now you have an excuse, and if you get a baby out of it, *bonus*."

"What if it makes things weird between us? Can we have a bunch of sex and then go back to being friends?" There's the rub. It's the question that's been haunting me since Jake's indecent proposal. I promised him I'd think about it, and in the five days since I've done nothing but think. And think. And overthink. On one hand, it's exactly what I want, and the intimacy of lovemaking over turkey basting appeals to me on the most basic level. On the other hand, what if it screws up me and Jake? Am I selfish enough to risk our friendship?

"Let me get this straight," Teagan says. "You don't think it's going to be weird to have his baby and be his friend, but if you have a few orgasms along the way, it might be too much to handle?"

"Can you orgasm with someone and just be friends?" I ask. I don't notice Levi at the table until Teagan turns to face him.

"What do you think, Levi?" Teagan asks. "Is it possible?"

Levi grins at her. "Wanna go into the restroom and find out?"

"Boy, don't tempt me. You have no idea how long it's been." She turns back to me. "I think the real question is whether you *want* to have orgasms with"—her gaze shifts to Levi and then back to me—"you know."

Levi folds his arms and stares at me. "To orgasm or not to orgasm? That's the question?"

I like how they say that as if I'm capable of orgasming with *anyone*.

"She doesn't hate the idea," Levi says to Teagan. "Look at those cheeks."

"Why are you even here?" I ask him.

"Levi has a Spidey-sense for women talking about sex," Teagan answers.

"It's true." Levi nods. "It's a gift, really. That, and I'm filling in for Jake tonight. Something came up, and he needed someone to cover the bar."

"Can you get us some drinks?" Teagan asks. "I think this conversation calls for tequila."

Wrinkling my nose, I shake my head. "Just beer for me. Do we have any of the vanilla imperial stout left?"

"Sure thing." He turns to Teagan. "And for you?"

"Well, if you weren't serious about the orgasms, I guess I'll have the imperial stout too."

"Sweet. Coming right up." He meets my eyes and the humor falls from his face. "Just think it through before you jump into his bed," he says softly.

"What?" I squeak. Was I stupid for thinking he wouldn't know who we were talking about?

He shrugs. "Drinks will be out in a minute."

"Yikes," Teagan says as Levi walks away. "I'm sorry. I thought I was being cautious."

I shake my head. "Don't worry about it. It's not a secret." And if we do this, it won't be.

My phone buzzes in my purse, and I pull it out to see a text.

> *Jake: Have fun with the girls tonight. I'll come by your place Friday. I'd like to review the benefits of turkey-baster alternatives if you're up for it.*

Teagan tips my phone down so she can read the screen, and

I don't stop her.

"What should I reply?" I ask.

She smirks. "How do you spell *bow-chicka-wow-wow*?"

Chapter THIRTEEN

JAKE

Since I offered to give Ava a baby, I've been keeping my distance. I need her to make this decision on her own and to have a chance to think it through. I hung out with Carter at his place until I was sure Ava would be gone, but the moment I walk into my bar, I know she's there. I *feel* it.

I immediately scan the room for her. Before I can spot her, I hear her laugh. I'd know that laugh anywhere—it's clear and unapologetic. The laugh of a confident woman who knows who she is and what matters to her.

The sound does something to me—warms me up and grounds me all at once.

She usually cuts girls' night short on school nights, so I'm surprised she's still here, camped out in the back booth with her friends. It looks like everyone made it tonight, and Ava is surrounded by all her favorites—Teagan, Nic, Veronica, Ellie, and even Shay. They're all laughing over something, but when Ava spots me, the laughter falls from her face. She watches me as I cross from the front door to behind the bar.

"How's it going, boss?" Cindy asks when I step behind the bar. She pulls a steaming rack of pint glasses from the machine under the counter.

"Great," I answer. But I don't feel great. I feel like a guy who just put his friendship on the line and is waiting for the other shoe to drop. "How's it been tonight?"

"Busy night. Went real fast. Levi was a big help, but I sent him home about thirty minutes ago."

"Great," I say, my eyes on Ava, who's still watching me. I wink at her and go about my business, as if having her attention isn't screwing with my brain, as if I don't want to pull her into the storage room, push her against the wall, and convince her with my mouth that this can work. That there's nothing she needs to say but *yes*.

I pull the receipts from the register and grab the deposit bag for tomorrow morning's bank run. *Just another day.*

I threw her world off balance with my proposal, but part of me wonders why it came as such a complete surprise. I told her how I felt before she married Harrison. Does she think those feelings went away over the last five years? Then again, we both pretend that conversation never happened, so maybe that's exactly what she thinks.

Ava whispers something to Teagan, and then Teagan turns her attention to me. Judging by her grin, she knows what I offered Ava. For my sake, I fucking pray Teagan's got my back on this.

Teagan climbs out of the booth so Ava can slide out. *Fuck me dead.* She's in red heels, jeans that hug her hips, and a sleeveless black tank that slides over her hips as she walks. I should get some sort of Oscar for keeping my poker face when she comes toward me dressed like that.

I watch her carefully, almost expecting her to stumble or at least sway in those killer red heels. Her stride is even and steady, and when she props her elbows on the bar and looks at me, her eyes are clear.

"Can we talk tonight instead of Friday?" she asks.

I arch a brow. *Not drunk but still willing to talk to me.* I'll take it. "Sure. Upstairs?"

Her cheeks flush bright pink. "Just to talk."

I lean on the bar across from her and lower myself so I'm level with her. "Don't worry," I say softly so only she can hear. "I'm not planning to fuck you right now." I look at my watch. "You'll be headed to work in eight hours, and the first time I get you naked, I'll require far more time than that."

Her pink cheeks flame brighter. "First of all, be quiet or someone will hear. Second of all . . ." She straightens and folds her arms, giving me a once-over before she lifts her chin. "You wouldn't know what to do with me for that long."

"Challenge accepted." I scan her face. Those soft brown eyes, flushed cheeks, gently parted lips . . . "Come on." I head to the back hall and the stairs to my apartment. I don't let myself turn back, but I can hear her behind me.

At the top of the stairs, I unlock the door to my apartment and hold it open for her. She walks in right past me, hitting the lights for us on her way. I close the door behind me and lean against it, waiting for her to start talking.

She wanders around my living room, her arms crossed, her gaze roaming around the space as if she's looking for answers. I wait, not wanting to rush her or what might be the most important conversation of our entire relationship. I expect her to have reservations. Hell, I like the idea of us having a baby together, and *I* have reservations. Most of them fall under the heading of What if She Never Feels This Thing I Feel for Her?

Suddenly, she spins to face me. "Are you serious about what you're offering? Because if this is your idea of a big joke, Jake . . ." There's so much vulnerability in her eyes that my chest aches.

"Shit. Of course I'm serious. Do you think I'd joke about something like that?" I want to cross the room and pull her into my arms. Instead, I press my palms against the door and force myself to stay put.

She swallows. "I don't know. I just can't figure it out. What's in it for you?"

I drag a hand through my hair and grimace. That's a loaded question, and she's not ready for the answer.

She rolls her eyes. "Sex, yeah, I get that, but you're not that hard up. This could change things between us. That terrifies me. You're my . . ." She chews on the inside of her bottom lip. "You're my *rock*."

"It doesn't have to change anything." But hell, I'm hoping it'll change *everything*, and for the better.

"I need to make sure you understand my situation. It's not as if we're going to be able to get drunk one night, sleep together, and get the job done. I mean, maybe? But . . ." She drops her gaze to her shoes. "The whole time Harrison and I were married, we were trying for a baby. We had no success. Obviously." She lifts her gaze to meet mine. "This might not be any different."

The look on her face makes something unravel inside me. It's as if even admitting there's a chance that her body won't cooperate causes her physical pain. And the idea that she needs to prepare me for this? As if her struggle to get pregnant might change how I feel about her, or that I won't want to get on board if I have to touch her more than once? That is insane. "Ava . . ."

She holds up a hand. "Harrison would get so frustrated with me. It got to the point that he didn't want to have sex with me at all unless he knew I was ovulating, which was tough to know, since I'm *broken*."

"You're not broken."

"You know what I mean." She tries to smile, but the effort does little but highlight the worry around her eyes.

I take a step closer, but she's still not close enough. She won't be until she's in my arms and wants to be there. She won't be close enough until she's come there on her own. "Let me get this straight," I say softly. "You were trying to have a baby, but you weren't really having much sex."

She draws in a breath, then nods slowly.

"And he wouldn't have sex with you, but then when you didn't get pregnant, he blamed it on you."

"In a nutshell."

Jesus. Leave it to fucking Harrison to screw her up like that.

My loathing for her ex-husband just reached a whole new level, but I keep my poker face in place and nod. "You're telling me that if this is going to have any chance of being successful, we'll need to have regular sex."

"And even then, there's no guarantee," she says.

"Right. So I need to understand *now* that we might need to have regular sex for months, and months, and *months*."

Red creeps up her neck and into her cheeks. "That's what I'm saying."

"That sounds terrible," I say, taking a final step forward, getting as close to her as I can without scaring her. She smiles for real this time and smacks my chest. I grab her hand and hold it there, and the contact is better than I imagined. "Your husband was an idiot, and I'm nothing like him."

"Okay." She swallows and nods, and the hand on my chest curls into my shirt. Her pulse flutters in her neck, telling me her heart's beating as fast as mine. "We're really going to do this?"

"We're really going to do this." My voice sounds too thick, and if she could cut just beneath the surface of my words, she'd see I'm planning for us to make so much more than a baby.

Dear God, let this work.

She clears her throat. "Do you think . . . I mean, should we get screened or anything? For infections or whatever?"

I step back and force myself to take a breath and remember I'm not going to rush into this. *Slow the fuck down, Jackson. This is a marathon, not a sprint.* "I'm okay with that if it would make you feel better."

She nods sharply. "It seems like the responsible thing, right? I mean, I haven't been with anybody since Harrison, so they're not likely to find anything but dust up there, but—"

I cough to cover my laugh—not at the dust joke so much as my shock that she hasn't been with anyone since Harrison. *And she's planning to sleep with me.* I won't let myself think that means more than it does. "I don't think vaginal dust mites are a thing, so you should be good. And I . . ." I drag a hand over my face, feeling a little awkward admitting the next part. "A girl I used to see called with a scare a couple months ago, so I've had a panel done. It was clean and I haven't . . . been with anyone since."

She cuts her gaze away. Not for the first time, I feel like an ass bringing up other women. Ava always acts sort of *slighted* when she knows about me seeing someone. Another reason I haven't given up on her, I suppose.

"One more thing," she says, bringing her eyes back to meet mine. "If at any point one of us wants to be done with this . . ." She searches my face. "If the sex feels wrong, or you change your mind about this crazy plan or anything, we can call it off. But we have to promise each other we'll *talk about it* so we can go back to being friends."

"I promise, Ava, but that goes both ways, right?"

She nods tentatively. "Are you sure, Jake?"

I arch a brow. "Did you miss the part of this conversation about the months and months of hot sex?"

Laughing, she releases my shirt and backs away. "We both know you could have hot sex with whomever you wanted whenever you wanted."

"You say that with such conviction, and yet you've never been in my bed."

She rolls her eyes. "That's right. Turn on the charm now. Maybe I'll eventually buy your lines." She eyes the door before swinging her gaze back to meet mine. "I bet the girls are jumping to all kinds of conclusions about what we're doing up here, so I should probably get down there. Talk to you tomorrow?"

I nod. "Night, Av."

I stare at the door long after she goes, willing my racing heart to calm.

Chapter FOURTEEN

AVA

I've never been so grateful to see the end of a school week.

Billy Joel Christianson—who was absolutely named after the singer—made my day hellish. Not only did he plagiarize his research paper, he tried to blame *me* for it. I told him his sources were acceptable; therefore, it was entirely my fault that he copied and pasted from them into his paper. Never mind the fact that we had a whole unit on avoiding plagiarism and how to appropriately paraphrase, summarize, quote, and cite your sources.

Billy Joel hasn't given me anything I haven't seen before, but his parents are big donors to the school. The cherry on my crap day sundae was being called down to Mr. Mooney's office and told I wasn't handling the matter delicately enough.

By the time I get home, I'm contemplating the merits of

spending my evening with the punching bag at the gym or the world's largest glass of wine on my couch. But when I pull up, I see Jake on a ladder tinkering with the gutters and realize neither of those plans are in the cards.

At the sight of Jake, my work stress reaches out to hold hands with my real-life stress, and they become one happy, united front, making me want to curl under a blanket and hide. I forgot he was coming over tonight. I put our agreement from my mind and *forgot* about having someone in my bed for the first time since my divorce.

Dread pricks at the back of my neck, and my stomach twists.
This will change everything.

No girl in her right mind would dread having sex with Jake Jackson. But no girl other than me is his best friend.

It's just sex, right? Our bodies were made to do this. I can lie back and think of England, as they say. Just get it done.

Except it's not that simple. I've never been one who could turn on sexually without turning on emotionally. And turning on emotionally with Jake is dangerous. I let myself think of him as more than a friend before and regretted it. What a sticky situation I've gotten myself into.

I pull my car into the garage and leave the door open so I can go outside and see what Jake's up to.

He sees me and flashes his signature panty-dropping grin. It's taken years of practice to become immune to that smile. I trained myself not to think about what it would be like to have him want me, worked hard to never wonder what he did with his dates when he took them home, or how it would feel to be one of those women. Am I ready to break down that wall? To let those thoughts creep into my consciousness? And if I do, will I ever be able to turn them back off?

The deluge of self-doubt makes me want to change our plans. I don't want to spend my Friday seducing Jake Jackson only to have him discover that I'm a dud between the sheets. I want him to stay for a movie and popcorn so we can talk trash about the eighteen-year-old trust-fund kid who thinks he can skirt the rules because his parents have money. But we have an arrangement. A deal that gives me what I want most. It's time for me to pull on my big-girl panties—or maybe time to pull them off.

"Hey, Jake." I offer a smile—not nearly as carefree as his.

He looks me over, head to toe. "Did something happen? Are you okay?"

I shake my head and wave away his concern. "Just a crap day. But it's Friday, so I have a couple of days to pretend asshole students don't exist. I'll be better." I scan the gutter he was working on. "What are you doing up there?"

"It was falling off again. Your soffit's rotting out. I'll get the materials and take care of it this weekend."

I shake my head. "You don't have to do that."

"With the rain we're expecting this week, I really do. If I don't, best-case scenario, you're going to have a lake in your flowerbeds. Worst, a flooded basement." He climbs down the ladder and wipes his hands on his jeans. "Stop looking at me like I'm offering you a kidney. I don't mind the work. The fresh air is good for me."

My belly warms. Jake has always been the kind of friend who takes care of me. I like to think it goes both ways, but I know I benefit more from his friendship than he ever has from mine.

And we're about to take that to a whole new level. "I can hire someone. You can get your fresh air doing something more fun."

"Av, I really don't mind. I know this isn't where you want to spend your money anyway."

I press my lips together. The truth is, he's right. And a job that'll take a couple of hours of Jake's weekend and fifty dollars in materials would otherwise cost me several hundred. "Thank you," I say. "It means a lot. It really does. How was your day?"

He shrugs. "Nothing special. Inventory at the bar, meeting with Brayden about getting some of the new brews bottled for distribution."

I grin. "Between your brewing and his business sense, Jackson Brews will be all over the country soon."

"Hope so. Want to order a pizza?"

Order a pizza. As in, spend our evening in. *Together. Alone.*

The warmth in my stomach cools then ties itself into a bunch of ugly knots. Is it just me, or does this suddenly feel awkward? Like everything either of us says is loaded with suggestion and innuendo?

Of course we're going to start trying. The whole idea behind Jake's plan is regular sex. I agreed to this. I wanted this. "Sure."

He steps forward and tucks my hair behind my ear, his eyes scanning my face. "Relax," he whispers. "I'm not gonna tie you to the bed and fuck you till you're pregnant, okay?" He drops his gaze to my mouth, and his lips part. "No matter how much I might enjoy that."

The knots in my stomach shimmy with delight at his words. I step back, swallowing. "I'm not worried."

JAKE

Ava came home wound as tight as I've ever seen her. She had a shit day at work, but it wasn't just that. She was spooked by seeing me at her house. I brought a growler of her favorite imperial stout from the bar, and after a couple of glasses, half a loaded veggie pizza, and three-quarters of a movie, she's on the couch smiling and relaxed, like she has not a care in the world.

And I can't stop staring at her.

Ava's curled up on one end of the couch, me on the other, her eyes on the movie, and mine on her. Attraction is such a strange thing. It seems impossible to me that I could have such an instinctive pull to her—that I could be *gutted* with wanting her when she's around—and she doesn't feel any of that for me. Something so elemental shouldn't be unrequited. I guess I don't believe it is. After all, here we are, planning to make a baby together. She wouldn't have agreed if she didn't feel *something*. And I wouldn't be doing this if I didn't believe I stood a chance.

She changed into pajamas while I ordered the pizza. While the black yoga pants and pink tank top wouldn't be considered seduction attire in any other circumstance, for me, right here, right now, I can't imagine her looking sexier.

"You have a busy weekend?" I ask, more to distract myself from my thoughts than anything else. "I noticed Cindy's covering your shifts the next two days."

She nods. "Yeah. Dinner at Dad's tomorrow and then

Harrison's baby shower Sunday afternoon."

I cough. "You're actually going to that thing?" Jesus. It was a dick move for Harrison to invite her to begin with, but I never imagined she'd feel compelled to *go*.

"I don't see how I could get out of it without looking like the jealous ex. Then Dad had Jill double-check to make sure I hadn't forgotten to RSVP, and I knew I didn't really have a choice." She frowns. "It might not be so bad, but it's a co-ed shower, so I'll have to see Harrison. That might be the part I'm dreading most."

If seeing the invitation screwed her up, I can't imagine how much an afternoon with the happy expecting couple will mess with her. "I want to go with you."

She laughs, as if my offer is a joke. "Yeah, sounds like fun, doesn't it?"

"It's a co-ed baby shower, isn't it?"

"You'd seriously go with me to this thing?" She rolls to her back and blinks at me, as if trying to process what I'm saying, then shakes her head. "I would have thought a baby shower with my ex-husband would be the equivalent of one of Dante's circles of Hell for you."

I grin. "Oh, it is, but it might be a little enjoyable, too . . . assuming I get to play the part of your boyfriend."

She grunts. "Why would you want to do that?"

I can only think of two hundred reasons off the top of my head, including but not limited to *any excuse to touch you.* "He was always jealous of me, Ava. He couldn't stand how close we were. You know he invited you to this thing to be a dick, so I say we strike back. I'll go with you and we'll pretend we're together. It'll make him crazy." *Pretend we're together* seems like such an odd thing to say to a woman who I'm planning to make a baby with, but that's par for the course in our relationship right now.

"I'd love for you to go with me, Jake, but I don't want you to feel like you have to."

"Don't say another word," I say. "I'll be your plus one." Her feet are by my legs, and I pull them into my lap.

She arches a brow as my thumbs dig into the pad of her heel. "A date to a miserable baby shower *and* a foot rub? What did I do to deserve this?"

"Who said you deserved it?"

She yanks her foot from my hand and kicks my thigh playfully. "I absolutely do. I've had a long day."

"In that case, relax."

With a sigh, she slides her attention back to the TV. There are certain things I've gotten away with in my years as Ava's best friend, and one of them is the occasional foot rub. While I've never been a *foot* guy, with Ava, any sort of contact gets me hard.

The first time I had an excuse to do this was after I forced her to do a 5k race with me. I hadn't realized she was wearing crappy five-year-old tennis shoes, and her feet were wrecked afterward. The foot rub was the obvious way to apologize for making her do something she hadn't wanted to do in the first place.

After that, the door was open, and from time to time I'd rub her feet after a long day at work or after she pulled a double at the bar for me. I never let it go any further than that. Never let my hand slide up her leg to work out the knots in her calves or feel the soft skin at the back of her thigh just above her knee.

But tonight, things are different. Tonight, I work my way up, rubbing her delicate ankles before kneading the muscle of her calf. I hold my breath, waiting to see how she'll react to my touch. She gasps when my hand goes a little higher and sweeps behind her knee. Then she flips from her side to her back, and the positioning gives me better access.

"You seriously could have been a massage therapist," she says, scooting toward me.

Her calf sweeps over my crotch and the really fucking obvious erection I have happening there, but she doesn't seem to notice.

"It's gotta be tough for guys who do that for a living," she says. "Rubbing on naked women all day."

"Yeah, sounds really tough." I trail my hand up to the back of her thigh and run my thumb along the outside of her hip—a spot I know gets tight on her because she's always fighting to get it stretched out.

She gasps, but this time it's not just a surprised gasp. This time it comes with that look of fear in her eyes. As if she's not sure what comes next and she's not sure she's okay with it.

"Relax." I don't want her to be scared. I want her to be as hungry for me as I am for her.

She pushes herself up with one hand and grabs my shirt with the other. When she tugs me down so I'm lying over her on the couch, it's my turn to draw in a sharp breath. Because she's pulling my mouth to hers. *Ava's soft lips under mine. Ava's body under mine.*

I follow her lead—first, just a brush of lips as I shift my position. She draws up a knee, allowing my body to settle over hers. She slides a hand into my hair and sweeps her tongue over my lips.

Fucking hell.

She could make me come undone so easily.

"Ava," I whisper against her lips, and her body trembles under my hands. I love this—her reactions, her uneven breaths. I want more. *So much more.*

My brain is trying to get too many steps ahead—undressing her, touching her everywhere, kissing her everywhere, laying her out on her bed and memorizing the way she looks tangled in sheets.

I push all that away and focus on now. The soft sweep of her lips against my mouth, her hands pressed against my chest and working their way down my body until— "What are you doing?" I still have my fucking shoes and shirt on, and she's unbuttoning my jeans.

"I'm ready," she says, then her hands go to her pants and she pushes them down her hips, exposing her pink cotton panties.

I climb off her and hold up my hands. "You're what?"

She sits up, her cheeks going pink. "I'm ready to have sex."

I narrow my eyes. "Are you even turned on?"

She shrugs. "I've got some lubricant in the bedroom. It's fine. Let's not make a big deal about this. Let's just get it over with."

I zip and button my jeans. *Get it over with.* Fuck. I'm ready to spend the night tasting every inch of her and seeing how many ways I can make her come, and she just wants me to *get it over with.*

How delusional was I to think this might have actually worked the way I wanted?

I drag a hand through my hair. "I think I should go."

"What?" She shakes her head. "Jake, I'm sorry. If you don't want to do this, I don't want you to—"

"That's not it."

She tugs her pants back in place, sits up, and looks at her lap. "I'm so bad at this," she whispers.

I feel like an ass.

I sink down to the couch next to her and tilt her chin until she meets my eyes. "When I'm finally inside you, it'll be because you want me there, because you're *begging* to have me there for reasons that have nothing to do with having a baby." Her lips part at my words, and her eyes go darker. "When I get inside you, you're going to forget why we even started this, and you're sure as fuck not going to need any lube. Got it?"

She nods, and her gaze drops to my mouth. *Fuck yeah, it does.*

I slide a hand into her hair and lower my mouth to hers. Her hands go to my shoulders, tentatively at first, then with more conviction, pulling me closer as the tension leaves her body. I suck on her bottom lip and she shudders, her nails curling into my shoulder blades. I slant my mouth over hers one last time, taking one more taste before pulling away. "See you in the morning."

Then I walk away, which is really fucking hard. But necessary.

Chapter Fifteen

AVA

I park in the circle drive of the McKinley McMansion and scowl at the house.

I cut the engine and force myself to climb out of the car. It's only a couple of hours. I can get through this.

"Ava!" Jill greets me on the front porch, her blond hair falling gracefully around her shoulders. "I'm so glad you could make it."

"I always do." Internally, I kick myself for that little jab at her daughter. I missed family dinner once, and Dad held it against me for months. Colton rarely bothers, but he and Dad are total oil and vinegar. My stepsister, on the other hand, can get away with missing whenever she chooses, and all is forgiven. Hell, Molly didn't even bother making it to my wedding. Not that I'm still bitter.

Jill wraps her arm around my shoulders and presses a kiss to my forehead. "How are you?"

"I'm good. What about you?"

"I'm great. Molly will be here any minute."

"How exciting!" I squeeze Jill's arm. I might not be excited about Molly's visit, but I am happy for Jill. I know she wishes she could see her daughter more often.

I follow Jill into the house, and the second my feet hit the marble foyer, I'm slammed with memories. My first Christmas here after the divorce, sitting in a corner with Colton and wishing we could have stayed home in our PJs with Mom. My thirteenth birthday party that I only had here because I thought it would impress the cool girls, and then feeling like a fake when it worked and they were so much nicer to me after. Then the eighteen months before college that I lived here and felt like an unwanted guest the entire time. I can't blame them. Jill, Dad, and Molly had been a family of three for seven years before I came along and rocked the boat.

"Too bad Colton can't make it tonight," Jill says over her shoulder. She leads the way into the dining room. "Your father is disappointed, but we understand that Colton's training is his priority right now."

"His priority should be finding a real job," Dad says from the hall.

Jill gives him a cautious smile as he barrels into the dining room and grabs the bottle of wine from the bucket where it's chilling and pours himself a glass. "Motocross is a real job, Nelson. Colton's doing great and has a whole team behind him." She takes the bottle from him and looks at me. "Wine, Ava?"

I nod. Judging by the volume of Dad's voice, I'm already a

few drinks behind. "Sure. Thanks."

She fills my glass to the top—God bless her—and winks at me as she hands it over.

"Have you had your interview for the job in Florida?" Dad asks.

I grimace. I completely forgot that he'd been putting out feelers on my behalf. "I haven't heard anything about it, Dad. Sorry."

He wags his finger at me. "They're calling. You just make sure you're ready."

I still have a job. But there's no need to remind him of that little fact. It'll only make me look ungrateful. "Will do, Dad."

"Hello?" comes a soft voice from the hall. "Mom?"

Jill brightens at the sound of her daughter's voice. "Molly, we're in the dining room!"

I take a long drink from my glass as the click of heels gets closer, bracing myself, but there's not enough room in this glass to drown out the feelings of inadequacy that overwhelm me in my stepsister's presence, and when Molly enters the dining room, I immediately feel like a forgotten part of the scenery.

"How was your flight?" Jill asks, wrapping her daughter in a hug.

"Don't smother the girl, Jill," Dad says. "She's been cooped up on a plane. She needs some space."

"I'm fine," Molly tells Dad. She wraps her arms around Jill and squeezes. "It was good." When she turns her attention on me, her smile is tentative, and I feel a pang of guilt. Molly hasn't come home much in the last five years, but I haven't done my part in keeping in touch either. "Hi, Ava. How are you?"

"Great." I hoist my glass of wine.

Molly chuckles softly. "I could use one of those too."

"Jill, pour the girl some wine," Dad says.

Jill obeys, and Molly takes the glass with the reverence of someone taking sacrament.

Molly is everything I'm not. She's brave and adventurous. She's blond to my dark and bold to my cautious. I know saying that my father always loved her more makes me sound like the whiny little girl who wanted her father's attention all for herself. But sometimes even the ugly things we feel are true, and Dad's affection for Molly always outranked and overpowered his affection for me.

"Have a seat," Jill says. "I'll get dinner from the kitchen."

"Grab another bottle of the '79 from the fridge while you're at it," Dad calls after her, taking his seat at the end of the table.

"May I help, Jill?" I ask.

Molly and I nearly collide, simultaneously filing behind Jill toward the kitchen.

"Girls, sit," Jill says sternly. "You're my guests." She flashes a glance toward my father, who's seated at the end of the table scrolling through something on his phone. For the first time since I've known her, I detect a hint of resentment from her toward my father. *Good for you, Jill.*

"Sit," she says again, and Molly and I obey, taking seats across from each other and sipping at our wine in the awkward silence.

"Still teaching?" Molly asks.

I nod. "Yeah. Still in New York?"

She nods. "Yep."

It takes Jill a couple of trips to get everything on the table. She tucks a couple more bottles of wine into the bucket of ice, then brings out a big bowl of salad and a platter beautifully arranged with breaded chicken breasts and roasted potatoes.

"This looks delicious," I say.

"I'm starving," Molly says. "Thank you, Mom."

Jill beams, and we fill our plates and pass food around the table.

"Molly, what's your announcement?" Dad asks when our plates are full. "We can't wait to hear your good news." He waves toward me. "Maybe it'll inspire Ava to do something with her life."

"I have a great life, Dad," I say.

"Of course you do," Jill says with a smile, then a scowl toward my oblivious father.

Molly cuts her eyes to her mom before looking at Dad. "I . . . I don't have an announcement."

Jill frowns. "But you said . . ."

"I said I needed to *talk* to you about something. There's no announcement."

Jill grimaces. "I'm sorry," she says softly. "I misunderstood. We can talk later. Of course."

"Nonsense. Don't keep us in suspense," Dad says. "What do you need to talk about?"

Molly puts her fork down and draws in a deep breath. "I need a loan. I lost my job, and I'm struggling to keep my apartment."

I can practically hear the tires screeching in my father's head as his fork drops to his plate and he stares at his favorite child. "What do you mean, you lost your job?"

I hold my breath. Dad always wished I could be more

athletic, then he got a daughter who was. He always wished I, his above-average daughter, could excel in school, and then he got a daughter who did. He pushed me to pursue something more practical than theater and literature, and when he married Jill, he got a daughter who did.

All that considered, I sometimes forget that Dad is just as tough on Molly as he is on me—maybe even tougher. She's his shining star.

There's a vulnerability all over her face as she avoids his steely gaze. I can't blame her. It's pretty intense. "We lost funding. There's no work. I'll find something else, but it'll take some time."

"But you already have applications out," he says. She stares blankly back at him. "Résumés, cover letters—that's child's play. You have so much great experience, and the world is your oyster. This shouldn't be an issue."

"I'm working on it." She bows her head and pushes her food around her plate.

My father takes a breath and exhales slowly.

I hate this for her. While I've always hoped for evidence that Molly isn't perfect, I know how it feels to be on the receiving end of Dad's disapproval, and it sucks.

"You have savings, though," my father says. "Money to live on until you find the next job? You always put thirty percent of your pay into savings. I taught you that."

"Dad," she says, exasperation clear in her voice now. "It's not easy for a single woman to live in the city on a non-profit management income. I don't have savings at all, and if I don't want to lose my apartment, I'm going to need some help until I find a new job." She looks to her mother. "I was hoping—"

My father's already shaking his head. "No. We made it very clear to you girls from the beginning that we would help you get where you're going, and then you'd be on your own. We're not going to be those parents who let their children fail over and over again throughout their lives with no consequences. At some point, you have to let the baby bird fly free, and if she falls, she falls."

Jill gasps, and her cheeks flush pink to red as she stares at my father across the table.

"Dad," I say. "That's harsh."

He shifts his gaze to me. "You've been through hard times. Did *you* ask for money after Harrison left you? With all the debt you racked up, I'm sure it would have been easier to ask us to bail you out."

My cheeks heat at that reminder. When I was married to Harrison, he encouraged me to take lavish spa days and go shopping with my friends. He handled the finances, and I had no idea that all those credit card bills were piling up, only getting the minimum payment each month. It was so important to Harrison that it *looked* like we had money to the outside world that he even let me believe it. He "let me" keep that crazy debt after we divorced, too. I wouldn't have felt right about him taking it on, but I couldn't help but resent Harrison's lack of transparency about our financial situation. My whole marriage was a lesson in lies by omission.

"If you did it, so can Molly," Dad says.

My stepsister looks utterly defeated, and I shoot her an apologetic smile. "I'm sure Molly will be fine, but that doesn't mean she doesn't deserve a helping hand. We all need help from time to time."

Dad scowls at me. "What's gotten into you tonight, Ava? My word is final."

I open my mouth, but Jill reaches across the table and brushes my arm with her fingertips. I see the warning in her eyes telling me to let it go for now. I have to grit my teeth to keep from saying more.

"Ava?" Jill says as we're cleaning up the kitchen. Dad retired to his office to take a business call, and Molly excused herself to her old room to shower. "Could I ask you a favor?"

I nod. My stomach's been in knots since dinner, and I would worry that I offended Jill by not eating her cooking, but it seems no one but Dad had much of an appetite. "What's that?"

"You know your father," she says. "I don't expect him to budge on this Molly thing, but I'm going to talk to him after he unwinds tonight."

After he unwinds is Jill's code for *after he has his whiskey*. Not sure whiskey's gonna help. He was already half lit when he went off at the dinner table. "It's nice of you to try," I say. I don't expect him to budge, either. My father doesn't *budge*. It's not in his personality. He makes a decision and he sticks to it. This might be an admirable quality in a businessman, but it's shit in a father.

"Well, if I'm not successful . . ." She looks away. "I have no right to ask this, but would you have money to loan Molly for a while? I have a little, but since your father handles our finances, it'll be tricky to get to it. I'll pay you back just as soon as I can manage."

I bite my tongue. My father doesn't "handle" the finances. He *controls* them. The difference is significant—I'm well aware from experience—and anger on my stepmother's behalf flares in the pit of my belly. But I'm angry for more than her. I'm angry for Molly. I'm angry for *me.*

I don't need to wonder how Dad will react if I'm successful in my plans and he discovers I *intentionally* became a single mom. I already know how he will feel. Tonight wasn't a revelation; it was a reminder.

"How much do you think she needs?" I ask.

"I'll find out, but I'm sure it's just temporary. You know Molly—something always comes around for her. She's never depended on anyone else." She snaps her mouth shut, as if she suddenly realized she just insulted me. I depended on someone else once, and it didn't end well. Then again, maybe she's thinking of how she depends on my dad.

"I could float her a small loan if you think that would help," I say softly. It'll come from my emergency fund, but I know between Jill and Molly, I'll get it back.

She exhales in relief. "I'm sure anything you can spare would make a difference. I'd like her to have a chance to get on her feet without it crushing her spirit. Your father doesn't realize how hard she's had to work to stay afloat these last five years. He doesn't know that she's had to make sacrifices for . . ." She shakes her head and squeezes my hand. "Well, it doesn't matter. I'm sure she'll appreciate your help as much as I do." The stress in Jill's eyes makes me feel like I just stepped off the tilt-a-whirl. She always brought calm to this household, but something's changed. "I'll let you know what your dad says when I ask him to reconsider, but..."

"I know. That's Dad."

She swallows and gives a tight smile. "He's not always easy to love, you know."

None of us are, I think. "He's lucky to have you."

"You don't have to say that," she says softly. She shakes her head and sighs as she squeezes my hand, and I wonder if she truly doesn't see the truth.

Chapter Sixteen

AVA

I let myself into the back of Jackson Brews and go straight to the walk-in cooler in search of Jake's famous "goat balls." I had no appetite at Dad's, but now I'm hungry and stressed, and I want comfort food. I find the breaded bites of fresh goat cheese on a sheet tray at the back of the cooler, slide it out, then head to the deep fryer.

Jake pushes into the kitchen just as I'm dunking the bites in the bubbling oil. He looks at the sheet tray then at me. "Rough night?"

I wrap my arms around my middle. "Nothing a little fried cheese and honey can't fix."

"I've got barbecue bacon donut burgers on the menu tonight." Jake leans against the counter. "Want me to put one together for you?"

I open my mouth to say no, but then shrug. "That actually sounds amazing."

He throws a patty on the grill next to me and studies me as it fries. "Do you want to talk about it?"

"About how my dad is a dick and probably an alcoholic, or about how I'm thirty years old and still can't reconcile my desperate need for approval from a selfish prick?" I pull the basket out of the frying oil and shake it.

Jake's expression softens. "Both? Either?"

"No thanks. Maybe another time. Tonight, I just want to eat my feelings, if that's okay."

He hesitates a beat then nods. "Plate of feelings, coming right up."

Jake has many specialties, but this Saturday night menu item is a local favorite—a bacon cheeseburger with frizzled onions and barbecue sauce, served on fresh glazed donuts from Ooh La La! Tourists always say it sounds gross, but then they order it anyway, too curious to pass, and always clean their plate.

I put my goat balls in a wax-paper-lined basket and drizzle them with locally sourced honey—the closest thing this whole kitchen has to "health food." Next to me, Jake puts together my burger, and my panic dissipates in the shadow of his calm. He grounds me. Always has. Even when he was a ten-year-old boy who made fun of my pigtails, he always knew what to say—or not say—when I was upset.

The day my Dad moved out, I held my chin high all evening. I had to put on a strong face for my mom, who was devastated. She went to bed early that night, emotionally exhausted. After she fell asleep, I snuck outside and climbed into the tree fort in

Jake's backyard. I was crying when Jake found me there, but he didn't say anything about my tears. He sat cross-legged on the plywood floor beside me and handed me a box of those things that snap when you throw them at the ground. We didn't say a word to each other, just sat in the fort and tossed them at the floor.

He knew exactly what I needed then, and has so many times after.

"Cindy's got the front covered," he says when he plates my burger. "Want to eat this in my office?"

I nod, grateful that he understands I'm not up for chatting it up with the barflies tonight. "I'm going to grab a water from the cooler. Want one?"

"Sure."

I get the bottles, and Jake carries my burger to his office. The space is utilitarian—a couple of desks, a computer for bookkeeping, and two tall filing cabinets. Jake keeps it meticulously organized, and the surfaces are clean and clear of the miscellany that clutters my home office.

I pull a chair up to his desk, and he sits on the opposite side, propping his chin on his fists and watching me.

"Do you want to share this with me?" I ask.

He shakes his head. "I already ate."

I look down at my food, then up at him. "Why are you staring? Did you poison the food or something?"

He shakes his head. "No, it's just that you rarely eat my cooking anymore. I thought maybe you'd grown an aversion."

I snort. "I wasn't blessed with your wicked-fast metabolism, so I *can't* eat your food very often." I lift the donut burger to my lips and take a bite. My eyes close as I chew and swallow. It's the perfect combination of sweet and salty. "Dear God, Ellie's right."

Jake frowns as he brings his water bottle to his lips. "About what?"

I grin. "She says you put the *come* in *comfort food*."

He chokes on his water. "Really now?"

"It's orgasmic," I say around another bite. Because *so good*. Swallowing, I nod. "I think she's right. In fact, we don't need to be awkward about having sex together, because you've already cooked for me. There's no sex act in existence that's better than your calorie-laden pub food."

"That sounds like a challenge."

"It's not a challenge. It's a fact." I shrug. "I'm sorry if that hurts your ego, but the food is just that good." Leaning across the desk, I hold the burger up to his mouth. "Tell me you don't think so."

He holds my gaze as he takes a bite, catching my fingers lightly between his teeth before he pulls back.

A flash of heat whips through my belly, and I can't take my eyes off him as he chews—the way his jaw works and the movement in his throat as he swallows.

I'm totally lusting after my best friend.

He flipped some switch in me last night, and now I'm seeing him with different eyes. That makes me nervous as hell. I never want Jake to fully understand how bad I am at sex, but if we keep heading down this road, he's going to. It's not that I don't know what to do. I have the mechanics down, *thank you very much*. I just struggle to stay out of my own head. I can't give myself fully to the moment—as I demonstrated so awkwardly last night.

I'm still holding the burger between us when he dips his head again, but instead of having another bite, he takes the burger from my hand and puts it on the plate. He holds my hand in his and draws my index finger into his mouth.

I gasp as he swirls his tongue around it and sucks hard. "Jake."

"Yeah?" He moves on to the next finger, and I hear my ragged inhale, because *hell*, that's hot. My insides are melting, and all my blood is in the fast lane to a single destination between my legs. I shift in my seat and squeeze my thighs together. "You have donut glaze all over your fingers," he says, as if this explains what he's doing to me. As if it's completely normal. As if he sucks sugar off my fingers all the time.

"Levi and Colton are racing in Detroit next weekend," he says. "Do you want to go with me? Watch the race? Go to dinner? Stay in the city overnight?"

"Yeah." I nod. But I'm not thinking about the race. I'm thinking about the scrape of his teeth on my fingertips. I'm thinking about a hotel room with Jake. I'm thinking of the words he whispered like an oath before leaving my house last night.

When I'm finally inside you, it'll be because you want me there, because you're begging to have me there.

I'll never again be able to take a bite of a burger without thinking about sex. "Will we . . . share a room?" Will we have sex? Will I kill the mood by panicking again?

"Is that okay with you?" He turns my hand and nibbles on my knuckles, the scrape of teeth followed by the hot tip of his tongue.

"Yeah, sure, why not? I mean, it's not a big deal, and it might be convenient to be in the same room when we . . . I mean, if we . . . I mean, it works, right? I just need to figure out what to pack and stuff. I never know what to wear to those things." *Dear Lord, make me stop talking.*

He looks me over, a smirk tugging at one side of his mouth as he drags his gaze down the length of me, as if he has x-ray vision and can see me through the desk and my clothes. "Why don't you wear those shorts you wear to garden?"

"My old cutoffs?"

He lifts his eyes to mine and gives a cocky nod. "Yeah. I *really* like those."

My cheeks heat. Jake and I don't say stuff like that to each other. There aren't moments in our relationship when he flirts with me or speaks in innuendo. That's not the kind of relationship we have. Then again, he's never sucked on my fingers before tonight either, and I'm not complaining about that, am I? "I'm not wearing my cutoffs in public."

Smiling, he opens my palm and presses a kiss right in the center—first lips, then the briefest touch of his tongue. My back arches. I want to catapult myself out of this seat and onto his lap. I want to claim all the dirty promises he's making with his lips and tongue.

"So those are only for me to enjoy when we're alone together?" he asks.

I blink at him. Straddling his lap would be heaven. I want the hard length of him pressed between my legs and his mouth . . . *What has gotten into me?* "What?"

"The cutoffs?" He shakes his head slowly. "You're so fucking cute when you blush. You know that?" He puts my hand down and stands. "But Cindy's going to kill me if I leave her out there alone much longer." He winks at me, then turns the knob to open the office door.

Another woman might let him leave then touch herself to relieve this pulsing ache between her legs. Another woman might tell him not to go and climb him like a tree. Another woman might not instantly ruin the moment with worry.

I bolt up from my chair and chase him out of the office. "You don't have to do this, you know."

He stops and turns in the middle of the kitchen. "Do what?"

I bite my lip and look away. "I don't know. Flirt with me, I guess. Seduce me with . . ." I swallow, a delicious chill running up my spine with the thought of his hot mouth on my skin. Are knuckles an erogenous zone? Because I'm pretty sure Jake just made them into one. "With your mouth. You don't have to. You're doing me a favor. It's not like I expect you to . . ."

"Because you have *lube*?"

My jaw drops, and I swing my gaze back to him and glare. "Oh my God, if you say that word one more time, I'll kill you."

He stalks toward me, something different in his eyes. Something darker and more intent than the playful Jake who sucked my fingers, and I back up until my legs hit the cold stainless steel of the walk-in cooler. He puts a hand on either side of my head and leans in, his body close to mine. Our gazes tangle for long, silent beats before he finally speaks. "I don't *have to* seduce you, or you don't want me to?"

I lick my lips. My heart is pounding, my body asking for so much more than I should ever want from Jake. "I don't think we need to over-complicate this."

His gaze drops to my lips. "Does it make you uncomfortable when I'm close to you?"

I swallow. "A little."

"Why is that, Ava?" He dips his head, and his mouth is so close to mine that speaking or moving at all feels intimate. "I know you feel this. I see it in your eyes." He tilts his head to the side and runs the bridge of his nose along the column of my neck. "In the flush of your skin," he whispers in my ear. "I hear it in the hitch of your breath. And before you threw the brakes on your own pleasure last night, I could *feel* it in the arch of your back, and the way your hips moved under me like you wanted to rub against me."

My eyes float closed. His voice is low and husky, and I want more of his words so much right now. "We're friends, Jake."

"We've always been friends. That's never going to change. But for the next few months, I'm going to be more than that, so it's time for you to get used to the idea. I'm going to do things to you that are a hell of a lot more pleasurable than a fucking burger can ever be. Don't fight it." He nips at my neck and sucks. When I release a soft cry, he groans into my ear. "*Christ.* You're going to be my undoing, Ava."

I'm not sure what he means by that, and I'm in no position to ask. If I weren't leaning against the cooler, I'm pretty sure I'd be in a puddle on the floor.

He backs up, and there's so much heat in his eyes that I don't know if I should shut this down before we do something we regret or drag him back into his office and shut the door. I'm walking on a dangerous precipice, and I'm terrified. I like the earth steady and solid beneath my feet, but Jake's offering the wind in my hair, the thrill of the fall.

His tongue touches his bottom lip as he gives me a final once-over. Then he disappears through the swinging door. My heart is hammering, and my skin is tingling, and I'm not even sure what the hell just happened.

JAKE

I push out of the kitchen and head straight to the taps. I need a drink, and water isn't going to cut it. *Jesus.* I could get off on nothing more than the little sounds Ava made when I sucked on her fingers, and my dick aches from the way her eyes went dark and her lips parted. I've never been short on fantasies when it came to Ava, but that little interlude just added a few dozen images to the list. And then she fucking ruined it by chasing after me to tell me I didn't need to seduce her. As if I'm just the stud who can show up a couple of times a week, get off inside her, and walk away.

Fuck that.

I pour myself a snifter of our imperial stout and drain half of it before turning back to the bar to play catch-up. My steps falter as I spot a beautiful blonde. She hops off her stool immediately when she sees me. "Jake! Oh my God! It's so good to see you!"

"Molly." I swallow, take a breath, and paste on a smile. Fuck, I'm rock hard in my jeans from touching Ava and then her stepsister suddenly appears, like fate is trying to remind me that I fucked up once, and that I lost the right to ever make Ava mine. "How are you?"

"I'm good." She stops, squeezes her eyes shut, and shakes her head. "That's bullshit. Sorry. You deserve better than that. I'm not good. My stepdad's an ass, my mom is a doormat, and my life's a mess."

"Sounds like not much has changed since last time we talked." I grimace the second the words leave my mouth. I really, really don't want to talk about *last time*. In fact, I'd rather we pretended last time didn't exist. "How long has it been?" I ask softly, but I know the answer. The last time I saw Molly McKinley was the night I found out Ava was engaged. The night I made the most epic mistake of my life.

"Almost five years."

"That's a while. I must have scared you off." I try to smile, but guilt makes my expression waver.

"I've come home a couple of times but never stayed long." She grabs her pint glass off the bar and hoists it in the air. "But now that I know the beer is as good as I remembered, I'll be sure to swing by next time I'm forced to visit." She looks me over slowly, and when she lifts her gaze back to meet mine, her pink lips are stretched into a smile. "I wonder if anything else is as good as I remember . . ."

Chapter SEVENTEEN

AVA

I clean up the remains of my dinner to give myself a chance to steady my breathing. I'm not ready to face Jake yet, so I sit in his office to scroll through my phone. If I were to walk out there right now, I'm pretty sure everyone who looked at me would know I have sex on the brain.

Sex with Jake.

Shit. Better not to think about it too much. Even if I want to. Even if I can't stop . . .

I'm scrolling through Instagram—something mindless to distract me—when my phone rings in my hand. "Hello?"

"May I speak with Ava McKinley, please?"

"This is she." My whole body tenses at the woman's use of my full name. Because this is such a small town, a parent of a student will occasionally get my phone number and call to yell at me for their child's grade—as if their child played no part in it—and after the Billy Joel Christianson incident on Friday, I should've known better than to answer a call from an unknown number.

"Ava! I'm so glad I reached you. My name's Penelope Grimly. I'm calling from Seaside Community Schools."

"Oh!" Not what I expected. But still awkward. "Hi?"

"Is this an okay time for you?"

"Um, I guess?" I shake my head. I didn't think my dad was lying about this, but I thought maybe he was overly confident. "I'm not busy right now."

"I promise to keep it short!" She laughs easily. "I hope you'll forgive me for calling you unannounced on a Saturday night. Martha passed your information on to me over dinner, and I was so excited to reach out to you about the opportunity we have here. I wanted to call as soon as possible." She makes a squeaking noise, as if she's putting the brakes on her own little speech. "Martha said you're in the market for a new job. She said she wouldn't forgive me if you took another position before we had a chance to make an offer."

"An offer?" I'm not only unprepared for this phone call, my mind's not right. I'm feeling warm and fuzzy from Jake's words in my ear, his mouth on my skin, and I'm on the phone with Penelope from Seaside Community Schools. *Good old Ava, always making her dad proud.*

"Nothing is definitive yet." Penelope gives another squeaky laugh. "Martha shared your résumé with me. She told me about your background and your experience with the children's theater in Jackson Harbor. You've built an amazing program there, and I'm so excited that you're considering joining us. I want to get the ball rolling on your application process."

I consider putting her off and explaining that there's been a misunderstanding, that, as far as I know, I still have a job next fall. But then I think about that news making its way back to my father. It's probably best that I play along. "Thank you for calling, Penelope—may I call you Penelope?"

"Yes, please do, thank you!" Her tone of voice isn't unlike that of a teenager receiving a promise ring from her first boyfriend. Either Penelope is totally impressed by what she knows about me or she's a great actress. Or maybe it's neither and she's just half squeaky toy. "Martha tells me that your mother lives near us. Is that true?"

"She's a professor at Pensacola State College."

"That's not far from Seaside at all! Less than an hour, depending on traffic. Does she like it down here?"

I smile when thinking of my mother in Florida—the freckles covering her cheekbones, her magnetic draw to the beach, the way she always tilts her face toward the sun. Mom was never overtly unhappy in Jackson Harbor, but she radiates joy in her new home. "She's been there for thirteen years, so I think it's safe to say she's a fan. It's hard to come back to snowy Michigan when you're used to the sunshine."

"Yes, I imagine. Most people who move down here can't imagine leaving, and Seaside is particularly close to my heart. I hope to get you down here for a visit soon so you can fall in love too."

Wow. What kind of favor do Dad's friends owe him? "I . . . Thanks."

"Listen, I don't want to keep you, so I'll cut to the chase. May

I email you some pertinent details? You can look them over and then we can schedule a call at a time that works for you."

"That sounds good. Thank you, Penelope." I give her my email address—curious about the position now, despite myself. I don't plan on leaving Jackson Harbor if I can help it, but Dad's right. It's always good to have a backup plan, and after my meeting with Mr. Mooney yesterday, I'd be lying if I said I felt as secure in my job today as I did the night of our date, when he told me I shouldn't worry.

I end the call with Penelope and shoot Dad a quick message to let him know she called and seems enthusiastic about me. I feel a twinge of embarrassment as I send the text—thirty years old and still trying to make my daddy proud. I slide my phone back into my purse.

My nerves feel frazzled and my heart is racing, and I barely did any talking. God save me if I actually have to go out on the job market and do interviews.

It's already after nine, and I want to get home early tonight, so I head out front to say goodbye to Jake. When I push out from the kitchen, I'm greeted with the sight of Jake standing across from Molly, his eyes wide as she chatters on about something.

Jackson Brews isn't *mine*. It'll never be mine. But I've worked here part-time since my divorce and feel a little ownership of the place as a result. So when I see my perfect stepsister sitting in the middle of a space I consider to be so completely *my world*, talking to *my Jake*, it throws me off balance.

Jake looks as if he's been knocked off balance too, but in a different way. Jealousy twists my gut. I'm in the simple black dress and flats I wore to dinner at Dad's, but Molly looks like she just stepped out of a fashion magazine. Her pink shirt is perfect for her fair complexion, and the low cut shows off her collarbone and the swell of her abundant cleavage—the only place you need to look to know Molly and I share no DNA. Her makeup is perfect, her hair a silky sheet of blond.

Jake practically jumps when he sees me, and I wonder with an acute pinch in my chest if he's regretting the things he said to me in the kitchen. In this moment, I forget what a dick my father was to her. In this moment, with Jake's attention swinging so quickly—magnetically?—back to my stepsister, I hate her a little.

It's not Molly's fault that she's practically perfect in every way, but it's pretty tough not to resent all that. Couldn't she just be pretty *or* smart? Vivacious *or* athletic? Why did she have to be everything? And why did I have to fall so damn short?

I shouldn't be jealous here. This is Jake. It's fine if he's attracted to Molly. What do I care?

Except that he's going to father your child. Except that he just whispered dirty promises in your ear so hot that your belly is still a little weird and fluttery.

"Molly," I say, trying to be a bigger person than I want to be. I let the kitchen door swing closed behind me and cross to where Molly's sitting so only the wooden bar top is between us. "Hey!" The word is stretched thin, but the smile she tosses my way tells me she doesn't notice.

"Ava, I was just telling Jake how awful dinner was. After you left, Dad tried to lecture me again and I blew up. We got in an awful fight and then he and Mom started fighting." She shudders. "I needed a drink." She shakes her head. "What a day it's been."

"I'm sorry about that." *There you go, Ava. Grab hold of that empathy you were feeling earlier.* "Dad's expectations can be impossible."

"It's my fault," she says. "I only agreed to visit because I thought it would be better to ask the favor in person, but I never should have told Mom I had something I needed to talk about. I should've known she would assume it was good news."

I swallow and shrug. "In her defense, it almost always is with you."

She rolls her eyes. "Yeah, right. I think I've given Mom more than a few gray hairs. I'm surprised Dad doesn't send me her salon bills."

"Dad won't budge on the loan, will he?" I ask, though I already know the answer.

She shakes her head. "I realize how bad this is to say when I'm here wasting money on alcohol, and I'm about to waste *more* money on a hotel when I'm officially a couple of strokes of bad luck away from being homeless."

"Homeless?" Jake's been standing by, a silent observer, but his eyebrows shoot into his hairline at this. "Shit. What happened?"

Molly waves a hand. "Lost my job. Can't find a new one—at least nothing that'll cover my rent in Brooklyn—and I'm running out of time."

"Can't you just move home for a while?" Jake asks.

I wince, but Molly gapes at him. "You want me to move back to Jackson Harbor?"

He shrugs. "You wouldn't be homeless."

I drag my bottom lip through my teeth. "He's right."

"Nope," Molly said. "It's not an option. I'm a New Yorker. You can take the girl out of the city, yada, yada, yada." She groans.

"I thought your parents were supposed to help when you were having hard times, but I should've known Dad would be all about the tough love."

"You can borrow some money from me," I say. Her eyes go wide, and Jake looks shocked too, but hell, I'm competitive with my stepsister, not hateful. "Jill said she'd figure out a way to pay me back. It's no big deal."

Molly squeezes her fists together and presses them to her mouth. "Oh my God! You are so amazing! Ava! What did I do to deserve you?" Her eyes well with tears, and my cheeks heat. Her words feel good, even if I don't deserve them. Her warm smile is full of gratitude and reminds me—yet again—that our so-called rivalry is one-sided.

"And you don't need to get a hotel room. You can stay at my place while you're in town." I practically throw a hand over my mouth, because I cannot believe the words that just came out of there. Maybe it's penance for years of unfair resentment.

"Get out!" Molly's blue eyes are bright. More gratitude I don't deserve. "Ava, you are seriously the best."

I wave a hand. "It's nothing. I have the room." I turn to Jake, really getting into my role as the good sister now. "You have business contacts in New York, don't you? Any chance you and Brayden could help Molly out?"

Jake blinks at me, then nods slowly. "I might have a lead on a job in the city," he says, turning to Molly. "I can get some details if you're interested."

"Of course!" She pumps a fist in the air. "Way to turn a girl's day around, you two!"

Jake's gaze ping-pongs between us. "I think this could work

out great, actually."

I force a smile. "Molly, I'm going to head home. Are you about ready?"

She tilts her head to the side. "I don't want to leave yet. Let's have a couple of drinks and hang out."

I shake my head. "I need some downtime. It's been a crazy week, but you can stay and I'll come get you later."

"No, no." Molly shakes her head vehemently. "I'm not going to drag you back out if you want to go home. If you give me the address, I'll just meet you at your place later. I'll get an Uber."

"Don't worry about it," Jake says, turning to me. "I can drive her home."

Molly beams. "We can catch up! That's a great plan. Love. It."

"I . . . Thanks?" Jake was never mean about Molly, never hated on her, but he always understood my resentment. When did they become *buddies*?

I'm irritated with my own irrational jealousy. I'm being an idiot.

"I'll see you tomorrow?" Jake asks me softly, and when I stare at him blankly, he says, "For the baby shower?"

"Oh, right! That's tomorrow." I nod. Mother Teresa in my guest room and Harrison's baby shower all in one day. It's gonna be a doozy. "Sure. Yeah, I'll see you then."

"I'll pick you up at noon."

"Okay." I stare at him for a beat, struggling with the possessiveness I've felt ever since I stepped out of the kitchen and saw him talking to my stepsister. *I don't want you to drive Molly home. I want you to kiss me like you did last night, but I want you to do it right here in front of everyone.*

He must not hear my telepathic plea, because he's already moved on, helping Cindy fill a tray with half a dozen of our popular house brew flights.

"Night," I say softly.

"Good night," Molly calls as I leave, and I know without a doubt she'd never ruin a perfect kiss by telling the guy she had lube.

JAKE

When Molly asked for her third beer, I decided it was time to take her home before tipsy turned into drunk. Before her little touches—on my wrist, my biceps, the back of my shoulder—turned into . . . more.

I knew Ava was dying to get out of there, so I offered to drive Molly home. Now that we're alone together in my car, I kind of regret it. The night is dark—the stars and sliver of moon covered by a thick sheet of clouds—and the car is too small. My mistakes weigh heavily on my tongue, keeping me from having the conversation I need to use this time for.

"You still smell good, you know that?" Molly says, turning in her seat and staring at me.

"Molly . . ."

She sighs. "Sorry. A girl can hope, right?"

I keep one hand on the wheel and use the other to squeeze the back of my neck. "Do you have any sales experience?" *Just pretend it never happened, and everything will be fine.*

"My background is in non-profit fundraising, which is the toughest kind of sales."

I nod and swallow. "Jackson Brews needs a regional sales rep in the northeast. I think you could be good at it if you were interested. I'm meeting with a few people when I go out there next month, but if you wanted, you and Brayden and I could sit down while you're in town."

"Like, an interview?"

I nod, my eyes on the road and avoiding hers, which I've felt glued to me since she got in the car. "Yeah."

"Sure. Thanks. I think . . . That would be awesome. I'm really grateful, Jake."

"No problem. I hope it works out." I flash her a smile.

She bites her bottom lip and trails her index finger down my arm. "Was there any other reason you wanted to drive me home?"

Shit. "Molly, I'm sorry if I gave you the wrong—"

Pulling away, she takes a deep breath and rolls her head to face the window. "Please don't. Don't give me that speech. It's embarrassing."

I pull into Ava's drive and cut the engine. The house is dark except for the single porch light.

"You're still in love with her?" she asks softly.

There's a big list of people I don't want to have this conversation with, and Molly is somewhere near the top.

"Does something like that usually change?" My voice cracks—my insecurities peeking out into the darkness.

"She rejected you and married someone else. For most guys,

that would do the trick. Especially after five years."

"She's not married now."

Molly squeezes my shoulder, and the dome light comes on as she opens her door. "Yeah. And you're not most guys. Night, Jake."

Chapter EIGHTEEN

JAKE
Five years ago . . .

She's marrying Harrison. She's marrying Harrison, and she doesn't want me.

I'm a mess. All I can do is repeat the ugly truth to myself again and again until rejection sits in my stomach like an undetonated bomb. I feel it there—a heavy obstruction ticking ominously with every second since Ava asked me to leave. At any moment, it'll explode and tear me to bits.

I do what any grown man does when faced with heartache and rejection. I go to the bar with the intent of getting as shitfaced as possible. I slide onto a stool, wave to Cindy, and order a beer and three shots of whiskey.

"You're not kidding around tonight, are you?"

I've been so wrapped in my own world, my thoughts racing at a hundred miles per hour, that I didn't even realize someone took the barstool beside me. It's Molly, Ava's stepsister. Her platinum-blond hair is down around her shoulders, her big blue eyes dancing with amusement.

"Hey, Molly," I say. Cindy slides my drinks in front of me.

"Let me guess," Molly says. "A girl has you twisted in knots, and you're trying to forget her."

"Wow. You're a fucking psychic," I mutter. I throw back the first shot and wince. I'm a beer guy more than a liquor guy, and that shit's intense.

"Do you want to talk about it?" she asks.

"Ava's engaged."

"I heard that."

I try to laugh and produce nothing more than a few pathetic puffs of air. "I'm not handling the news very well." I'm surprised to hear myself say it—surprised I say anything at all. I didn't come here intending to talk about my problems with anyone, let alone Molly, who's practically Ava's nemesis. The girls get along, but sharing a father—step or otherwise—they've always been incredibly competitive with each other. It's a competition Ava's sure she loses again and again, but I've never believed that.

"Are you going to tell her how you feel?" Molly asks.

"Already did." I take the next shot, and this time the trail of fire into my stomach feels great. If I have to feel the *tick, tick, tick* of the bomb lodged there, I'll drown it in booze. "I told her I loved her." The words are a dull, serrated blade scrubbing down the center of my heart. "She did *not* appreciate me sharing that information."

"Jake." Molly curls her hand around my forearm and squeezes. "I'm sorry. I can see how you feel about her, but maybe it's better this way. Who knows if it would have even worked out between you two? And this way, you won't ruin your friendship."

"I think that ship's sailed." I take a breath. "I'm pretty sure I ruined my friendship the moment I decided to kiss her."

She draws in a breath. "You kissed her," she says softly. "Wow."

"Too little, too late," I mutter.

"She'll get over it."

I shrug, as if I don't give a shit, and then take the next shot, proving I clearly do.

"Aren't you going to ask what problems *I'm* trying to drink away?" Her lips twist into a smirk.

"I wasn't planning on it." I'm acting like a dick because I'm in a dick mood.

Molly doesn't seem to mind. "Right. Well, I'm going to tell you anyway because no one else wants to hear it." She pauses a beat and then meets my eyes. "My father—stepfather, whatever—is an asshole who tries to control my life, and my mother's a doormat. I'm terrified of starting grad school in New York. Everything feels like it's kind of . . . falling apart, and I really just want to be close to my mom right now, but I can't because I can't tolerate my stepfather."

"He is a dick, but Ava said he adores you."

She tenses and stares at her drink, her jaw tight. "I wish he didn't *adore* me. He's the whole reason I almost killed myself to finish undergrad in three years instead of four—always pushing, pushing, pushing. And when I pushed back . . ." She turns to me and shakes her head. "Whatever. It's fine. I'm being a coward."

"You're not." I sigh. "And what you're feeling is normal. Everyone gets homesick. You're going to grad school for a reason, right?"

"Yeah, to impress my father."

"Ride it out. You can always come home."

She tilts her head to the side and smiles at me. "I wish I were like Ava and wasn't afraid to tell him what I want. She doesn't let him rule her life."

"Doesn't she? Isn't that why she's marrying Harrison?" Suddenly, I wish I were a smoker. Going outside and pulling poison into my lungs sounds like a fucking great time at the moment.

She shrugs. "I think she loves Harrison. But if she cared what Dad thought, she never would have majored in drama or stayed in Jackson Harbor. He wanted her to be an engineer." She laughs and shakes her head. "Man, the fights they had her senior year of high school . . . He shouted, and she froze him out. I envied her so much."

"If it makes you feel any better, I'm pretty sure she envies you too." I wave to Cindy again. "Two more shots," I say, and when Cindy slides them onto the bar top in front of me, I offer one to Molly. "To forgetting," I say, tapping my shot glass against hers.

"Are you just being nice to me to spite my sister?"

"Not at all." I've never been mean to Molly, but I've always kind of given her the cold shoulder in a show of solidarity to Ava. But why should I do anything for Ava anymore?

She doesn't want you.

"Okay, then," Molly says, swaying a little on her stool. "I have a confession to make."

"What's that?"

"When I was in high school, I had the biggest crush on you."

I blink at her. Molly was what you would call a "cool girl" in high school. She was a cheerleader and on the debate team. She was a straight-A student and always welcome in the "in" crowd. She was also four years behind me and my best friend's brat little sister.

"You did not," I say. "You were a baby when I was in high school."

She dips her head and looks up at me through her lashes, a crooked smile pulling on one corner of her mouth. "I did, Jake. I thought you were hilarious and so freaking cute. And then you went to college and . . ." She skims her gaze over me slowly as she shakes her head. "Well, it only got better from there."

"Oh, so now the truth comes out. You liked me after I started working out."

"And before," she says.

I laugh softly. "My ego needed that tonight, so thanks."

"Ava's crazy for not wanting you." She drags her bottom lip between her teeth. "If I were her, I'd at least give it a shot." She taps on my shoulder. "One. Wild. Night."

I scan her face—pretty blue eyes, rosy cheeks, and parted pink lips. "Are you coming on to me, Molly?"

Her pink cheeks flame brighter. "Do you want me to?"

Ava calls Molly *Mother Teresa*, but when Molly was at Jackson Harbor High School, the guys around here had a different nickname for her. Something much less innocuous. I wonder if Ava ever knew they called her stepsister *Blow Job Molly*.

She shakes her head and averts her eyes. "Of course you don't."

Hell. "We've been drinking, and considering my seriously

bruised ego, I'm not sure I can trust my judgment right now."

She swallows, and her gaze drops to my mouth. "I could never tell you how I felt because you were Ava's, but if she knows how you feel . . . if she pushed you away anyway . . ." She lifts her eyes to meet mine. "I'm not the evil stepsister for telling you now, am I?"

"You leave tomorrow."

She nods. "I do. So maybe we should make the most of tonight."

I just stare at her, at a loss for words. Molly is sweet and smart. Despite her sketchy reputation in high school, everyone wanted her. She's fucking beautiful, and she's . . . *not Ava.*

Silence stretches between us, as if she's waiting for me to make my move or say my piece. When I don't, she releases a puff of air and slides off the stool and heads to the bathroom.

"Molly," I call after her.

She holds up a hand, signaling for me to leave her alone. I feel like a world-class dick. I know too well how it feels to be rejected by someone you've been in love with for years. It's not a feeling I'd wish on anyone. And, hell, I'm only pushing Molly away because I don't want to betray Ava. How ridiculous. I can't betray a woman who isn't mine and doesn't want to be.

Molly disappears into the bathroom, and long minutes pass as I stare at the door waiting for her to emerge.

"Shit," I mutter. She's not coming back. Because I'm an asshole who just made her feel shitty. I head across the bar and down the hall to knock on the door to the women's restroom. "Molly?"

No response.

I knock again. "Molly, I'm sorry."

When she emerges, her eyes are wet with tears, her chin held high. "Sorry about what? You didn't do anything wrong."

I don't know what makes me do it. Guilt? Desire? Loneliness? But I slide a hand into her silky blond hair and lower my mouth to hers.

She gasps against my lips. "Jake . . ."

I kiss her. I kiss her with all of the emotions I've had bottled up all day. Hope. Fear. Disappointment. Heartache—so much fucking heartache. And when she kisses me back, it feels *good*. For once, I'm not alone. For once, I'm not being pushed aside as just a friend. For once, I'm needed as desperately as I need Ava.

The whiskey is hot in my blood and her hands are crazy all over me, and when someone clears his throat trying to get past us, I push her against the wall and double down on this mistake.

There's more kissing. In the back hall. In the alley. More booze and laughter. Then we eventually stumble up to my apartment above the bar.

The next thing I remember, the sun is pouring in my bedroom window. I bolt upright, dread crawling over my skin like a thousand invisible bugs. Molly is curled into the sheets beside me. She's naked, judging by her bare shoulders and the way the sheet's draped across her. One slim arm is on top of the covers and reaching in my direction.

I kissed Molly. I remember kissing her. And I remember more alcohol. Flirting. I have flashes of being outside the bar, holding her against the brick as her hands roamed all over me. And after that? After that, everything gets blurry. Flashes of bare skin, roaming hands, clothes thrown to the floor. *Fuck*.

After years of wanting Ava and having her fail to see me as

anything but a friend, it felt good to have Molly's hands on me. I couldn't have Ava, but the stepsister she's always believed was so much better than her threw herself at me. I knew it was sick and twisted, but somewhere in my petty, self-pitying mind, it actually made me feel better about myself. A *fuck you* to the universe. *To Ava.*

At least, that's what I thought four shots and a couple of beers in. This morning, nothing is better. Everything is worse. Molly's blond hair lies across her cheek, her sooty black lashes making her look like something out of a photoshoot.

I want to get out of here before she wakes up, maybe leave her a note that says, *Let's pretend this never happened.* But I also want to refrain from being the world's biggest dickhead. I can't have it both ways.

"Hey." She's awake, blinking the sleep from her eyes as she takes me in. "You look like you've seen a ghost. Are you okay?"

Not okay. What the fuck did I do, and how many times did I do it? "I'm fine."

She scrapes her fingers down my chest and smiles. "Last night was . . . wow."

I drag a hand through my hair. There's no way I'm getting out of this without being the asshole. "Molly, you're amazing. You're gorgeous and sweet, but last night . . . I'm so sorry."

"Whoa . . ." She sits up, clutching the sheet to her chest. "Hey, save me the speech, okay?" Her face goes stark with disgust. "I leave today. You don't need to worry about me clinging to you or . . ." She looks down to her lap before bringing her eyes back up to meet mine. "I won't tell Ava."

Those words flood me with relief. I don't want them to matter.

I don't want Ava or anything she thinks to matter, but that doesn't change that it does. What happened last night would make Ava hate me. She'd be angry. Maybe even refuse to speak to me again.

Yesterday I was so sure my relationship with Ava was over on every level. When I walked out of her apartment, I thought I was walking away from her. I was sure I couldn't continue to be her friend when I wanted so much more. But this morning, in the light of this stupid-ass mistake, I realize more than ever that I don't want to lose her.

Terror grips my stomach. Loving Ava doesn't mean all or nothing. It means I'll take her in my life however I can get her. Even if it kills me.

"Molly . . ."

She puts one hand on my chest, holding her sheet in place with the other. "Last night was a bit of a dream for me. My only regret is my timing. If I'd told you how I felt before she rejected you, this could have been about us instead of about her." She shakes her head. "But then, this probably wouldn't have happened at all, would it?"

I search her face and try to imagine how I would have responded if she'd come on to me months ago. Or years.

She's probably right. Without a broken heart, I wouldn't have touched her.

"I'm leaving." She says it with more conviction now, and I'm struck by how beautiful she is. What guy wouldn't feel lucky to wake up with her in his bed? What guy wouldn't trip over himself to try to have a relationship with someone like Molly?

A guy who's in love with someone else.

"Could you leave the room so I can get dressed?" She

looks away. "I know that sounds stupid after last night, but I'm feeling . . ."

"No, I get it." I nod, climb off the bed, and grab my jeans from the floor.

She keeps her gaze on the wall the whole time I dress. Only when I reach the door does she stop me.

"Jake?"

I turn, and she studies me for a beat.

"My sister's an idiot."

I shrug. "Maybe I'm the idiot." An idiot for wanting what I can't have. An idiot for ruining any chance at it ever happening in the future.

Chapter NINETEEN

AVA
Present day...

"Where *the fuck* is Jake Jackson?" The front door clangs against the wall as Colton storms into the house.

I push aside the stack of papers I'm grading to shake my head at my brother. His face is red, his eyes are blazing, and his hands are in fists at his sides. When he sees me on the couch, his shoulders drop a little from where they were bunched around his ears.

"Where is he?" He goes to my bedroom door and reaches for the handle.

"Have you checked his apartment?" I ask wryly. In her chair across the living room, Molly folds her legs under her as if she's settling in to watch the show. Seriously, I don't want Colton to beat up Jake, but Colton gets like this all the time. He's a drama queen who's riled up by the stupidest things. Jake probably said

Levi was a better racer than Colt or something equally innocuous.

He spins on his heel and turns to the kitchen. "Don't try to protect him. Where is that motherfucker?"

I look at my watch and shrug. He's probably on his way to Brayden's for brunch, but considering Colton has murder in his eyes, I'll just keep that information to myself.

Molly clears her throat. "He hasn't been here since he dropped me off last night."

Colton freezes at the sound of her voice. Turning slowly, he blinks at her. "Molly."

She smiles. "Hey, Colton. What's up?"

He blows out a puff of air. "*You* were out with Jake last night? Who does this son of a bitch think he is, messing with you both?"

Molly laughs. "The only place Jake Jackson *messed* with me last night was in my dreams." Colton and I both stare at her, and she shrugs. "He's hot and sweet and gorgeous and smart and . . ." She turns up her palms. "I can't be held responsible for the images my subconscious provides while I'm sleeping."

Colton grumbles something under his breath, but I'm too busy processing completely irrational jealousy to make it out. He turns to me. "I want to punch him."

"I noticed." I take a sip of my coffee. "Is there a reason you're ready to kill my best friend?"

He glares at me. "You know why."

I shake my head. "Nope. I really don't."

"Jake talked you into sleeping with him instead of going to the sperm bank. I'm going to kill him."

Oh, shit. "Who told you that?"

"I caught Levi and Ellie whispering about it and made them

tell me."

Anyone who's known my brother longer than thirty seconds could guess this would be his reaction to the news, but I guess it was bound to come out eventually. I play it cool. "I thought you were on board with me having a baby?"

"I support you becoming a mom because that's what you want. That motherfucker is taking advantage of you just so he can get you in bed."

"It's not like that," I say.

Molly's gaze ping-pongs between us, her eyebrows climbing higher with every exchange.

"This is exactly why I flipped out when I saw him in bed with you the other day," Colton growls. "I knew you wanted a baby, and there he was, so *conveniently.*"

I roll my eyes. Molly looks half horrified and half fascinated. "He wasn't *in bed* with me," I explain. "He was sitting on the edge of my bed."

"Not the most effective way to get a woman pregnant," Molly mutters.

"I felt it in my gut when I saw him there," Colton says. "I knew he was going to use your wish for a baby to get you in bed. You know he's always wanted you, Ava."

"That's not true." The pull of longing that thought brings with it makes me squeeze my eyes shut for a beat. I worked *so hard* to get my feelings for Jake in check. It hasn't been an issue for years, but suddenly they're flooding back like they never left. "Jake doesn't *want* me. That's not what this is about."

For the first time since Colton walked in the door, Molly returns her gaze to the book she was reading.

"He's just helping me," I whisper. I don't want to have this conversation in front of Molly. Hell, I don't want to have it *at all.*

"*Helping,*" Colton says. "Meaning he screws you and then goes on about his business while you raise a baby alone?"

"He hasn't screwed me at all, Colt," I blurt, and for this I get another look from Molly. "He's . . ." What? Taking it slow? What am I going to tell my brother? *Don't worry, bro. Jake is going to make sure I'm hot for him before he fucks me.* I'm pretty sure this would only make Jake look worse in Colton's eyes.

"But Ellie said—"

"Yeah, well, Ellie should have kept her mouth shut." I take a breath. "Colton, relax. I'm not a little girl. Jake is helping me out. We're giving this a shot before I spend my savings on fertility treatments."

"Yeah, real selfless of him," he mutters.

"You're the one who told me I should go after what I want."

He folds his arms. "I thought you were taking the more *clinical* approach. I don't like this. It feels sleazy."

I squeak in my exasperation. "If anything, I'm taking advantage of *him.*"

He threads his fingers through his hair. "Fuck."

Convinced he's no longer determined to bloody Jake's face, I turn my attention to my stepsister. "Molly, please don't say anything to Jill and Dad."

"So you and Jake aren't . . . together?"

I shake my head. "He really is just my friend." *My friend who sucked my fingers and whispered dirty words into my ear. My friend who put ideas so hot in my head that I was aching in my sheets last night.*

"He's going to get you pregnant," she says slowly, measuring the words. "Like, as a favor?"

"It sounds stupid, but it's not a big deal."

"If he's sleeping with you, it's a big fucking deal," Colton says.

"If you have a *baby* together, it's a big deal," Molly says, her words a little sharper than before.

"I don't want to talk about this with you two." My phone rings, clattering against the end table as it vibrates, and I'm so grateful for the interruption that I snatch it up. I recognize the Florida area code and swipe to accept the call. "Hello, this is Ava."

"Ava! It's Penelope. I'm sorry to bother you again. I wanted to let you know that I emailed over the paperwork with the job description and some details about the school. I hope you'll look it over and let me know a good time for us to bring you down for an official interview."

Molly and Colton are both looking at me, and I climb off the couch and wander into the kitchen so they can't see my face while I talk. It's not like my reactions are going to give away the contents of the conversation, but I know Colton would freak about the possibility of me moving. "Thanks, Penelope. I'll look for it."

"That's great. Talk soon?"

I nod, even though she can't see me. "Talk soon." I end the call, and when I turn around, Colton's in the kitchen with me, studying me.

"What was that phone call about?" Colton asks.

"Nothing."

"Ava, since when do we keep things from each other?"

I grunt. "Since always?" I love Colton and I do tell him a lot, but I'd confide in Jake long before him.

"Was it the job in Florida?"

I gape at him. "How did you know about that?"

"Dad told me. He thought maybe I'd remember the area well enough to help you get settled."

My father is so determined that he knows what's best for me and my career that he's already mentally moved me down to Florida. "Well, don't get ahead of yourself. I'm trying to keep all my options open in case I get laid off this summer, but as of now I don't have any plans to move."

He folds his arms. "You, Ava Drama-Is-My-Life McKinley, don't want to move to Florida to teach nothing but theater classes to a bunch of private school kids?"

Nothing but theater classes? No composition? No grammar and rhetoric? I look to my computer and wonder if that's what I'll find in Penelope's email. "My life's here, Colton."

But it's not much of a life, is it? It's days working at a private school for a man who has so little respect for me that he'd put his hand up my dress. The nights working at Jake's bar are fun, but they aren't the way I imagined I'd be spending my time at this age. Then coming home to an empty house? That's the hardest part.

"The way you tell it, the job sounds a little too good to be true," I say. "I think Dad pulled some mob-level favors to get a school to woo me before I've even had an interview."

He shrugs. "Maybe he did. You know Dad. Nobody wants to disappoint him."

"Present company included?"

He releases a puff of air. "Fuck that. I *live* to disappoint that man."

I wave a hand. "This conversation is so premature. First of all, I have a job here. Second, this lady is just going through the motions as a favor to Dad."

"You think Dad's worked magic, when the truth is he had Jill send your résumé. Any magic is yours. It's who you are and what you've accomplished that they're after. Not Dad's approval."

My heart swells. My little brother can be a self-centered jerk sometimes, but here he is noticing my accomplishments. "Thanks, Colt. That means a lot."

He lowers his voice. "And if you do get pregnant? How do you think Dad's going to handle that? Do you really want to be here for that fallout?"

He's right. It would be nice to start my life fresh in a town away from my ex-husband, his beautiful new wife, and all the judgmental stares of everyone who knows I wasn't good enough to keep him. But if I have a baby, I can't imagine being anywhere but Jackson Harbor. Sure, I'd have Mom close in Florida, but one woman can hardly substitute for the support system I have from thirty years living in Jackson Harbor.

"I don't know." It's the most honest answer I can give him.

"I hate the phrase *failed marriage*." I turn away from my window and blink at Jake. I didn't mean to say that out loud, but the twenty-minute drive to my ex-husband's baby shower has had my mind twisting in knots as it travels down memory lane.

Jake takes his eyes off the road for a beat to flash me a sympathetic smile. "I never thought about it, but I guess it is kind of shitty."

I shrug. "It might be fair—I failed to make it work—but I still hate it." In truth, my marriage feels like nothing more than a series of failures. My failure to communicate effectively with my husband, my failure to be the kind of wife he always imagined having on his arm at business dinners. My failure to get pregnant . . .

When you're planning a wedding, friends and family shower you with gifts to prepare you for your new life together. Champagne glasses for when you celebrate anniversaries. A stand mixer for Christmas cookies. Picture frames for your memories.

No one prepares you for the failures. *"This is what you should do if your husband doesn't want to sleep with you, and this is how you should handle it when he looks at you like he feels stuck and is disappointed."*

"Why do you say *I*?" Jake asks, shaking me from my thoughts. "Shouldn't it be *we failed* to make it work? Doesn't Harrison get to take his share of the responsibility here?"

"Well, yeah." I wave a hand. "It takes two people to get married and two people to screw it up, right?"

Jake reaches across the console and puts his hand on my thigh. It's not a sexual touch, but suddenly I wish it were. I want the Jake from last night who pinned me against the cooler and told me he knew he turned me on. I want the reminder, the reassurance that he meant it and that this is going to happen. I want the distraction.

Intellectually, I know this isn't an either/or situation, and that

Harrison having a child doesn't mean *I* don't get to have one, but on some selfish gut level, it feels that way. I'm angry that he gets this dream we had together while I'm still floundering so desperately in my attempts to grasp it that I'm going to cross lines with Jake that probably shouldn't be crossed. I need the reassurance that this crazy plan isn't going to send my life into a tailspin.

I put my hand on top of his, willing him to sense what I need. The panic is growing in my chest, and I want him to pull over and drag me into his lap. I want him to kiss me until this heavy fear dissolves completely, until my brain is so cloudy with lust that I can't examine what we're doing too closely. I don't want to admit that our plan is reckless and probably a terrible idea, that it might be smarter to accept that being a mom isn't in the cards for me.

Jake cuts his eyes to me and frowns; maybe telepathy isn't failing me this morning, because he pulls the car over and throws it into park. "Hey," he says softly. He takes my chin in his big hand and turns me to face him. "*Breathe,* Ava."

"I'm fine."

He shakes his head slowly, searching my eyes. "Do you forget that I know you?" he asks, and the tenderness in his expression threatens to break something inside me. "You're not fine, and you don't have to pretend with me."

He dips his head, but I don't get the passionate kiss I wished for. Instead, I get the soft brush of Jake's lips across my forehead.

I close my eyes, and I *breathe.*

Chapter Twenty

AVA
Five years ago . . .

Jake Jackson kissed me last night.

I keep waiting for those words to jar me. For it to feel weird. Because it should feel weird when your best friend kisses you.

Instead, I can't stop thinking about the way he slid his hand in my hair, the graze of his thumb along my jaw, and the heat in his eyes as he lowered his mouth to mine. I can't stop thinking about how easy it was to open under him and how, when his tongue touched mine, my heart wanted to climb out of my chest and into his.

I'm in love with Harrison, and I consider myself incredibly lucky to have found someone who's such a good match for me. I've never been the girl with a steady line of boyfriends, and I've never found it easy to connect with the guys who asked me out. But Harrison and I work. I'm excited about the life we're going to have together, and when he asked me to marry him, I didn't hesitate a single beat.

Then Jake showed up at my door and kissed me. That kiss unlocked feelings I've stored away for years, and now the ring on my finger feels like a lie.

I had such a painful crush on him when we were in high school. Maybe before that, too. But during our senior year, he was the rock that kept me sane when living with my dad and feeling like I didn't belong made me want to run away.

That year, I spent hours agonizing about how I could tell him that my feelings for him had grown into something more than friendship. I'd catch myself staring at him when we were hanging out at his house. When he and his brothers would play football in the backyard, I'd watch the way his body moved under his clothes. He was tall and lanky then, nothing like the man he grew into, but in my eyes, he was perfect. When he'd steal the ball from his brother, he'd look my way and wink as if he'd done it for me, and my heart would pound wildly. I'd think, *Someday Jake and I are going to end up together.* I believed it, and instead of finding the courage to tell him how I felt, I waited for the day that he might feel it too.

When we started college, I was still waiting, but Jake didn't seem to be in any rush to change our relationship. We both dated other people, and sometimes I'd lie to myself and pretend I wasn't madly in love with my best friend. Sometimes I'd even believe the lie.

Then he had this girlfriend, Erica, who didn't like that he spent so much time with me. She wasn't the first to make that complaint, but she was the first girl he tried to change things for.

One night I went up to Jake's apartment over the bar to hang out, and I heard them in there together. I heard my name. I heard him laugh.

Erica said she felt like the other woman because he spent so much time with me, and he said he didn't see me that way. He told her he spent so much time with me because he was a family guy, and I was like his sister.

In that moment, I realized I was waiting for a guy who'd never want me. He always went after the curvy girls, the blondes who looked like fifties pin-ups, whereas I was rocking the body of a 1920s flapper—my curves barely there, my breasts too small.

That night, I stood outside his apartment, vaguely aware of the cacophony of the busy bar below me while the sound of Erica's laughter cut through me like a scalpel. Standing there, sliced open and raw, I gave him up. I let him go. I took all my girlish fantasies of us as a couple and locked them away somewhere deep inside myself, somewhere I could pretend they never existed.

Then yesterday, he kissed me.

He kissed me and told me he was in love with me, and this morning I can't stop thinking about it.

I have to tell Harrison. I can't keep this a secret. Jake *kissed* me, and his touch was so intense that I'm sure when Harrison looks at me this morning he'll see it on my skin, see thoughts of Jake in my eyes. Harrison needs to know that this ring feels too heavy on my finger, that I'm having second thoughts. Maybe we should back up a few steps and slow down.

A woman shouldn't plan her wedding while thinking of another man's kiss.

AVA
Present day...

The best way I can describe how badly I want a child is to say I've always seen myself as a mother. A lot of girls do, but it wasn't just that I thought having children was something I was *supposed* to do or something I might like. It was part of my identity before I was old enough to understand how it all worked. Like every other little girl who plans to be a mommy, I grew up believing that my ability to bear children was a foregone conclusion. I was so sure that once Harrison and I started trying, we'd be able to get pregnant. After all, if I'd spent years before putting a lot of effort into trying *not* to get pregnant, getting pregnant should be easy, right?

In reality, it wasn't so simple, and month after month, motherhood was a dream kept just beyond my reach. When my body wouldn't cooperate, my heart felt raw with the effort of wanting. Try after try left me with an empty nursery and empty arms, and the vacancy in my womb grew unbearable. It felt as if the more I wanted a child, the further it fell from my reach, until I was grieving the loss of a child who'd never been conceived. The magnitude of that grief built a wall between me and my husband until he was so lonely he sought comfort in another woman's arms.

And look how happy they are now. Harrison's chest is puffed with pride, and his wife is *glowing*. She's the picture-perfect expectant mother today, wearing a light pink chiffon dress with a big bow at the top of her baby bump. And I hate her desperately.

The baby shower is at a local winery, which seems a little thoughtless to the mother-to-be who can't partake, but that would be consistent with Harrison's personality. If a baby shower at a winery speaks of his social class and importance more than a baby shower somewhere else, then that's what he's going to want, regardless of the preferences of the mother of his child.

It's a crisp early spring day, and the dining room doors are open to the patio. The place looks amazing—tables dressed with white cloths and pink napkins folded into little cranes at each spot. The centerpieces are made of light pink peonies and white roses, and look like something you'd see at a high-budget wedding. In fact, the whole party rivals some of the nicer wedding receptions I've attended. Lunch was four courses, each served with its own wine pairing, and the cake is as tall as Jake's niece.

The baby shower probably would have made me sick to my stomach if I didn't have Jake here by my side, quietly whispering his commentary on the food, décor, and the behavior of the parents-to-be.

We've just been served cake—an Ooh La La! creation and, so far, the best part of this day—and we're sipping at our fresh cups of coffee when Harrison makes his way to the empty seat beside me. He props his elbows on the table as he takes us in.

"I'm so glad you could make it, Ava," he says in his best salesman voice.

Jake slings his arm over the back of my chair and scoots toward me.

I smile. "Yes, I wanted to congratulate you in person."

Jake squeezes my shoulder.

Harrison's gaze darts between my face and Jake's, then settles on Jake's hand on my shoulder. "I see you're still dragging poor Jake around." He shakes his head. "I've gotta hand it to you, Jake. You're a better sport about it than I am. I don't even like going to these things with my wife, let alone just a friend."

Jake smiles next to me, totally unfazed by Harrison's attempt at cruelty. "I'd go anywhere with Ava," he says. "I mean, we can have a good time watching paint dry, so if she wants company at your baby shower, I'm happy to oblige. Besides, I get her to myself all next weekend, so I'm trying not to be too greedy."

"Is that so?" Harrison shakes his head. "Well, you two have a good time." He pushes back from our table and walks to the next.

I feel small. Like I've been caught playing a game. My ex knows better than anyone that there's nothing between me and Jake. Harrison and I were together for years. He saw that Jake and I were the perfect example of how a man and a woman could have a truly platonic relationship.

I look down at the napkin I've crumpled into a ball in my lap. The happy pink taunts me. *They're having a girl.*

"Hey," Jake says. He takes my chin in his hand and tilts my face up to his. "Don't let that asshole get you down."

I swallow hard. "I was foolish to think he'd care."

"He does care, Ava. Seeing me here with you is making him crazy. I bet he's watching us right now, isn't he?"

I take my eyes off Jake's to look over his shoulder. Harrison's still at the table beside ours. He's nodding as if he's listening to the conversation, but I catch his gaze on us before he yanks it away.

"The only foolish thing," Jake says, bringing my attention

back to him, "is that you still *want* him to care."

"I . . ." I wince and shake my head. I wish I didn't. Harrison's opinion of me and my life shouldn't matter at all. "It's immature, but I want him to feel like he lost something good when he walked away from me."

"He might never say it, but he knows he did." The fingers on my chin fan out, sliding over the sensitive skin under my ear before moving back up into my hair. I know what he's doing and how this looks from Harrison's perspective, and though it's small and probably proves I'm petty, I'm grateful. "You wanted more than you got out of that relationship. You gave more than you received." He strokes a thumb along my jaw. "But I promise you, there are better things coming."

Affection swells in my chest. Sometimes people say nice things to make you feel good, but you know in your heart you don't deserve the kindness. But when someone you've known this long wishes you well, when someone who knows all your flaws, shortcomings, and neuroses believes in you, it means more. "Thank you."

He hums, his eyes dropping to my mouth. "I'm gonna kiss you now, Ava."

I hear my quick inhale. "Now?"

His eyes remain on my lips as if he needs to catalog every millimeter he wants to taste. "Yeah. It's not going to be the kind of kiss I want, but the kind I want will have to wait for when I have you alone." He dips his head and sweeps his lips across mine.

Tingles radiate through my limbs. A spiral of warmth coils in my belly, and he does it again, lightly nipping at my bottom lip before pulling away. I take a fistful of his shirt, trying to keep him close. I'm so full of sensations and longing for *more* that I can't breathe.

"That should do it," he says. He slides his mouth to my ear and whispers, "He never deserved you."

And I'm so caught up in the feeling of Jake's lips on mine and the hot pull of desire in my belly that it takes me a beat to realize who he's even talking about.

Chapter TWENTY-ONE

JAKE

I unlock the front door of Jackson Brews and pull it open for Molly. "You're early."

She grins as she steps inside. "I wanted a chance to talk to you before Brayden joined us."

I tense, but I suppose this was unavoidable. If I was enough of an idiot to get drunk and screw Molly five years ago, I have to be willing to talk about it now—and be willing to own up to the mistake to Ava. It feels more important than I want it to, but yesterday she let me kiss her in front of her ex-husband and a couple dozen people who were a part of her married life. I don't know if it felt significant to her, but the significance of the moment wasn't lost on me.

"Yeah, I need to talk to you too." I wave to one of the tables and shut and lock the door behind her. The bar won't open to the public for two hours, so Brayden and I will have plenty of time to give Molly the rundown on what we'd need in a regional sales rep.

Molly puts her purse down on one chair and pulls out another to sit. "I want to talk about you and Ava," she says.

"If you're going to give the 'hurt my sister and die' speech, you should know Colton already beat you to it." I rub my shoulder, still a little sore from where his fist connected when he saw me at the bar last night. That whole conversation would have gone a lot better if I could have been honest with him instead of rolling with the whole "trying to help my best friend get pregnant" story. But the truth? That I want Ava to give us a chance? That I'm going all in for one last shot at making her love me back? I kept that story to myself. I don't want Ava knowing what this is about for me. Not yet. I can't risk her freaking out.

"What exactly is going on between you two?" Molly asks.

"It's complicated."

"Complicated because you're still in love with her and she still doesn't feel the same about you, or complicated because you're going to let her *use* you for a baby?"

Her words are a punch to the gut, and I wince. "Jesus. Don't say it like that. It's not like I don't know what I'm getting myself into here."

She turns to look out the window. The street outside is quiet, with only a few people walking by on their way to work or their Monday morning yoga class down the block. "Has anyone told you this is a terrible idea?"

Colton, Levi, Carter, Ellie—pretty much everyone who knows what I offered Ava has taken a moment to inform me that I'm a fucking idiot. "It's come up a time or two."

She keeps her eyes on the window. A woman walks past carrying a rolled-up yoga mat. "Good."

I feel like a jerk. The night we hooked up, Molly admitted she'd had feelings for me for a long time, but I never would have guessed that she'd been holding on to those feelings since. "Is this about us?" I ask. "Because, Moll, we haven't seen each other in almost five years."

She tugs on a lock of her hair. "I know."

"I'm really sorry I let that happen. I should have never—"

"Don't. Please. I don't want your regrets." She shakes her head and lowers her voice. "Not when I have none of my own."

I could offer excuses. Platitudes. Bullshit. But that all feels wrong and insulting. "This thing with Ava . . . You're right. I'm still in love with her. Maybe I'm an idiot, but I'm taking a chance to see if maybe, if she lets herself, she can feel something in return."

"What are you going to do if it works?"

"I'm going to fucking *rejoice*."

She shakes her head. "I don't mean if your plan works. I don't mean what happens if you end up together. I mean what happens if you *don't* end up together, but you have a baby. Are you just going to carry on with your life knowing you have a kid out there? Pretend you aren't a father?"

"I would never walk away from my child." I swallow. I've kissed Ava a couple of times and made some promises, but she hasn't pushed me about when we're going to follow through. I imagine that's because she's nervous about it. I am too. Nervous that she might only want the child I offered. Nervous that she might feel like I've changed the terms of our deal when she finds out this all comes back to how I feel about her. "I'm taking it slow, and she's okay with that. So I'm hoping things will shift between us as we move forward, and she'll . . ."

Molly smiles softly. "You're hoping she'll catch feelings?"

"Something like that."

She traces an invisible figure eight on the wooden tabletop. "I guess this is a bad time to tell you I've never forgotten about you. I know what happened between us might not have seemed like a big deal to you. Everyone knows Molly McKinley's an easy lay—"

"I *never* said that."

She shrugs. "Maybe you didn't, but enough people did. I just wanted you to know you weren't just a warm body on a lonely night. You've always been special to me."

"I'm sorry, Molly." I hate that she has feelings for me that I can't return, but more than that, I hate that I fed those feelings on any level—even if I told myself it was only physical, even if it was just one night.

She shakes her head and traces the same pattern over and over. "Not as sorry as I am."

"About what happened that night . . ." I feel like an insensitive prick for bringing this up right now, but I don't have a choice. "I know we agreed not to tell Ava, but considering how things have changed, I need to tell her now."

"Don't," she says. She shakes her head and locks her pleading eyes on mine. "Jake, please don't. It's a bad idea."

"Why?"

"It was *one night*. You were drunk, and she was engaged to Harrison."

"If it doesn't matter, then why can't I tell her?"

"You know she won't like it."

"I can't argue with that." More than not like it—I'm afraid that my mistake will make Ava obsess again about this idea that Molly is everything she isn't and was supposed to be. I'll explain how it happened and why. I'll tell her that it didn't mean anything. But I have this rotting feeling in my gut that none of that will matter to Ava. *What if this is how I lose her?* "I don't like this hanging over us. I don't like keeping secrets from Ava." I hesitate for a beat. "I don't like making *you* my dirty secret. It's not fair to any of us."

Molly rubs the locket on her necklace and then squeezes it in a clenched fist before taking a breath and nodding. "Just let me think about it, okay? Let me think of a way to . . ."

I mentally finish that sentence. *To soften the blow? To protect your relationship after Ava learns the truth?* "You're as afraid of losing her as I am," I say.

Her eyes water. "We can't tell her yet. Things are so new and fragile between you two."

"And you as well?" I ask.

She nods. "Please, Jake, I'm begging you not to tell her yet."

There's a knock on the glass, and I look over my shoulder to see Brayden at the door, reaching for his keys.

"I don't like the secret," I say, quickly now, because his key's in the lock.

"And *I* don't like that you picked her over me even when she took herself out of the running." She shrugs as Brayden pushes into the bar. "Sometimes we have to deal with things we don't like."

AVA

Molly's at the table, papers spread out in front of her, tears rolling down her cheeks. I immediately think of the weeks after my husband left me when I was confronted with not only the worst heartache of my life but with the reality of the debt he'd gladly handed over. I felt stupid for the assumptions I made and guilty for embracing a pointlessly lavish lifestyle.

"Molly, are you okay?"

She startles and sweeps all the papers into a pile. "You're home early."

"Yeah. Sorry." I turn away, understanding that she doesn't want me to see whatever she was studying.

"It's your house. You can be here any time you want. I just thought you had children's theater auditions or something tonight?"

I shake my head, and when I turn back to her, she's sliding the stack of folded papers into her purse. "I'm meeting Jake's niece to help her with her audition piece, but I'm not heading over there for a couple of hours. Are you okay?"

She gives a shaky smile. "I'm fine. Great, actually. I met with Jake and Brayden today, and they're going to hire me as their new northeast regional sales rep. It's totally different than anything I've done before, but I'm actually pretty excited about it." She blows out a breath. "I'm just indulging in a little pity party that my life didn't turn out the way I wanted. I thought I'd be juggling social engagements, and instead I'm juggling bills."

"This is why *adulting* became a verb."

She laughs. "Oh my God, you're an English teacher. You're supposed to hate that."

"Not at all. In fact, I don't know why it hasn't been a verb for centuries. Our parents had to deal with this shit too, didn't they?"

"Yes, but they'd tell you they weren't as coddled as children as we were, and that's why adulthood wasn't a brutal a wakeup call for them."

"Whatever," I mutter. "They weren't saddled with student loan debt before they even got started."

"Preach!"

We laugh, and something tugs in my chest—grief for a missed opportunity. Molly and I could have been friends, but I let my own insecurities form a wall between us. I wish I could say it's the only time in my life I've done that, but it seems to be a habit of mine. When I feel unworthy, I push people away. In a way, that's what I've been doing with Jake for years. Maybe I didn't push him out of my life, but I always put limits on what I believed our relationship could be.

Her phone clatters against the kitchen table as it buzzes, and she grabs it and swipes the screen. "Hello?"

Maybe I should leave the room, but worry creases her features, so I stay.

"How high is it?" She squeezes the locket on her necklace and looks at the ceiling. "Dammit. No, don't apologize. I understand." She cuts her gaze to me and then looks at the clock on the stove. "I'm supposed to fly home in the morning, but I'll see if I can get a red-eye tonight." She shakes her head. "Don't. You know I didn't want to come anyway. The sooner I leave, the better." She flashes me an apologetic smile, then lowers her voice. "Um . . . I can't right now? Yeah. I'll call back when I know something. Yes. You too. Thank you." She pulls the phone from her ear and ends the call.

"Is everything okay?"

She taps on her phone and nods as she stares at the screen. "My friend's son is sick, and she has to work. Daycare won't take him with a fever." She taps the screen and puts the phone to her ear. "I need to get back."

I frown. She's going to get an earlier flight to take care of a friend's sick kid? "You two must be really close."

She nods, then turns away as her call connects. "Hello, I need to speak with someone about changing my flight?"

My own phone buzzes in my purse, and I pull it out to see a new text message from Nic.

Nic: Lilly and I are at the store. She wants to know if you prefer your hot chocolate with rainbow marshmallows or jumbo marshmallows.

I grin. Nic is dating Lilly's dad, and it's the best thing that ever happened to both the kid and the father. I've loved having her in my life too.

Me: Rainbow, obviously.
Nic: Obviously. See you in a couple of hours.

When I slide my phone back into my purse, Molly's wrapping

up her call and some of the tension has left her eyes.

"I'm going to fly home tonight," she says. "I can't thank you enough for letting me stay here. One of the reasons I can't stand coming home is because Dad gets to me. It was a relief to be here and not have to have him judging my every move."

I grimace. "I always thought you two had such a great relationship. Actually, I was . . . I was always kind of jealous, because he seemed to love you so much more than me."

Her eyes go wide. "Are you kidding? I could never measure up to his sweet Ava. You were reliable and thoughtful, and most importantly, you didn't spread your legs for every guy who came around."

"He said that?"

"Almost verbatim." She draws in a long breath and exhales slowly. "Anyway, it was a relief not to have to deal with that so much this trip, and with any luck, before I come home again next time, Mom will wake up and leave his drunk ass."

Maybe it makes me a disloyal daughter, but I hope she's right. Jill deserves better. "Next time being in another five years or so?"

Laughing, she shrugs. "Maybe. What's here for me?" She crosses the kitchen and wraps me in a hug. "Thanks again. Good luck with the whole pregnancy thing."

I give her a quick squeeze and then step back. "Be honest. Do you think I'm crazy?"

"For using your best friend to get a baby you plan to raise on your own? Yeah. I think you're nuts." Her expression softens. "But you're steady, reliable Ava. I'm sure you've thought this through."

"I have. I really have."

She hoists her purse onto her shoulder. "See? It doesn't

matter what I think."

I swallow hard. She's right. It doesn't matter, but it would feel nice to have a couple more people on my team. "Do you need a ride to the airport?"

"No, I'm going to call Mom and have her drive me. She'll want a little time with me anyway."

"Good luck with the new job and everything. Can I call you when Jake and I are in the city this summer?"

She beams. "I'd love that."

She goes to the guest bedroom to pack, and I feel like I've made some steps toward building a relationship with my sister.

Chapter TWENTY-TWO

AVA

I've never been very into motocross aside from being excited every time Colton makes it through another race uninjured, but when I do go to the races, I always have a good time. Today was no different. Ellie, Jake, and I stood by the winding dirt track, drinking beer and cheering our heads off. The nerves I felt while packing my bags this morning fizzled the second the race started, and now I'm warm from the sun and lazy from the beer.

When Jake and I get into our room, I collapse on the bed, bone-deep exhausted but happy. There's nothing like a day with your best friends to feed your soul.

"You had fun?" Jake asks.

"Yes." I stretch my arms overhead and arch my back. The last few weeks of the school year are always hectic, but there's an extra layer of tension around Windsor Prep as everyone waits to find out who's going to lose their job. I needed to unwind. "Does it always feel this good to take time off work? Because I think I've been missing out."

He chuckles. "That's what I've been trying to tell you." He leans against the wall and watches me as if he's waiting for me to say something or do something. I feel that old sexual awkwardness creep in. *I'm sharing a room with Jake, and we're supposed to make a baby.*

Things were never awkward between us before, but now I've confused everything, and he has too, dammit. I just thought we'd have sex—compartmentalize the baby-making and the friendship, keeping them separate. He's the one who's muddied the two, and my old feelings refuse to stay buried where they belong.

Maybe I should have expected that, but it's not what I was asking for, and it scares me more than a little.

I kept myself busy all week so I didn't have a chance to think too much about spending Saturday night in a hotel with Jake. Monday, I met with Lilly to help with the audition piece she's already nailed, then Tuesday I had the children's theater board meeting. I caught up on grading on Wednesday and worked at Jackson Brews on Thursday and Friday.

I hoped my shifts would include a repeat of Jake pinning me against the cooler, maybe some of that knuckle foreplay he's so good at, or even him giving me a preview of what was to come this weekend. Instead, he was scarce, and I barely talked to him all week other than to confirm our travel plans. But now we're here, and I'm nervous and greedy for what happens next for reasons that have very little to do with the baby I want.

"Wanna order a pizza tonight or go out?" I ask, more to have something to say than because I'm hungry. We're supposed to meet Ellie, Colton, Levi, and some chick Levi's seeing at the club across the street at ten, but suddenly, the five hours between now and then seem to stretch too wide. They're too filled with possibility.

"Let's go out," he says. "I can make reservations."

"What about that tapas restaurant down the block?"

He already has his phone out, tapping the screen. "Got it." He slides his phone back into his pocket. "I made a reservation for six. Wanna shower or anything?"

"That's probably a good idea. I must stink from a day at the track." I roll to sitting. Climbing off the bed feels like it requires way more effort than it should. I'm either going to need a cup of coffee or a nap if we're staying out late with everyone tonight. I'm out of energy.

Grabbing my overnight bag, I head to the bathroom. I start the shower to warm it, but when I turn to close the door, Jake's standing in the way, watching me.

I frown at him and wave to the shower. "Did you want to go first?"

He shakes his head. "Nope."

"Okay . . ." I look at him, and then the door. "Do you wanna leave so I can do this?"

"Nope."

"Jacob Jackson, you are *not* planning to stand there while I take off my clothes."

He smirks. "I'm not? Are you sure about that?" His gaze sweeps over me. Heat races through my veins followed by a chill of anticipation. He folds his arms. "You don't want me to see you naked. Is that the problem?"

"I don't know why you'd want to," I blurt, then realize it sounds like I'm fishing for compliments. I wince and wish I could take the words back. It's not that I'm ashamed of my body. It's just that I don't have much to look at. My breasts are barely there, my ass only a hint of curve. There's nothing to get excited over.

He chuckles. "Holy shit, Ava. I'm a dude—a heterosexual dude at that. Seeing you naked is . . ." His grin spreads. "Let's just say I think about it a lot. *Daily*."

I gape. *Daily*? Does that mean since we made this plan or before?

"But if you want me to leave, I can do that. I'll just liquor you up tonight and try again."

"Try to get me naked or try to have sex?" My voice squeaks. We're going to do this. I'm sure we are, but I need to prepare myself. Mentally. "Because if this is just about seeing me naked, I don't want . . ." *I don't want to disappoint you.* "There's just . . . not much to see."

"I *will* see you naked before I'm inside you. It's this silly little prerequisite of mine." He walks toward me, and there's a challenge in his eyes that makes me feel bolder than I should.

"So we're going to"—I swallow—"start trying tonight?"

My heart's racing when he bends his head down and leans his forehead against mine. "Do you have any idea how gorgeous you are? How beautiful you looked in the sunshine with that big grin on your face?" He cups my jaw in his hand and groans. "I couldn't stop thinking about tonight. About sharing that bed with you."

"Really?"

"Oh, yeah." He slides his hand into my hair and wraps it around his fist. He tugs gently, and pleasure sparks up my spine. "Are you going to let me touch you?" The words are a hot whisper against my ear, and everything in me is tight and begging.

"Yes." I practically pant the word.

He pulls my earlobe between his teeth, and his hand trails over my collarbone and down to cup my breast. "And you'll let me look at you?" His thumb grazes my nipple, and hell, now I *want* to be naked. Even the thin layers of my bra and T-shirt are too much to have between us. "Let me explore you?"

I nod, and I think I might whimper. Am I really expected to form words right now?

"Think on that for me." His hand slips under my T-shirt, and *shit*, I want more. His palm runs over my belly. His fingertips dip under the waistband of my jeans. "Think about it in the shower. At dinner. When you dance tonight." He drops his face to the crook of my neck and takes a deep breath.

Then he steps away and he's walking out of the bathroom, pulling the door shut behind him.

He gets his wish. I think about him while I close my eyes under the spray, my body pulsing, my mind spinning fantasies about him pressing me up against the tile shower wall, the heat of his bare chest pressed against me as his hands explore.

I wash my hair and shave, taking the extra care of a woman who's preparing for her lover. I'm thinking of him when I climb out of the shower and when I dry my hair. I'm thinking of him when I choose a short black dress and the slinkiest underwear from my bag.

When I step out of the bathroom, he's changed into a fresh pair of jeans and a crisp black dress shirt that's open at the collar and rolled up, revealing his forearms. *Those forearms.*

A sound bubbles up from my throat that I think might be a purr.

Jake looks me over. His slow, raking gaze trailing from my feet and up my body is its own kind of seduction. "Ready?"

I swallow. "I really am."

JAKE

Usually I wouldn't be interested in the thumping music of the nightclub and the throng of bodies crowding the dance floor, but it's good to see Ava let loose. She and Ellie have danced since we got here, and Ava's gotten more into it with each subsequent song. Her arms are in the air, her hips rocking back and forth as if the music is vibrating from inside her.

"Thanks for coming this weekend," Levi says from beside me. We're leaning against the railing that surrounds the dance floor, and his date is . . . somewhere. I don't know. I haven't paid much attention to the giggling redhead.

I nod without looking at him, because I can't take my eyes off Ava.

"It's always nice to have a few extra people around so I'm not just the third wheel," Levi says.

This time, I cut my eyes to my brother. "You can't be a third wheel if you have a girl hanging on your arm, Levi."

He shrugs, an unspoken *you know what I mean*. And I do. The women in Levi's life come and go, but Ellie is as much a fixture of his world as his friend Colton is. She has been since she and Colton started dating.

I know he loves them both. But I'm also realizing his feelings for Ellie might be heavier than any of us realized. Unrequited love is a bitch. Hopefully he handles it better than I did.

"How's the big plan going?" Levi asks.

On the dance floor, Ellie loops her arms behind Ava's neck, and Ava throws her head back in laughter as Ellie dances against her. "It wasn't the smoothest start, but I'm getting there."

"Getting in her pants or in her heart?" he asks, then holds up two hands when I scowl. "The difference seems significant, is all."

"As I'm all too aware." I drain my beer, then slide the empty bottle back onto the table. I don't want to talk about this shit tonight. "I'm going to go dance with my girl."

Levi arches a brow. "You dance?"

"I do tonight." I head onto the floor and pull Ava away from Ellie and into my arms as if I do it all the time. Ava gasps, her eyes going wide, and I press a palm to the small of her back and hold her body against mine. Because I can. Because she's given me permission to touch her tonight. Because I've waited for this for years, and I know not letting myself take things too far might be the hardest damn thing I've ever had to do.

She laughs and shakes her head. "What's gotten into you? You never dance."

I take her chin in my hand and turn her face up toward mine. Her laughter falls away, and her eyes search my face. I dip my head down and rub the tip of my nose over hers. "Just dance."

She probably can't even hear me. The music's so loud in here and the crowd grows thicker around us with every song, but dancing is in Ava's blood. She loops her hands behind my neck and shifts her hips, so close that her body brushes against mine with each movement.

I can't think about us falling apart. I can't think about her never seeing me as more than a friend or about her starting a family without me. So I just think about this: Ava dancing in my arms. Her body close and warm. *Soft.*

I place the flat of my palm against her belly and drop my nose to the crook of her neck to take in her smell, her heat. I use my free hand to trail up and down her side, only hinting at every inch I plan to explore.

And when looking into her eyes makes the sting in my chest too sharp, I spin her in my arms and pull her back against my front. She reaches one hand back behind my neck, keeping hold of me as we dance. She craves the same contact I do. I have to believe it means something.

Chapter TWENTY-THREE

AVA

Jake's dancing with me. Maybe it's the alcohol talking, but I swear this feels like sex. The way his hands move over my body, gripping my hips, the graze of knuckles over my stomach, his breath at my neck then my hair tugged lightly in his fist . . .

I've never had sex with Jake, but I can imagine if we ever make it there, this is what it'll feel like—a relentless desire for *more, more, more,* each touch making my body plead for the next, each caress making my skin hum. The thought makes me want to rush this and slow it down all at once.

Dinner was good. We didn't talk again about the things he said to me in the bathroom, and I didn't ask again if he planned on sleeping with me tonight—a question I realized he never actually answered.

We talked about typical Jake and Ava things: business at the bar, school, his mom's treatments, how perfect his niece is going to be on stage this summer. I understood he was making me wait. And I liked it. But now that his hands are on me and his body is against mine, I'm done waiting. I spin in his arms so I can see his face. I feel *good* after a couple of drinks, and more relaxed than I have in months. Maybe years.

Jake scans my face before meeting my eyes. "You're drunk," he says, his voice rough.

"I'm . . . *relaxed.*"

"Relaxed but not drunk?" he asks, searching my face. "Tonight, the difference matters."

"Buzzed, not drunk," I promise. I rise onto my toes to get my mouth closer to his ear. "Take me to bed."

He runs his thumb over my bottom lip and nods. "Yeah."

I wave to Ellie, to Colton, to Levi and his date. Jake keeps hold of my hand the entire way to the door. His strides are long, and I practically have to jog to keep up with him. I brace myself to chase after him the whole way to the hotel, but his steps slow the second we reach the sidewalk, as if the cool air outside the club has sobered him and made him less frantic.

I squeeze his hand. I *want* him frantic. I liked the way he was racing out of there with me. I was imagining he couldn't wait to get me alone, and I want that to be true. I'm just not sure it is.

We stop to cross at the light, and he's so quiet it's killing me. His whole body is tense. Is he regretting this? Wishing he hadn't made promises or whispered in my ear?

"Jake?" I'm still holding his hand, and I squeeze. This is where I should give him the out. *You don't have to do this. It's okay if you've changed your mind.*

Before I can get the words off my tongue, his hard eyes meet mine. He shakes his head as he presses his index finger to my lips. "Don't."

What does that mean?

I don't have much time to analyze the word before he's tugging me across the intersection, into the hotel, and across the lobby. The second the elevator doors close behind us, I'm pressed against the wall, his mouth on mine. His hands are greedy and seem to be everywhere at once. One is in my hair and the other's at my hip, tugging at my dress until his fingers splay over my bare thigh. He traces the strap of my thong from the small of my back to under my belly and down between my legs, where I know I'm wet. Does he feel that through the lace? Does he understand that I suck at this? That my body sometimes locks up and that at any moment my pleasure could morph into panic? That my overactive brain could start a destructive spiral and ruin everything?

My worries evaporate at the feel of his knuckles along the fabric between my legs. "Do you want me to touch you here?" The question is a husky whisper against my ear. "Put my mouth on you here?"

I never thought I was into words, but Jake's are the best kind of foreplay, and I want more. "Yes. Please. I want you. All of you."

"I'm not going to fuck you tonight, Ava."

I suck his bottom lip into my mouth and moan as I release it. "Please." I know I'd never have the courage to speak like this if it weren't for the drinks. I'm grateful for the buzz making me bold. I *need* the courage tonight. "I'm begging. You said that's what you wanted."

His palm snakes up my dress and flattens against my belly as his fingertips slide into my panties and he cups me. "I like hearing you say that. I like knowing you want me."

The elevator dings. The door slides open, but neither of us moves.

"Tonight isn't about anything but you and me. Do you understand what I'm saying? I'm touching you tonight because I *want* to touch you. I'm going to make you come just because it feels good, and because I've had too many fucking fantasies of getting my mouth between your legs to pass it up now."

I shudder in his arms, faintly aware of the doors sliding closed. "You don't have to—"

"Fuck *have to*. Tonight is about *want*. You hear me?" He shakes his head slowly, studying me. "Anything you want. But no sex. That's something we both have to wait for."

I nod my understanding, and part of me is grateful. I want Jake to touch me. I want this to be about us and not about my big plans—and he's giving me that without me ever asking for it. He knows I need it because he knows *me*.

He punches the button on the wall, and the doors slide open again.

My legs aren't much better than noodles beneath me as he leads me out of the elevator, but I somehow make it to our room. He opens the door for me, and before it has the chance to swing closed behind him, I grab a fistful of his shirt. "I want it to be good for you, too."

"Good." He grabs my dress in both his fists and yanks it over my head. I don't have time to feel nervous about him seeing me in my bra and panties because one second he's tossing my dress onto the floor, and the next he has me pressed against the wall. His hand slides between my legs, rubbing the lace over my clit.

"You're wet," he murmurs against my mouth. "So fucking wet." He kisses his way down my neck and across my collarbone—a symphony of lips and teeth and tongue that signals hunger more than seduction and leaves me feeling desirable in a way I've never felt in my life.

He drops his head to my breast and sucks at me through my thin bra. When I cry out, he pulls his head away and pinches my nipple between his finger and thumb. "I'm going to have so much fun discovering all the ways I can make you come," he murmurs. His mouth trails lower, skimming over my belly, his tongue grazing my navel until he's on his knees before me with his hands on my ass and his forehead resting against one hipbone.

I slide a hand into his hair. "Jake, you . . ."

His eyes are hot when he tilts his face up to me, and the intensity there makes the words clog in my throat. He shakes his head. "Don't you fucking dare give me a *you don't have to* speech right now. I already told you, tonight is about pleasure, and I want to feel you. I *want* to taste you. So don't tell me to stop unless you don't want this."

"I want you to . . ." My voice wobbles on the words. "I want to feel your mouth on me." I'm so nervous about letting the words out that they're too soft. He holds my gaze for five thunderous beats of my heart, and I think he might not have heard me at all. But in a flash, I see that he did. I see it in his eyes and hear it in the guttural rumble of his groan. He heard *every* word.

"Fuck yes." He dips his head to nuzzle me between my legs. He groans, and I feel the vibration of the sound right against where I'm hot and wet. Where I'm aching. His fingers curl under the string of my thong, and my legs shake as I wait for him to pull it off.

Instead, he stands, eyes all over me. "You want this on when my mouth is on you?"

I shake my head.

He steps back. "Then take it off, baby." His eyes trail over me—the modest swell of my breasts, the flat of my stomach, my thighs. "Let me see you."

I unhook my bra with shaking hands. I'm already wearing so little that there isn't much surprise left, but I'm still as nervous as a virgin bride. I want to be everything to Jake. I want to be his fantasy. When I slide the straps down my arms, delicate lace cups fall to the floor, and his nostrils flare.

"Fuck yes." His eyes are all over me. "So fucking perfect."

I catch his eyes as I loop my thumbs into the straps at my hips and tug until this last scrap of covering falls to my feet, then I step out of my shoes.

"This is happening." He shakes his head slowly, eyes scanning every inch of my face—trying to read me or memorize me. Both?

I swallow hard because I can't believe it either, and I'm scared to admit even to myself just how long I've wanted this. "I like the way you look at me."

"How'd you think I'd look at you?"

I shrug and swallow the words lodged like a fist in my throat. Now's not the time for insecurities. This is a moment for bold passion and frantic touches, but Jake wants to know, and it feels important. "I've always wanted to be *more*." I take a step toward him and wave a hand down my body. "More hips, more boobs, more ass."

"Nah," he says softly. "You don't need more of anything." He lifts a hand to cup my breast and grazes a thumb across my nipple. His greedy eyes are all over me. "This is you, Ava. Do you know how many times I've gotten myself off imagining you showing me this body? Imagining you letting me touch it?"

"Really?" My voice cracks on the word—like a shell breaking and releasing my fears to puddle at my feet.

"I've pictured you so many times that you'd think I would have gotten it right." His Adam's apple bobs as he swallows. "And yet you're even more beautiful than I imagined."

My insecurities fade away, replaced with boldness from the awe in his eyes. "I've thought about you too."

He lifts his head, his eyes locking on mine. "Have you?"

I nod. "Every night this week I've touched myself thinking about the things you said to me." I lick my lips. The admission leaves me exposed, but I like the feeling. This is what it's like to strip myself bare for Jake. To show him where I'm most vulnerable. "I don't normally do that so often, but you've made me . . . Jake, you put ideas in my head. Made me want things."

"This week?"

I nod. "And in the shower . . ."

His chest expands on his deep inhale. "And what about before this week?" He grazes my collarbone with his index finger, then traces a line down between my breasts, over my navel, and between my legs, where I'm swollen and needy for him. "Before this week, did you ever touch yourself thinking about me?"

Desire is ungrounded electricity between us, snapping at the air and looking for connection. "Yes."

"Once? Twice?" He cups my jaw in his hand and rubs my bottom lip with his thumb.

"Too many times to count." I give a shaky smile. "You've starred in my fantasies for years. Even when I didn't want to admit it to myself, you were there."

He growls and nods. "I would've been. You only had to ask."

I open my mouth to question this—or maybe to object—but he leads me to the bed, and I don't care about anything else. "Lie back, beautiful."

I do as he says, but he's unbuttoning his shirt, so I only go down to my elbows, wanting the view of his broad shoulders, the display of ink on his skin. He drops his dress shirt to the floor, then yanks his undershirt over his head and throws it aside. The sight of him makes the ache between my legs coil tighter. Bare chest. Tattoos. Hard muscle under soft skin.

"I like that." He nods to me. "I want you up on your elbows when my mouth is on you." He strips out of his jeans, and my breath catches at the sight of him. His strong legs. The dark hair that trails under his navel and into his boxer briefs. The thick erection beneath them.

He's gorgeous. And right now, he's mine.

"Come here." I reach out a hand. As he takes it, I hear the muffled trill of his phone from his discarded jeans. "Ignore it."

He grins. "I don't have anything nice to say to someone who'd interrupt me right now." He climbs over me, and I lie back, welcoming the weight of his body between my legs, the press of his erection through the cotton of his briefs.

He kisses me again, and I lift my hips and cry out at the pressure of him against my clit. How can I be so close to coming apart? He's hardly touched me, but I feel my body skating along a precarious ledge. I press my hips down into the mattress to suppress the instinctive grind.

He mutters a curse against my ear. "Don't stop."

I grip his shoulders and curl my nails into his skin. "I'm afraid I'll . . ." My hips jerk under him, and heat whips down my spine. "Jake . . ."

"Just let yourself feel good." He circles his hips, rubbing himself against me, and God it's good. It's heat and pressure and elation, and I want more and less all at once. He sucks at the tender skin of my neck before returning his mouth to my ear. "Do you have any idea how hot it is to see you this turned on? To have you naked under me and know you're about to come against my cock?" He sucks my earlobe between his teeth, and I hear my own sharp cry. *God, that mouth.* "I can't wait to get inside you."

His words are my undoing. They cut away the last of my restraint and push me over the line between pleasure and release. I rock against him through it—wild and unashamed, my entire body a collection of tiny explosions.

He kisses my neck. My ear. My jaw. The tip of my nose. "You're so beautiful."

I drag in one gulp of air after another. I can't believe I just did that. I can hardly get myself off on a good day, and orgasms with a partner have been rare at best in my experience. But I just dry-humped Jake until I saw stars. "Wow." I uncurl my fingers from his shoulders and wince. He's going to have marks from my nails. "Sorry."

A phone rings again, but this time it's mine. We both ignore it.

He pushes himself up on one arm so he's looking down at me. "What are you apologizing for?"

I shrug. "For digging my nails into your shoulders? For finishing before we really got started?"

He grins. "I can handle some battle scars if it means hearing you moan like that." His eyes search my face. "And I never said you were finished."

A booming knock echoes through the room. "Jake! Get your ass here now!"

Chapter TWENTY-FOUR

AVA

Jake tenses, and I frown. "Is that Levi?" I ask.

"I think so." Jake sweeps a kiss across my lips. "I'll be right back."

I nod, and he studies my face for a final beat. When Levi pounds again, Jake climbs off the bed and tugs on his jeans, not bothering to zip them. He grabs a hotel robe from the closet and tosses it to me with a wink before he rounds the corner to get the door.

I scramble off the bed and pull on the robe. I try to listen, but I can't make out their murmurs until Jake says, "Okay. I'll meet you in the lobby."

Funny. Two minutes ago, I was naked and rocking under Jake, but when he comes back around the corner and gathers his shirts off the floor, I feel awkward and self-conscious. His shoulders are tense, and stress is written all over his face.

"Mom's in the hospital." He tugs his undershirt on over his head.

I blink, and my worries about me and Jake fizzle away, replaced with concern for Kathleen. "What happened?"

"She fell—broke her ankle and hit her head pretty good. Shay found her passed out on the floor in her bathroom. They're still in the ER, but they're getting Mom a room." He tugs on his shirt, but he doesn't look at me. He's already on his way home.

My heart swells and aches all at once. Some guys would call to check in and then crawl back into bed, but this is Jake. Steadfast. Loyal. Reliable. He's there for his family whether they need him there or not, and if there's anything he can do to help, he will.

And he's the same for me.

Shivering, I tighten the robe around me.

"Ellie and Colton will take you home so you don't have to miss your brother racing."

"Sure."

Jake throws his toothbrush and outfit from the track into his bag and zips it up before turning to me. He's been all business since Levi left, but his expression softens as his eyes meet mine. "Hey." He drops the bag and comes around to my side of the bed. He cups my jaw in his hand as he studies me. "Are you okay?"

I shiver again. "I'm fine."

His lips quirk, but there's no humor in his eyes. "You only say that when you're not." He strokes the back of his hand up the side of my neck. "I'm sorry I have to go. I promise I'll make it up to you."

"I know you will." *Because that's who you are.* The back of my eyes sting with tears, and I just want him to leave before I cry. "I hope Mom's okay," I whisper.

He closes his eyes and leans his forehead against mine. "Me too."

Then his mouth is on mine, gentle at first, before turning coaxing and deeper, and when he pulls away we're both breathless, both staring at each other. Am I the only one who has some thinking to do, or has he been rocked by tonight as well?

"I'll text you when we get back to Jackson Harbor," he says softly. "Try to have fun tomorrow."

I don't trust myself to speak, so I nod. He sweeps a final kiss across my lips before slinging his bag over his shoulder and heading out the door.

I listen to the heavy door click closed and crawl into bed, where I draw my knees to my chest and squeeze my eyes shut.

Jake offered to give me a child because that was what I wanted. I was going to let him because my wish to be a mother made me blind to my own selfishness, and maybe more than that. Maybe on some level I knew I wanted the nights with Jake too. But suddenly, I'm greedy for more.

AVA

Five years ago . . .

Looking my fiancé in the eye isn't easy. I told him that Jake kissed me, that Jake said he was in love with me. That confession alone wouldn't have been so bad, but I'm a full-disclosure kind of girl. When I told him, I confessed that I kissed Jake back, that I felt something I shouldn't feel.

Harrison looks at me differently now, and tonight the questions in his eyes mirror the questions in my heart. I slide the steaks onto plates and toss sliced tomatoes, peppers, and olives into the salad.

Harrison is very traditional, and he waits at the dinner table while I serve. He's said that's how he was raised, and he always thought there was something special in the way his mom treated his father. He believes that's the secret to their lasting marriage. When I saw his mother in action, I decided I'd give Harrison the same treatment she gave her husband. Tonight, however, having him watch me as I bring the plates and bowls to the table, I feel less like the adored spouse and more like the chastised servant.

That's just your guilty conscience, Ava.

When all the food is on the table and I'm finally in my seat, he pours me a glass of wine.

"Have you thought any more about a wedding date?" he asks.

"Maybe we shouldn't set one yet." My voice gets caught on the emotion in my throat and hitches, and then my eyes fill with hot tears. I love Harrison, and I'm so angry at Jake right now for ruining days that should be full of excitement and celebration. I'm also mad at myself. If those old feelings hadn't come rushing to the surface the second his mouth came down on mine, I'd have been able to brush this off. I'd be planning my wedding right now instead of hurting the man I love.

"Because of Jake?" Harrison asks.

I shrug. We both know the answer to that question.

"Ava, I love you," he says. "And I thought you loved me."

"I do!" My chest squeezes. "Of course I do. But if I have feelings, I should . . . It's not fair to you."

"He's manipulating you to control you."

I blink at Harrison. That doesn't sound like Jake at all.

Harrison rubs the back of his neck and leans back in his chair. "I didn't want to upset you, baby, but maybe you need to know. After you told me what happened, I confronted Jake."

"You did?"

His eyes meet mine, and he nods slowly. "He kissed my girl. I couldn't do nothing."

"Harrison, what did you do?"

He draws in a long breath. "I didn't hurt him. Don't worry." He shakes his head and looks away. "I went to the bar, ready for a fight. I was so angry. I called him on what he did. What he said to you. And do you know what he said to me?"

My heart is in my throat. I haven't talked to Jake since I sent him away three days ago. "What did he say?"

"He said you were his best friend, but his feelings stopped there. He told me you are nothing more than a sister to him, but he'd have said anything to you to keep you from marrying me." He holds up a hand. "I'm not discrediting your feelings, but I think *you* need to understand his."

Nothing more than a sister. My gut twists around the blade of those words, and the pain makes my breath shudder.

"I'm not saying he doesn't have feelings for you, but I don't think they're the feelings you want him to have," Harrison says. "Before you break my heart and walk away from our life together, I want you to think about the fact that this guy never looked at you twice before I put a ring on your finger. I want you to think about his words. He admitted he'd have said *anything* to you to keep you from marrying me. What kind of friend is that, Ava? Are those the words of a man going after the woman he loves, or are those the words of a selfish child who thinks his playmate is being taken away?"

The blade twists again and again in my stomach until there's nothing left. I feel empty inside, hollowed out. I push my plate away. My appetite is gone. "How can you still want to marry me after all this?" I ask. "I love you, Harrison, but I don't want to misrepresent what I'm feeling right now."

"You're *confused*," he says.

I nod. Hot tears roll down my cheeks. *I'm so confused.*

His chair squeaks against the tiled floor as he pushes it back and steps to my side of the table. He turns my seat so I'm facing him but stops me when I try to stand. Lowering himself to his knees in front of me, he cups my face in his hands and looks up into my eyes. "We love each other," he says. "I'm not going to pretend this hasn't hurt me, but I don't want to lose you either."

My head bobbles as I nod. "I don't want to lose you."

His big thumbs swipe at my cheeks, wiping away my tears. "Then marry me, Ava. Set a date. Make me the happiest man in the world."

Chapter
TWENTY-FIVE

JAKE
Present day...

Ava: Thank you for this weekend. I was looking forward to it all week, but then it was even better than I'd hoped. You know how to make a girl feel special, Jake. Let me know how Mom's doing.

The text came sometime this morning while I was passed out in a chair in Mom's hospital room. Levi and I arrived around three a.m. I made Ethan go home to be with Nic and convinced Shay she needed sleep if she was going to help with Mom today. Carter had gone back to the station to finish his shift before we arrived, but Levi, Brayden, and I have lingered at the hospital all night, unwilling to leave Mom alone despite optimistic reports from the nurses.

It's just me and Mom now—Levi and Brayden went down to

the cafeteria to scrounge up some breakfast—but any minute, the room will be flooded with my siblings. I take advantage of these last moments of peace and let myself read the text over and over again.

"You look like you're trying to solve the world's problems over there," Mom says.

I look up from my phone and blink at her. She was awake when Levi and I made it into town last night, and thank God for that. I don't think I would have slept a minute if I hadn't been able to hear her voice and see her smile. By the time I got here, she was laughing about her fall. She'd been changing a light bulb in the bathroom and hopped off the stool and landed wrong.

"Forgot I wasn't sixteen anymore," she said with a laugh.

The doctors thought she suffered a mild concussion from hitting her head on the counter when she collapsed, and they wanted to keep her overnight for observation. This morning, they'll take her into surgery to set the ankle and put in screws to make sure it heals right.

I smile at Mom. She might be in a hospital bed and have a colorful bandana covering her bald head, but she looks healthier than she did after her last treatment four weeks ago. There's more color in her cheeks—less misery in her eyes. She has more energy. Now, if we could just get her appetite back so we could put some meat on those bones, I might feel the optimism I keep reaching for and missing. "Good morning, Mom."

"Good morning, Jakey," she says, using the old nickname from my childhood. Mom and Shay were the only ones who could get away with it. I'd take a swing at anyone else who called me *Jakey*. "What's got my boy so worried?"

I open my mouth to lie, to tell her I'm not worried about anything, but then I decide against it. "Ava," I admit.

"Oh." She studies me for a silent beat. I wonder if Mom knew I was in love with Ava before even I did. Probably. She knows all her kids better than we know ourselves.

I wave a hand. "It'll be fine. I think we need to talk when she gets back in town. That's all."

"Someone told me she's trying to get pregnant and you're going to help her."

With a little huff, I drop my head into my hands and shake it, groaning. "Who told you that?"

"I get a little of my information here, a little there. I put it all together and then coerce your siblings until they fill in the blanks for me."

I don't have the energy to be pissed at anyone for that right now, so I let it go. Anyway, trying to explain to my mom that I'm using my best friend's wish for a baby as a way to seduce her and trick her into falling for me boils it all down in a way that makes me feel a little slimy. "Well, don't worry about it. I'm being careful."

"Do you really think this is the only way you can have a chance with her?"

"Have a chance with whom?" Shay asks, walking in the door with a stainless-steel carafe.

Grimacing, I stand from the chair I've occupied for the last four hours and stretch to straighten the kinks in my back. "I don't want to talk about it."

"Jake's trying to get Ava pregnant so she'll give him a chance," Mom tells Shay.

"I'm not trying to—" I groan and press my palms to my eyes. "I don't want to have this conversation with either one of you."

"You know better than to think we're letting it drop." Shay pulls a sleeve of disposable coffee cups from her purse and hands one to me. "Talk."

I take it, grateful, and pour myself a cup of coffee. I can tell by the smell of it that Shay made it—it's bold, rich, and contains enough caffeine to wake a dead man. "She's looking at me as something other than her friend for the first time in . . ." I shrug and look helplessly at my sister. "The first time ever, I guess."

"Risky as hell," Shay says, and when I shoot her a warning glare, she holds up both hands. "I'm not going to interfere, and I didn't say I didn't think it was worth it. I just think it's risky." She pours her own cup of coffee and shrugs. "I understand why it's a risk worth taking. It's Ava."

"That's true," Mom says. "It's Ava."

I feel like a bug under a microscope, and I want to squirm. Instead, I drink my coffee and stew. I'll have to wait until Ava gets home, but we'll talk. Maybe she'll let me kiss her again. Maybe we can pick up where we left off in the hotel room. Because this is working. What's happening between us isn't just about the baby for either of us. She knew we weren't going to have sex, and she wanted to be with me anyway. If I can keep nudging her, I might finally get the chance I've been waiting for.

"Do you remember when you were sixteen and dating that Emily . . ." Mom snaps her fingers and screws up her face in concentration. "What was her last name? The blond cheerleader? She was older than you."

"Emily Higgins," I supply.

"Oh, I remember her," Shay says. "Pretty but no sense of humor."

Mom smooths her sheets over her stomach and smiles softly as if lost in the memory. I have no idea where she's going with this. "You and Emily couldn't keep your hands off each other." She grins at me. "I threatened to make you wear my oven mitts on your hands every time she was in the house, remember?"

I laugh. One time, she didn't just threaten. She taped those mitts on me and told me my girlfriend could only go down in the basement with me if I wore them. Mom underestimated Emily, though, and that night turned out *just fine* for me. I couldn't pull a pan out of the oven without getting hard for months after that.

Shay laughs. "Oven mitts never scared the girls away from your boys, Mom."

Mom winks at her, then turns back to me. "One night you were in the basement, doing God knows what. Ava came over from next door, went down there, and raced right back up the stairs."

"I remember," Shay says. "Carter found her out in the tree fort. He brought her inside and up to my room. Her eyes were red, and her face was streaked with tears. God, she was miserable. She swore up and down that her tears had nothing to do with Jake, but no one bought it."

"I made her those cookies she always liked," Mom says, "and Carter put on that Jim Carrey movie—the one where he becomes God and gives everyone what they pray for."

"*Bruce Almighty*," I supply. No actor can make Ava laugh like Jim Carrey, and I love that laugh. Before I heard her come, it was the best sound I knew.

Mom nods. "Yes, and by the time you and Emily came back upstairs, she was laughing and happy, but we all knew how much it hurt Ava to see you with someone else."

I swallow hard. I've never heard this story before. Back when I was sixteen, Ava truly was *just* my best friend. Or at least that was what I thought.

"You two have been inseparable since you met," Mom says. "Even before you considered yourselves friends, you couldn't stay away from each other."

Shay grunts. "I couldn't believe she wanted anything to do with you. You were always playing tricks on that poor girl."

I stare into my coffee, grateful for the familiarity of it. We might be stuck in the hospital, but having a cup of Shay's coffee in my hand makes me feel like we're at home. "Well, she was fun to tease."

"Of course, being the old lady that I am," Mom says, "I always wanted you two to stop skirting around the issue and tell each other how you felt."

I look up at Shay, then at Mom. "I already tried that, Mom."

She arches a brow. "Have you? Directly?"

I nod and absently pull my phone from my pocket to look at Ava's text again. I hover my thumb over the picture of her that appears next to the words. "I told her the day I found out she was engaged to Harrison. I went to her apartment and I kissed her. I told her I was in love with her."

Mom's completely silent, and I can't tell if it's shock or sadness, but I take Shay's silence as commiseration. She was the only sibling I told about that day—the only one I trusted to hear the story and not hold it against Ava.

When I look up, Mom has her hand pressed to her chest and her eyes are sad. "Oh, Jakey."

"My timing was bad," I say. "I get that. But sometimes . . . I don't know, Mom. Sometimes I think I'm just being dense. Holding on to her. But I can't make myself let go."

And then there was last night. When she confessed to touching herself and thinking about me. Too many times to count.

"Do you *want* to let her go?" Mom asks. "Would you be happier?"

"No." I shake my head. "Not at all." But I don't want to scare her away either, and I don't know if she's ready to learn that my feelings for her have never changed. And I don't know if she'll be able to forgive me when she finds out about my night with Molly.

Shay squeezes my shoulder then refills my cup. "Hang in there, brother."

I meet her eyes, grateful. "Thanks."

AVA

"Why are you in a crappy mood this morning?" Ellie asks.

We're at the breakfast buffet in the hotel lobby. We were supposed to meet Levi's date here, but she decided to get together with some friends who live in Livonia, just outside Detroit. My brother's already left for the track and we'll see him over there later. So it's just Ellie, me, and my bad mood the size of Texas.

She grabs the carafe of coffee and fills her mug. "These walls aren't very thick, you know, so I have pretty good reason to believe you should be in a *spectacular* mood."

I try to laugh, but it falls flat. "I thought you were still at the club when Jake and I came back."

"We weren't far behind you." She squeezes my wrist and gives a small smile. "I'm sorry he had to leave. That sucks."

I shake my head. "It's not that. I just had bad dreams all night."

She wraps her hands around the mug and holds it to her chest as if she's using it more for warmth than to drink. "Nightmares?"

I shrug. "I don't know if I'd call them nightmares, but kind of. I was having dreams that I was pregnant, and I was setting up the nursery but I was at Jill and Dad's house. They were giving me all these rules about how I had to raise my child, and how the baby had to be quiet when we had dinner parties. The whole time I knew I didn't want to be there, but it was like I had nowhere else to go."

"What was that about?" she asks.

Ellie only moved to Jackson Harbor a few years ago, so while she knows a lot about my family and life, she doesn't know all the details. "Remember how I told you I moved in with Dad when I was finishing high school."

"Yeah, and you had to live with Mother Teresa."

"I felt like a burden the whole time I was there. It was like he was making an exception by letting me stay. Like he was doing me a favor by letting me live in his house with his real family. The better family. In my dream, I was the unwelcome guest again. The burden. But this time I had a baby."

"Oh, shit. Your subconscious has the subtlety of a bulldozer, sweets."

"I know, right?" I shake my head.

"Jake is nothing like your father," Ellie says softly.

"I know. I do." In every way that counts, I'd say Jake's entirely different. Except that I feel like I'm seventeen again, knowing my whole life is about to change and that the easiest path is to let someone who doesn't really want me take me in. Last night, Jake made it clear that he's attracted to me, but is that enough? Admitting that he's thought about me naked is a far cry from wanting to have a life with me.

"So why the insecurity?" Ellie leans forward on the table and studies my face. "I know I wasn't on board with the idea of you becoming a single mom, but honestly, I didn't realize how serious you were about this. I think you and Jake would make great parents."

Parents. That makes it sound like we'd do it together, side by side. "Jake didn't sign up for parenting with me," I say, my voice cracking a little on the words. Audible heartbreak. "That wasn't our deal."

"But you have to believe he'd be involved, right?"

I nod, feeling the unwelcome heat of tears pricking my eyes. "I know he would. Jake doesn't take family lightly either. When he rushed out the door to be with his mom, I realized what should have been so obvious from the start—there's no way he's going to give me a baby and not feel responsible for both of us for the rest of his life."

"He'd be your rock," Ellie says. "Maybe even more. You two are so good together. The chemistry between you on the dance floor last night . . ." She shakes her hand as if it's been burnt. "Scorching."

"I don't want to become an obligation he can't ignore. I can't spend the rest of my life like that. I want better for myself and for my child."

"So what does that mean?"

I draw in a ragged breath. "I think it means I need to postpone Operation Pregnancy for the immediate future." I blink away tears. "I can't believe I've been so stupid. I just wanted what I wanted so badly that I didn't think it through. I don't think I wanted to." I shake my head. "How *dare* I ask him to give me a child?"

"You didn't ask—not sober, at least." She squeezes my wrist again. "Jake offered. And I promise you, *he* thought it through. He knew what he was doing when he made you that offer."

I look away. I know exactly what Jake was doing—he was giving me what I so desperately wanted. He was taking care of his family.

If I have a baby on my own with the help of the fertility clinic instead of him, it'll be the same. Jake will be right there to help me every step of the way. Because that's who he is. But at least that way he'd be able to walk away when he met someone else. He wouldn't have the *forever* kind of obligation a child of his own would give him. "I don't want him cornered into a life with me like Dad was when Mom moved. I don't want to feel like I did when I was seventeen. I never want to feel like that again."

She shakes her head. "Jake wouldn't make you feel that way, though. He wants you around, Ava. He's been your best friend forever, and there's a reason for that."

My best friend. But last night we opened Pandora's box, and now I don't know if I can handle going back to the status quo. "My dad got me a lead on a job," I say, desperate to stop talking about Jake. "He's convinced I'm going to get laid off."

"Jerk," she mutters.

I sigh. "Totally, but that's Dad."

"What's the job?"

"I'd be teaching theater and drama, and starting a new children's theater from the ground up." I laugh softly. "I can't even imagine a life without endless composition papers. This would be all theater and teaching kids who love it." I sit up straighter. "Their budget for plays and musicals is insane, and even though they only called me because of Dad's connections, they act like they're really impressed with me and my experience. They want me to interview."

"That's amazing. What's the holdup?"

"The job's in Florida."

"Oh," Ellie says. "Wow."

"No kidding." I let out a breath. "It's near my mom, so there's that, but I always assumed I'd spend the rest of my life in Jackson Harbor, know what I mean?"

She nods. "I do. I didn't grow up there like you did, but it even feels like home to me."

"Yeah, but what's keeping me here? Every time I have to see Harrison with his baby, it's going to kill me." *And if I stay in Jackson Harbor and have a baby on my own, Jake's going to sacrifice his own life to be my rock.*

"You're seriously considering this."

"I don't know. Maybe?"

She squeezes my hand, and I can see the anguish on her face. I know she wants to say more. She wants to tell me that Jake and I can work it out, but to her credit, she doesn't. Instead, she waves to the waitress and asks for two mimosas.

CHAPTER TWENTY-SIX

AVA

"Sydney, I got your application, and you're good to go." I scroll down my list, making sure I've talked to all the students in drama club who want to help with the children's theater this summer. "Lance, I still need the permission slip from your parents, but other than that, you're good to go."

"On it," Lance says.

"May I help at auditions tomorrow?" Sydney asks, packing up her things.

"I'd love that." I grin at her. "Are you prepared to deal with a bunch of incredibly hyper and nervous grade-school kids?"

She shrugs. "I wish someone had let me get on stage when I was little. I think it's cool that they're getting into it so young."

Lance sticks around with Sydney as the other students file out. "I can come too," he says. Then he remembers to look apathetic and shrugs. "I mean, if you needed help, it wouldn't mess with my plans or anything."

I grin. Drama club met after school today, but since we've already wrapped up the spring Windsor Prep performance, the weekly meeting is more of a planning hour for these last few weeks of the year. "I can always use extra hands on audition days."

"Miss McKinley?" I look up to see Mr. Mooney sticking his head in the door to my classroom. "May I see you in my office before you leave today?"

My stomach sinks. Being called to the principal's office isn't any less terrifying when you're an adult. "Of course. I'll be down in about fifteen minutes."

Mr. Mooney doesn't even attempt a reassuring smile. Instead, he gives a tight nod and walks away.

"Are you in trouble?" Lance asks.

"Is it about the layoffs?" Sydney asks.

I wave them both off. "You two worry too much. Go ahead and get out of here. I'll see you at the theater tomorrow."

They look skeptical but gather their things and leave my classroom. I'm glad when they're gone, and I no longer have to fight to keep my smile in place.

It's been a long day at the end of an even longer week. A meeting with Mr. Mooney wasn't on the agenda, and I can't imagine it's likely to make an already tough week any easier.

My phone buzzes, and seeing Jake's name in the text notification makes something knot in my stomach.

Jake: I've missed you this week.

I've been avoiding Jake—easy enough to do. The children's theater is beginning its inevitable takeover of my life, as it does this time every year, and the end-of-the-school-year grading seems never-ending. But now it's been six days since he walked out of our hotel room. I'm bound to see him when I'm out for girls' night tonight, and maybe again when Lilly comes to her audition tomorrow. We've texted a couple of times, but he's been busy too. Kathleen had surgery on Sunday and was released from the hospital but needs a little extra help getting around.

> *Me: I've been so busy. If I don't see you at the bar tonight, I'll try to catch you tomorrow morning.*

I bite my lip and force myself to hit send. I need to see Jake. I need to admit to him that I'm hitting the brakes on Operation Pregnancy . . . at least for now. I'm just not sure how to have that conversation. What will that mean for me and Jake? Will we go back to how we were before? Is that possible or have I ruined everything?

> *Jake: Oh, you'll see me tonight. In fact, I might pull you away from the girls. Give me fifteen minutes in my office. I promise you won't regret it.*

A thrill rushes down my spine and my thighs tighten at those words, and I have to squeeze my eyes shut for a beat. Part of me—a very selfish, undersexed part that's lusted after her best friend for longer than she'll admit—wants to hold off on telling Jake. I know letting him give me a baby is a capital-B, capital-I

Bad Idea, but having him flirt with me and touch me has been nothing short of a fantasy. I don't want it to end. I know I turn him on, and he's admitted he's been attracted to me for a long time, but is that enough? Is either of us willing to give Ava-and-Jake a try without a baby as an excuse?

I type three different replies before I settle on a cryptic *We'll see about that*, and tuck my phone back into my purse.

I take my time packing my things, needing the few minutes of alone time before facing Mr. Mooney. Last week, I let my plagiarizer have another chance on his research paper, and even though I'd bet money he had someone write it for him, I couldn't prove a thing, so I graded it, and everyone but me seemed pretty pleased with that outcome. Today must be a different unhappy student. Or worse, unhappy parents.

Just a day in the life of a private school teacher.

I roll my shoulders back and head to Mr. Mooney's office, knocking twice on the frame of the open door before poking my head in. "Mr. Mooney?"

He gives me a tight smile from the other side of the desk and waves me in. "Please, Ms. McKinley, have a seat."

"Thanks," I say softly. My hackles are up, but I need to assume the best until I know there's a reason not to.

"As you know," he begins, "we've been having to grapple with some pretty difficult choices with all these layoffs."

I wait for him to say more, but he just looks at me, and as the seconds tick away, I realize what he's not saying, and I freeze. I knew layoffs were coming, but I naively believed what he told me that night at Howell's. I thought I wouldn't be affected. But he's staring at me as if he's waiting for me to understand something.

He wants me to guess it before he has to say it out loud.

I won't give him the satisfaction. "Okay?"

He sighs heavily, his annoyance weighing in the air as unmistakably as his cheap cologne. "I've always appreciated your work ethic and your rapport with your students. But as you know, we have to look outside the classroom, too. Miss Quincy has taken our cheerleaders to state championships two years in a row. Not only is it an invaluable experience for the girls and a pathway to scholarships, it's good for the school. Girls want to come here because they want to be on that team."

My stomach sinks. "But I have seniority."

"This is a private school, Miss McKinley. We've never used years of service as a metric for teacher evaluation."

"But what about the theater program? Those kids—"

"Do you really think the theater program is going to bring kids to this school?"

I lean forward, feeling desperate. "If you'd give me some money to work with, it might. The cheerleaders have gotten everything they've asked for and more, and meanwhile the theater kids are expected to put on major productions with nothing but the paltry budget they get from fundraisers."

He holds up a hand. "I could have waited until the end of the school year to deliver this news, but I'm telling you now as a professional courtesy. I knew you'd want to prepare yourself."

I shake my head. This isn't just about me and my job. Every year, kids find themselves through the drama club. They forge friendships and develop confidence. They create something they can be proud of. "We've already started planning next year. These kids are counting on me."

"Mr. Wick will take over the drama club."

I gape at him. Mr. Wick is the orchestra instructor who hasn't taught a drama class in the entire time I've been here. "Mr. Wick hates theater. He mocks the kids who want to do it and resents having to put his orchestra in the pit for our musicals."

"Enough, Ava. I've done you a favor by telling you sooner than I needed to, and frankly, your behavior is making me regret that decision."

Protest after protest surges up my throat, but I swallow them all back and focus on keeping the burning tears at the back of my eyes from making their way down my cheeks. "This is all just a very big shock."

"I want you to have as much time as possible to find a new job. We had to make hard decisions, and I don't like that any more than you do. I don't want you to disrupt the last two weeks of our school year because you're *pouting* about not being chosen."

I'm *pouting*? This is my job. It's my *life*. I've given this place everything for eight years, and now I'm pouting?

"I hope I can trust you to handle this properly with the students. The last thing we need is you making us look like the bad guys."

"I'll do what's expected of me. Just like I always do." I push my chair back and stand. "Is that all?"

"It is." He folds his arms and leans back in his chair. "I'm sorry I don't have better news, Ava, but you and I both know you already have one foot out the door."

"What's that supposed to mean? I've been fully dedicated to Windsor Prep since I graduated from college."

He arches a brow. "Why would I keep on an employee who's

considering jobs in Florida when I could keep the ones who *want* to be here?"

"Knock, knock!" Ellie calls from the foyer, her heels tapping on my hardwood floor.

Shit. I completely forgot it was girls' night. I'm in sweatpants and a ratty old T-shirt, and am feeling as prepared for a night at Jackson Brews with the girls as I am for a walk across a beauty pageant stage.

"What's wrong?" Ellie asks as soon as she spots me. "Ava, what happened?"

I wipe my cheeks. "I lost my job."

"No!" Ellie's face crumples. "Seriously?"

I nod. "I knew they were doing layoffs. It shouldn't come as a *complete* surprise."

"Yeah, but they're getting rid of one of their longest-serving, most dedicated teachers?"

I shrug. "It was me or Miss Quincy, and she's got the cheer team, which brings in all the money."

"Well, you've got the drama kids."

I cut my eyes to Ellie. "Who bring in no money."

"Because they don't give you any support. Cheer gets all the funding!"

"I love you," I whisper. I know she's just parroting the things she's heard me complain about, but it doesn't matter. Right now, it feels really good to have her on my side.

"That asshole," she says. "He's had it out for you ever since you refused to let him feel you up on that blind date. That's what this is about. He has a personal vendetta against you."

"He found out about the job in Florida," I whisper, and my cheeks flame hot with anger, frustration, and humiliation. I wasn't even trying to look for another job, but my father's belief that I'd be the first to be let go came back and bit me in the ass.

"Crap." She sinks down on the couch beside me, and I lean my head on her shoulder. "What are you going to do?"

I swallow hard and draw in a ragged breath. "Wallow in self-pity tonight, spend my afternoon at Jackson Harbor Children's Theater tomorrow, and spend Sunday trying to figure out what my options are."

"Your options meaning Florida?"

I shrug. "That's one possibility, I guess. I don't know. I was considering it, but I hate feeling like I'm being cornered into making such a big decision."

"Get dressed. Let's go out. You need a drink."

I shake my head. "I can't do it tonight, Ell. I love you guys, but I'm only giving myself one night to feel sorry for myself, so I'm going to make the most of it."

She kisses the top of my head in an uncharacteristically maternal gesture. "Okay, but next girls' night, you're coming whether you want to or not."

"Understood."

She squeezes my hand again. "Want me to swing by after? I could bring ice cream, and we could make a voodoo doll of Mr. Mooney."

"I appreciate the offer, but I think I'll go to bed in a bit."

"Okay. Love you, Avie."

"Love you too, Ell."

Shortly after she's out the door, my phone buzzes. I half expect it to be a text from Ellie insisting I come to girls' night. Instead, it's Jake.

> *Jake: The girls are getting started without you. Everything okay?*
> *Me: I decided to stay in.*
> *Jake: That's my loss. I was really looking forward to my fifteen minutes.*
> *Me: Maybe another time?*

My thumbs hover over the keyboard as I hesitate, considering whether to tell him about the layoff. Usually, Jake's the first person I tell when something big happens in my life, but I don't want to tell him this. He'll swoop in to try and find a solution. He'll pull strings to get me a job, pay my mortgage when I'm not looking, and then, months later, I'll realize that the balance of our friendship has once again fallen to favor me and I'll feel like shit about it.

I will tell him. I have to. But first I need to decide what's next for me, and I have to make that decision alone. Jake won't want me to leave Jackson Harbor.

I'm wondering if that's part of the reason I should.

Chapter TWENTY-SEVEN

JAKE

Me: Confession time? I've had all week to try and haven't managed to make it more than five minutes without thinking about you naked and moaning under me. The only thing keeping me from showing up in your room in the middle of the night is the need to maintain the illusion that I'm not a creep.
Ava: I've thought about it a lot too. I've been thinking about a lot of things this week.

Blood rushes to my dick at those words, and I grimace as I scan the crowded bar. Ava's been at auditions all day, so she probably isn't up for company tonight, but fuck if I don't want to show up at her doorstep right now and hear some very specific details about her *thoughts*.

> *Me: Up for a call? I can hide in my office for a few. Don't mind texting but would rather hear your voice when I learn all about what's been on your mind.*
>
> *Ava: I can't call. I'm meeting someone, but it's my turn for a confession.*
>
> *Me: Please, go on . . .*
>
> *Ava: I'm putting the brakes on Operation Pregnancy.*

I blink at my phone and reread her last text three times before the next one comes through.

> *Ava: We can talk more tomorrow, but I wanted to tell you.*

I'm not sure if this should feel like a victory or a defeat. On the one hand, when I finally do sleep with Ava, I have no intention of being the stud called in to share his seed before being sent away. In that sense, I'm glad she's putting her plans on hold after our night together.

On the other hand, I don't know if the end of Operation Pregnancy means the end of my excuse to seduce her.

Maybe it's an opportunity to confess it was never more than an excuse.

My fingers hover over the screen as I mentally compose and dismiss dozens of replies. I'm equal parts relieved and panicked. I have no doubt Ava still wants a child. She's just decided it's better not to try for one. Or has she decided it is better not to try for one *with me*?

> *Me: Swing by and have a beer with me.*

I regret that reply the second I send it. *Too damn casual.* I don't want her to think that this decision is nothing to me. So I send another.

> *Me: Or I can come by your place. Whatever sounds good to you. We should talk.*
> *Ava: Maybe I'll come by Jackson Brews after my date.*
> *Me: Date????*

I grimace at the four question marks looking back at me from my text. If I wanted to play it cool, I could have left off a few of those.

> *Ava: I forgot I scheduled two SUC dates at once. Just got the reminder about tonight and didn't want to be the bitch who stood someone up.*

I officially hate text conversations. Is it really that she doesn't want to stand someone up, or does her decision to end Operation Pregnancy mean she's back on the market?

I tried to give her space this week. Last Saturday night was intense for her. It was for me, too—intense and fucking amazing. We both put ourselves out there. Admitted this attraction isn't new on either side. It was everything.

> *Me: Enjoy your date. Be safe. Call if you need me.*

I have to believe her plans to take the focus off pregnancy might mean something good for us, but until we get to talk *in person,* I can't assume anything.

AVA

*I*f I hadn't scheduled my first two Straight Up Casual dates at the same time, and if I didn't have a serious guilt complex at the prospect of standing someone up, I'd be spending my Saturday night at home, not at Howell's downing another shot of tequila and praying to every deity I've ever heard of that this experience is better than my last.

I'd like to blame the tequila for the heat pooling in my belly, but I know Jake's texts are responsible. I *like* the idea of him thinking about me. I *like* the idea of him showing up in my bed in the middle of the night. My only problem is that I don't know if the attraction he proved so clearly last weekend extends beyond sexual desire. Does he want a real relationship with me? And do I want one with him when I don't know where I'll be living come fall?

Ending Operation Pregnancy in a text was cowardly, but I was afraid I wouldn't do it at all if I didn't do it now. And if the sexy texts stop now? That'll tell me all I need to know about where Jake stands.

I study the contents of my drink and wait for a date I'm not the slightest bit interested in having. This is the last one. Thankfully,

Ellie was cool about it when I told her I was transferring her gift to Teagan.

I might as well make the best of tonight, though, so I will myself to imagine a good outcome to this date. A handsome guy with a big smile who looks at me with stars in his eyes. Someone with a steady job, who values family and knows how to make me laugh.

Someone a lot like Jake.

The thought makes my chest pinch, and I take a long pull of my beer. Jake isn't just a prime example of the kind of guy every girl deserves; he's my rock.

Since Saturday night, when I realized how thoroughly I was taking advantage of him, I've been trying to brace myself for a life where I hold myself up a little more on my own and depend on Jake a little less. It won't be easy.

When Carter Jackson walks in the door of Howell's and spots me and the Straight Up Casual placard on my table, I want to crawl under the nearest rock. If he knows that Jake and I were jumping headlong into Operation Pregnancy only a week ago, seeing me here with another guy tonight is going to make me look like an ass.

I am an ass.

This is so stupid. I should have just called and canceled this date. I've lost my job, might be moving to Florida, and have feelings for my lifelong best friend that I don't really know what to do with. I have no business dating right now.

Carter grabs a shot from the bar, throws it back, then strides across the room to me. He thrums his fingers on my table. "Straight Up Casual?" he asks with an arched brow.

"If you mock me for this," I say, "I'll tell every single woman in town that you have a small penis."

He holds up a hand and then clears his throat. "Okay, first of all, they know better. Second of all, I'm not mocking you." He looks around. "I'm pretty sure you're my date, Ava."

I glare at him. "Are you freaking *kidding* me? They set me up with my boss four weeks ago, and this week it's my best friend's brother?"

He winces. "They set you up with Mr. Mooney?"

"Yeah. Not the best night of my life, let me tell you."

"Shit." Grimacing, he scratches his head. Like the rest of the Jackson boys, Carter is incredibly hot. He has dark hair and eyes, full lips and scruffy cheeks, and a thick, muscular build that's a testament to his hours at the gym and his firefighter training. "Well, this is awkward."

"Little bit," I agree.

"I thought . . ." He clears his throat and looks around again. "I thought you and Jake were . . . I heard something about a baby?" His voice squeaks on *baby*, and my cheeks heat in embarrassment.

"I called that off." I sigh. "It was a crazy idea, and I came to my senses."

"Right. It was . . . well, unconventional, I guess." When he brings his eyes back to meet mine, his expression softens. "You can't be my date, Ava," he whispers. "No offense, but I just can't do that."

Thank God. "Because I'm like a sister to you, or because I took all your money last time we played poker?"

When he grins, little lines pop up by his eyes. "I forgot about that. Damn, I still think you cheated."

"I don't have to cheat. I'm just good." I wave to the waitress with a grin. "But how about I buy you a drink to make up for it?"

Chapter TWENTY-EIGHT

JAKE

Sunday brunch with my family is supposed to be the part of my week I can always look forward to. At least, that's the idea. But sometimes—like this morning—I'm in a shit mood, and would rather sit at home and zone out with some video games than have to look my siblings in the eye and deal with their well-intentioned judgments of my life.

This morning is like every other. Brayden's kitchen is crowded with people, and eight conversations seem to be going on around me at all times. Though I adore Ethan's girlfriend, Nic, seeing him and her wrapped around each other makes me want to punch something. Because I want that. It's what my parents had. It's what I grew up believing I could find so easily, and then I found myself wanting it with a woman who doesn't want it with me.

I've had lots of girlfriends and made plenty of attempts to get the fuck over her, but I have nothing to show for it but a best friend who went on a drunken blind date last night, a fucking *week* after I had her naked under me in a hotel room.

I ran into Ava's nosy neighbor at the coffee shop this morning and was informed Ava didn't get in until after two a.m. *"I was up—this arthritis doesn't let me sleep more than a few hours at a time—and I saw her coming in. She was so happy and frazzled! I think she must've met someone pretty special. She didn't say so, but I recognized that look in her eye. I was young once too, you know."*

It was all I could do to not walk out of Ooh La La! and go straight to Ava's to remind her how she responds to my hands and mouth.

"Well, good morning, Jake," Shay singsongs when she catches me scowling at the coffee pot. "Aren't you a ray of sunshine this morning!"

"I'm training a new bartender," I grumble. It's the reason I worked later last night than I intended, but it has very little to do with my desire to maul the nearest punching bag. "He's an idiot who doesn't know the difference between an imperial stout and a milk stout. Why the fuck do you want to work at a brewery if you don't know the difference between basic beers?"

"Language!" Mom says. She's at the counter putting the finishing touches on finger sandwiches, a cast on one foot, a crutch under her arm.

"Sorry, Mom," I mutter.

"Forgiven. The boy should know his beers if he's going to work for the Jacksons."

"Sure, blame your mood on the bar," Shay says, passing me a

steaming mug of coffee. "That's cool."

I frown at her, but she's already moved on to helping Lilly with her plate. I roll my shoulders back and grab a plate of my own. I'll go through the motions this morning and cut out of here as soon as I can.

I shouldn't have stayed away this week. Giving Ava space was a mistake. She's a thinker, and she probably thought herself into knots worrying about what we did last weekend.

"Uncle Jake, I got a part in *Charlotte's Web*!" Lilly says, bouncing on her toes in front of me.

"I heard that!" Shay says. "Congratulations, Lill! Or should I say Fern?"

"That's awesome!" I smile at my niece, and it's probably my first sincere smile of the day. "Great work."

"I told Ava she didn't need to give her any special treatment," Ethan says softly at my side.

I shake my head. "She wouldn't need to. Lilly is made for the stage."

"Mom, let me get that," Carter says, lunging forward and grabbing Mom's plate.

Mom sighs heavily but lets him take it. "Just when I was starting to feel like I could do things for myself again, I had to go and break my ankle."

"Pretty clever way to keep your kids waiting on you," Brayden says, winking at her.

Some of my tension fizzles away as we all head into the dining room and take our seats. *Family. This is what matters.*

But on the heels of that thought is the thought that Ava should be here. She's already part of this family—has been for twenty years—but she got out of the habit of coming to Sunday brunch when she was with Harrison. I should have pulled her back in the second he walked out her door.

"Carter had a big date last night," Levi says.

Mom beams. "A date!" Mom says, and you can practically see visions of future grandbabies dancing in her head.

I'm not the only one who thought we'd all so easily find what she and Dad had. Sometimes I wonder if she worries she did something wrong. Here we are, all of her six children grown, and only one of us is in a serious relationship.

"I didn't know you were seeing anyone," I say to Carter.

Carter shoots Levi some serious stink-eye, and Levi chuckles.

"Carter's doing the Straight Up Casual thing," Levi says.

Mom tsks. "I don't want to hear about you boys having casual sex."

"That's not what that means, Mom," Carter says, cutting his gaze to me for a beat before returning it to Mom. "It's a company that sets people up based on their profiles, and then sends them on blind dates together."

He leaves out the part about the liquor, but I figure Mom doesn't need to know about that anyway, so I don't chime in.

"You do these blind dates a lot?" Mom asks.

"Last night was my first time," Carter says, clearly reluctant to share details.

"Was the girl nice at least?" Mom asks.

Levi cracks up, as if he can't hold in his laughter anymore. "It was Ava," he blurts.

"Excuse me?" Mom says.

"Ava and Carter were matched up last night," Levi says. He

turns to me. "So I guess you give her the baby and Carter gives her the dates? Is that how this works?"

All the eyes at the table go to me. Except Carter's. That fucking chicken-shit coward keeps his gaze on his plate.

What the fuck was Carter doing with Ava until two a.m.?

"Rumor has it they had a *really* nice time," Levi says, stretching out the words. "Laughing together at Howell's until last call. Really cozy in their booth."

I wait for Carter to deny it or say something to lead me to believe I shouldn't be pissed, but he stays silent, so I push back from the table and leave the dining room.

"Jacob?" Mom calls after me.

"Leave him be," Brayden says.

"He's sulking like a teenage girl," Levi says. "I told him this whole thing was a bad idea from the start."

"You're being a troll," Shay says.

"*Somebody* needs to kick his ass into action," Levi says.

I don't hear anymore because I go into the backyard, narrowly resisting the urge to slam the door behind me on the way out. I feel like I'm stuck in the Twilight Zone. My best friend was naked in my arms last week, and last night my brother went on a date with her and kept her out till all hours. What in the *actual fuck* am I supposed to do with this?

When I hear the swish of the door opening and closing again, I have my hands fisted, my face tilted toward the cloudy midmorning sky.

"Are you seriously doing this?"

I can't look at Carter right now, so I stay in place and drop my gaze to my shoes. "Doing what?"

"Acting like I'm gonna steal your girl?"

"She's not my girl." My voice is rough, as if every word's being scraped against the cheese grater that's rubbed against my heart since Ava's birthday. Why does this have to be so damn complicated? Why can't she just love me back?

"Okay," Carter says. "Fine. I mean, I like her. Always have. Maybe *I'll* give her a goddamn baby."

I spin on him. "You think you're funny?" One step forward and then another. Carter throws his hands out from his sides and rakes his gaze over me, and I realize I have my chest puffed out, my shoulders back, my fists clenched as if I'm going to throw a fucking punch.

"No, I don't think I'm funny," he says. "I *think* you're in love with Ava, and it's past time for you to do something about it."

"Oh, gee. Why didn't I think of that?"

Carter meets my glare and holds it. "Don't you get sick of spinning your wheels? Don't you feel stuck?"

"I like my life. I don't mind if I'm stuck."

"Well, while you're happily standing still, Ava's not." Carter looks away. "She's moving."

I frown. "What? Why would she move? She loves that stupid little house."

"Not moving to another *house*, Jake. Moving to another city. Maybe another state. Wherever she can find a job."

"What? That's crazy. Why would she . . ."

The layoffs, I realize, as Carter says, "She was laid off from Windsor Prep."

Finding out that Carter went on a date with Ava was a punch to the gut, but this is the opposite. Learning about the date hurt, but now I'm numb. As if there's no ground beneath my feet, no world around me. *No air in my lungs.* I feel nothing but this vague sense that any minute now I'm going to crash, and I know in that moment I'll feel everything.

Why didn't she tell me?

He rubs the back of his neck. "Levi's being Levi and starting trouble. Ava and I stayed out late talking. Just talking. I know she's your girl, and I'm not a dick."

"She lost her job?" My voice cracks. I've been spoiled. I've always had Ava close. Even when she married Harrison, I didn't really have to let her go.

"She doesn't want you to take the problem on as your own, but I think you and I both know why she doesn't want to tell you she might move."

I narrow my eyes at him. "We do?"

"Telling you makes it real. She doesn't want to leave you, Jake. Whether or not she feels the way about you that you do about her, I don't know. But she *does* care about you. You need to do something before she walks away."

AVA

I didn't expect to spend my Saturday night talking until two a.m. with Carter Jackson. But the Jacksons have always been like family to me, and once Carter and I got over the awkwardness of having been set up together, we relaxed and had a good time.

I didn't even realize how badly I'd needed someone to talk to until Carter and I started catching up. Then it all spilled out of me. He's a good listener—always has been. He's the quietest of the Jackson brothers, next to Brayden, who's cornered the market on tall, dark, and silent. I talked, and Carter listened, and before we knew it, we were closing down the bar.

It wasn't the kind of date Ellie had hoped for me, but it was a good night. I'm glad we found ourselves there together, even if all it meant was catching up with an old friend.

Nevertheless, it left me really tired, even at noon. I'm nursing another cup of coffee and actively fantasizing about a nap when I hear the scrape of a key in the lock and the sound of heavy footsteps headed toward my kitchen.

Jake appears at the table, pulls out a chair, spins it around, and straddles the back of it. "Hot date last night, huh?"

Of course. It's Sunday. Jackson family brunch. I bet my date with Carter was great fodder for conversation. "Totally hot," I say. "He's probably my soul mate."

Jake grunts and flicks his gaze down to the stack of papers in front of me before bringing it back up to study my face. "Why didn't you tell me?"

I frown. "That I was set up with Carter? I haven't even seen you."

He shakes his head, and I realize what he means. *My job. My move.* I feel a bit betrayed. While I never told Carter that he couldn't tell Jake, I thought discretion was implied.

"Carter told you?"

He sets his jaw and nods. "You lost your job and didn't say a word to me."

"You'd have tried to fix it, Jake. Look at you, sitting there with the wheels turning in your head already trying to come up with a solution. I need to do this on my own." I swallow hard and drop my gaze to the table. "And I need to do the baby thing on my own, too. I can't let you fix everything that's wrong in my life."

"You still want a baby. You just don't want one with me?"

My heart twists. "Everything's so confusing right now. I think you're great and I know you'd be an amazing father. But the truth is, I didn't really think about the consequences of our plans."

"Consequences?"

"If we have a baby together, there will be consequences for that child. For *you*. If you found someone and it didn't work because of me, because of a *favor* you did for me, I couldn't live with myself. I'm sorry I never thought it through."

"You're worried about *me*?"

His shock makes me shrink in shame. Of course he's only thinking of me. Because he's Jake. I swallow back the emotion that's trying to bubble into my voice. "You give me more than I deserve and I . . . I'm going to try to be better. To take less of you."

"I never asked you to take less," he says under his breath. "Never."

"I know. You wouldn't. That's why I need to do better and not let you give so much." Emotion is a ball of cotton in my throat, suffocating me. I feel like I'm breaking up with him, and that's so ridiculous because we've never been together. Not for real. "One day, you're going to find someone who's as awesome as you are. Someone you want to spend your life with."

He lets out a sardonic laugh and shakes his head. "You think

I haven't already found her?"

I stare at him, hope building inside me even as I try to push it down.

"Christ." He pushes his chair back and stands then tugs me out of mine. "Come here."

He draws me against his chest, and in the next moment, his hands are in my hair and his mouth is on mine. I've wanted this since the moment he walked out of the hotel room, and feeling his mouth on me now is enough to make all my worries disintegrate.

When he pulls away, he holds my face in his hands and meets my gaze. "I want *you*. I've spent the last few weeks trying to make you see me as more than a friend for the first time in our entire lives."

"But you . . . I thought . . ." I can't seem to put words together, or even thoughts. "I know we're attracted to each other, but what about our friendship?"

"Christ, Ava, I'm *in love with you.* So in love with you that I stood by your side while you married another man. So in love with you that I can't move the fuck on until I know without a doubt in my mind that you don't feel this too. I'm pretty sure I was born in love with you, and every moment we're together, this thing I feel becomes more of who I am." He shakes his head slowly and scans my face. "I don't want to scare you away, but I can't pretend anymore. I want you, and if you think there's any chance . . ."

"I want you too." I nod wildly. "I love you, and I want . . ." A shudder moves through me. "I'm terrified, Jake. You're the best thing I have, but I want more."

He pulls me to his chest and kisses the top of my head. "We'll take it slow. Okay? As slow as you need."

Chapter TWENTY-NINE

AVA

"What kind of health food do you have on the menu tonight, Jake?" Teagan asks with a wry grin.

"I was going to serve a nice kale salad with chicken breast, but then I remembered I don't serve food that tastes like punishment and self-loathing."

"Hardy-har-har," she says.

This afternoon was Veronica's baby shower. Nic arranged for a sweet little party at Ethan's house where we spoiled the big-bellied woman with all the material things she'll need for the next several months. It was the first time in years I can remember going to a baby shower without an ache of longing in my chest. Finally, I believe everything is going to work out as it should. Time will get me there. With Jake.

The mother-to-be was exhausted after her big day, but the

rest of us wanted to hang out more, so we came to Jackson Brews and claimed our favorite booth at the back.

"For you," Jake says to Teagan, "I'm offering deep-fried Oreos with ice cream and hot fudge. And if you ask really nice, I'll dig up a Twinkie to put on top."

"Is he kidding?" Teagan asks, looking around the table. "I honestly can't tell if he's kidding."

Shay rolls her eyes. "He's probably only half kidding." She turns to her brother. "What's on the menu, Jake? We're hungry."

"Doing street tacos tonight," he says, pulling a few folded menus from his back pocket.

Brayden has given Jake lectures on more than one occasion about how profit margins would go up if he'd keep a fixed menu, but Jake doesn't like to do things Brayden's way. Brayden says it's because Jake hates money, but the truth is Jake takes pride in his rotating menus and would be bored by the monotony of standard pub fare.

"Oh, these sound *so good*," Shay says.

"Agreed," Teagan says, then shakes her head. She points to a description while scowling at Jake. "Avocado is perfect just as it is. There is no reason to deep-fry it."

Personally, I've had the taco with the deep-fried avocado and the drizzle of cilantro ranch, and as sinful as it is, once you've tried it, you can't blame Jake for serving it. *Heaven.* "I'll have two of the Avocado Ranchers," I say, grinning at him.

"Yeah, you will." He winks at me.

The other girls give their orders, and Jake scribbles notes down on his pad before tucking it into his back pocket. "Anything else?"

"Privacy?" Ellie asks. "You haven't walked away from this table since your woman got here."

My cheeks heat, and Jake shrugs. "If you'd let me take her to the back for five minutes—"

"No!" the girls chorus.

Jake chuckles, then dips his head to bring his mouth to mine. The kiss is chaste by most standards—two pairs of lips touching, no tongue, no groping—but the way his mouth lingers against mine makes my blood heat. "You look fucking *amazing* tonight," he whispers in my ear. "I'm feeling really sorry that I promised to take it slow, because I'd love to strip off everything but those heels and—"

"Oh my God! Leave already!" Shay screeches, and I look across the table to see her shudder. "I can't hear what you're saying, but I still feel like I need a shower."

Jake winks at me, then heads to the kitchen to prepare our food.

"So, how's *that* going?" Teagan asks.

My gaze darts to Shay, who's the only person at this table of my friends I haven't talked to about my Sunday afternoon with Jake six short days ago. She folds her arms and watches me. "I'm curious too. He's certainly happier."

"Of course he's happier," Nic says. "He finally got the girl."

"And you're happier," Teagan says. "Lost her job but can't stop grinning. *Somebody's* getting laid."

Ellie snorts, and Shay grimaces. "Remind me to find some friends who don't fuck my brothers. There are some things a girl just doesn't need to know about her family members."

"So you're doing it," Nic says, squeezing her hands together and grinning. "This is happening."

"They're actually *not* doing it," Ellie says. "She got me all excited about being an auntie, but at this rate we're all going to see the dawn of the next century before those two actually copulate." She props her elbows on the table and leans forward. "I think they missed the day in health class when they taught about how the penis has to go *inside* the vagina for babies to get made."

Shay drags a hand over her face. "Maybe I'll leave, and you can text me when you're done talking about my brother's penis?"

I dip my gaze and focus on my beer instead of all the curious eyes pointed in my direction. "We're taking it slow." I nibble on my bottom lip. "It's been nice, actually. I was in such a rush to have a baby, and I still *want* that, but . . . there are a few other things that have taken priority."

"That doesn't mean you can't have sex," Ellie says. "Because condoms?"

Nic smacks her arm. "Stop it. I think it's sweet."

It turns out Jake was serious when he said we'd take it slow. He hasn't done anything more than kiss me since that afternoon in my kitchen. That and some heavy over-the-clothes petting against the bar after we closed last night. He kissed my neck and whispered dirty words, then rubbed me through my jeans until I came. I wanted to go to bed with him so badly afterward that I nearly screamed when he kissed me goodnight and sent me home.

"We've both been really busy," I say. "Slow makes sense." Even if it is making me crazy.

"You're coming to the cabin with us next weekend, right?" Nic asks.

I bite my bottom lip and nod. I've been to the Jackson family cabin many times before. It was a home away from home for me when I was a teenager. But this is the first time I'll be there as Jake's girlfriend—and it will be the first time we've spent the night together since we confessed our feelings. "Is it stupid that I'm nervous?"

Shay laughs. "Yes. Totally stupid. You two have been a couple for two decades without even realizing it. Nothing's changed."

"Colton and I can't make it," Ellie says. "His team needs him in town to test out the new bike they've been working on. So if Jake wears out your hoo-ha and you need a timeout, I won't be there to protect you."

Teagan groans. "Please never refer to a vagina as a hoo-ha ever again."

"Just because your vagina is sad doesn't mean I can't give mine a happy name."

♡

"You hanging in there?" Jake asks me on Friday night. We snuck outside after dinner, and we're standing here with our backs against the house, our faces tilted up to the sky. The night is warm, and the blanket of stars over the cabin is the perfect reminder of why I love this part of Michigan so much.

I nod. "I feel like this is the first chance I've had to catch my breath all week."

We're at the cabin with his family, and there's nowhere else

I'd rather be.

This week has been one unbelievable and emotionally exhausting turn of events after another. Tuesday, I did a Skype interview for the job in Florida. It turns out that Colton was right, and it isn't just Dad's influence that had them coming after me with such gusto. Seaside Community Schools is looking for a candidate who can start a summer theater program from the ground up—which is exactly what I did in Jackson Harbor, except in Seaside the children's theater director position would be paid, whereas here my long hours are done on a volunteer basis.

Then today was my last day at Windsor Prep. My drama kids cried and so did I, but I reminded them that we'll see each other all summer while they help with the children's theater.

Colton's right about my fear of change. I've always been that way, and now it's no different. Jake encouraged me to take the interview for the Seaside position, even if we don't know where the move will leave us. He wants me to make an informed decision, and I just want an excuse to rule out anything that takes me away from him.

Jake's hand finds mine, and I hold my breath as he slowly threads our fingers together and strokes the back of my knuckles with his thumb.

I feel like I've been waiting *forever* for us to make love—which is crazy, because if someone had asked me a few weeks ago, I would have lied and said I wasn't interested in sleeping with Jake at all. Now, all he has to do is walk into a room and I'm warm from my cheeks all the way down to my toes, aware of my body in a way I haven't been in a long time—maybe ever. I hadn't even realized I'd stopped thinking of myself sexually, but I had, and now I'm a bit obsessed. I think about it all the time—his hands, his mouth, how it will feel the first time he's inside me.

"What's going on in that mind of yours?" he asks.

"I'm wondering if you're ever going to do more than kiss me," I say, gathering every bit of my bravery. "If you ever plan to finish what you started at the hotel."

He releases my hand and turns to stand with a leg on either side of mine. He leans over me, his hands against the side of the house. "I promise I'm going to finish what I started." His gaze sweeps over my face before he slowly lowers his mouth. I draw in a breath as his lips sweep across mine. *God, it's good.*

Every cell in my body seems to expand at his touch. It's like flowers blooming or the sun rising or butterflies breaking free from their cocoons—he does that to me all over.

One hand slides under my shirt and up my side. "But if you're wondering if I'm going to do it here," he says, his thumb stroking the underside of my breast, "the answer is no. I can't. There are too many ears around, and the first time I'm inside you, I'm going to make you come so hard you can't help but scream."

My breath catches and my back arches, my body desperate for more of his touch. "What if I'm not a screamer?"

His lips quirk. "We'll see . . ."

"What if I disappoint you?" I mean it to sound like a joke, a reference to the idea of me screaming when I've never screamed during sex in my life. But instead, the words sound a little shaky. A little too vulnerable. A little too insecure. I'm afraid I'm going to disappoint him in so many ways, and I think we both know it.

"You couldn't possibly."

"That night was an anomaly for me. Usually . . ." I swallow. "Usually it's not so easy."

"It was pretty easy when I was rubbing you through your jeans." His lips quirk. "Not that I'm complaining. It was hot as hell."

My cheeks heat at the memory. "But sometimes I just can't," I whisper.

"You let me worry about that, okay?" He shakes his head slowly. "All that matters is that you're enjoying yourself—orgasm or no orgasm, there's no possible way you could disappoint me." He cups my breasts, his thumb stroking across my bra and catching my hard nipple. I bite my bottom lip to catch my moan, and he smiles. "And anyway, I haven't decided what I want to do yet."

"What do you mean by that?"

"Considering how long I've wanted to get inside you . . ." His gaze drops to my mouth. "How many times I've fantasized about having you in my bed. . . I want to make sure the first time is as amazing for you as it is for me. So I can't decide if I want you under me—your knees pulled up around my waist, so you can feel me deep inside you—or if I want you to ride me." He pinches my nipple. "Then I could suck on these perfect breasts while you got yourself off on my cock."

My breath catches, and I press into his hands. "I like your mouth on my breasts."

"I noticed. But then I've thought about taking you from behind—God knows I'm going to make sure that happens eventually—with your ass in my hands as I drive deep and make you stroke your clit for me. It'll be fucking amazing to take you like that."

His words are the light to a fuse that races across my skin and sets every nerve ending on fire. *Yes, please.* I want everything. All of it.

"But not the first time. The first time, I want to see your face. I want to watch all the pleasure wash over you and see what you look like when you come."

I lean forward, pressing my face into his chest, and groan.

"I've been trying to go slowly," he whispers, "but it's the hardest fucking thing I've ever done. I want you so badly."

"Then take me." Do I sound as desperate as I feel? His words have me twisted in knots. Every muscle from my shoulders to down between my legs is tight with longing.

"I will. And that's a promise." He takes my hand and leads me away from the house. "Come on a walk with me?"

I nod and intertwine my fingers with his as we wander through the darkness.

The Jackson family cabin is forty-five minutes inland from Jackson Harbor, away from the tourist draw of the shoreline of Lake Michigan and the lights of the city. The cabin is tucked off the road and into the woods on a nice piece of property with a small lake. We've spent so many summer days out here swimming and fishing, and winter days sledding down the hill by the pole barn. The far side of the property has a dirt bike track where Levi and Colton train with their motocross team.

Jake leads me away from the house and down the path to the little beach area in front of the lake. When I see it, I stop walking and press my hand to my chest. "Jake."

I can make out his grin in the moonlight, and my heart

squeezes hard with love. Lanterns line the path to the beach where there's a blanket laid out in front of a small campfire.

"Come on," he says. "I think there's a bottle of wine waiting for us."

Wordlessly, I follow him down to the sand and sit on the blanket in front of the fire. He pours us each a glass of wine.

"Do you like it?" he asks. He lowers himself to the blanket beside me, and I try to find my voice.

"I love it. How did you . . . When?" He hasn't left my side since we arrived tonight.

"I made Carter help. He owed me some favors for going on a date with my girl."

Laughing, I shake my head. "This is so amazing. Thank you."

"You're amazing," he says softly. "This is the first weekend we've gotten to spend as a couple, and you didn't even hesitate when I asked you to spend it with my family."

"Of course not, Jake. They're . . ." I turn, looking up toward the house. "They're my family too."

He studies his wine and then takes a long pull from his glass before meeting my eyes again. "I don't want you to move to Florida. You belong here with us. But if you decide that's what you want, we're gonna figure it out, okay?"

I nod, emotion clogging my throat. "I don't know what I want yet." I don't want to leave, but I don't want to be that girl who dismisses amazing opportunities for a guy. I did that with Harrison. If my relationship with Jake is going to work, it can't be like my marriage was.

"Hey." Jake pulls my glass from my hand and sets it in the sand next to his. "You don't have to know yet. We'll figure it out."

There are so many unknowns in my life right now, but in this moment, his promise is enough to quiet the worry inside me.

He sweeps his lips over mine, leading me to lie on my back as he slowly slides his hand down my body. When he inches the hem of my skirt up my thighs, I giggle. "I'm beginning to think you planned this."

"You think?" He grins against my mouth as his hand inches up the inside of my thigh. When his fingers brush the satin between my legs, I lift my hips off the ground, and he takes advantage of the moment to tug them from my hips and down my legs in one smooth movement.

I gasp and look up toward the house.

"Don't worry about them. They know this spot is for us tonight. We won't be bothered."

I study his face and shake my head in wonder. I'm really here with Jake. "Do you remember when we came out here after finals our senior year?"

His fingers lazily stroke over my hip. "The night you got trashed and passed out right here on the beach? Yeah. I remember. I slept by your side to make sure you were okay."

"I was going to tell you how I felt that night." The fire flickers and snaps behind me, casting shadows over his face as his grin falls away. "I'd had feelings for you for so long, and I'd finally worked up the courage to tell you."

"And then I met you out here with a girl," he says flatly. "*Fuck.*"

I shake my head. "Her name was *Sadie,* and I hated her. She was so beautiful."

He shakes his head, and I see torment in the lines around his eyes. "I would have sent Sadie home in a cab if I'd known. She broke up with me after that weekend anyway. She didn't like that I spent the night with my drunk friend instead of in bed with her."

"Why did it take us so long to get here?" I ask, still remembering that night. I was drunk and jealous but also a little triumphant that he was with *me* and not her.

He lowers his head and brushes his lips over mine. "I don't know." He kisses me again, longer, slower, deeper, his hand slipping between my legs and skimming across my sensitive skin. "What matters is that we're here now."

His thumb finds my clit, and I close my eyes. I'm wet and aching. "Yes," I whisper.

"You feel so fucking amazing," he says against my ear. His fingers slide over me again and again, teasing my clit and circling my opening. When he slides a finger inside me, I arch my back and gasp, and he sucks my earlobe between his teeth. "So amazing."

"I wanted this that night," I confess on a broken exhale. "I passed out in your lap imagining you might touch me like this."

"I thought about touching you too. I watched you sleep and wondered how it would feel to kiss you, wondered if you were drunk enough to let me or if I was enough of an ass to try when you were so wasted. By then, I'd already touched you a million times in my imagination." He slides a second finger inside me, and I have to bite my lip to keep from crying out. "Rock into me," he says. "Fuck my hand like you moved against me at the hotel."

I obey, slowly moving my hips and relishing his groan of approval in my ear, and I'm lost. He strokes me again and again, teasing my clit with his thumb and whispering encouragement as

I tighten around his fingers.

After I come apart, he kisses me with so much tenderness that I'd melt if there were a single solid piece of me left.

"I love you." I slide a hand into his hair, loving the feel of his breath on my neck and his hand flat and possessive against my belly.

"I love you too, Ava."

The fire crackles beside us, and the moon reflects off the water. I don't know what's in store for me next, but I know tonight is perfect.

Chapter Thirty

JAKE

Sleeping next to Ava is fucking killing me.

I meant every word I said last night. I'm not going to make love to her here. I don't want her to feel inhibited in the slightest when I'm finally inside her. But sleeping in the same bed together, waking up with her body curled into mine, her ass rubbing against my morning hard-on, and the memory of her orgasm pulsing around my fingers. . . I'm about to lose my goddamned mind.

I sweep her hair to the side and lower my mouth to her neck. I won't wake her up, but I can't walk away without putting my lips on her. I press a kiss to the tender skin beneath her ear then force myself out of bed before my hands start something I can't finish—at least not with my mom and sister on the other side of the wall.

I go straight to the shower and turn it hot, as if I can wash the lust from my brain. I can't stop thinking about the way she looked at me last night while we were standing against the house and I described everything I wanted to do to her. Hell, I don't *want* to stop thinking about it. Her eyes were dark with lust, and her lips were parted and waiting as she hung on my every word. Her body swayed closer to me with each whispered promise.

Taking her to the lake and touching her there was a longtime fantasy of mine, and when she crawled into bed with me hours later, having her in my arms tested my limits. It was all I could do to resist rolling her over and pinning her hands behind her head as I kissed my way down her body. I want to taste her. I want to know the feel of her losing control when my face is between her legs and she can't hold still.

I fought the fantasy last night, determined to keep my promise, but now I wrap my hand around my dick and stroke. I imagine pulling her nipples into my mouth until she moans and begs for more, parting her legs with one thigh, the wet heat of her greeting me as I slide inside. I grip myself harder as I remember how she squeezed around my fingers, the arch of her back and the lift of her hips as her body bucked into me.

I let the water spray over me, and I rub up and down my shaft. In the fantasy, her knees draw up around my waist, and I slide into her. Her hips come off the bed as she pulls me deeper and deeper into her body.

In terms of fantasies, it's pretty tame—her body under me, her eyes locked on mine—but I'm so fucking turned on because it's so close to my reality. She's afraid she's going to disappoint me, but all she has to do is want me in return and I know it'll be more than enough. Ava with me and turned on *is* my biggest fantasy.

I grip my dick harder and quicken my strokes, tilting my face up to the spray.

I don't know what makes me open my eyes, but when I do, Ava's standing on the other side of the glass shower door, watching me. She's wrapped in my dark blue robe, her hair pulled into a sloppy bun on top of her head. I didn't think I could be more turned on than I was imagining her two seconds ago, but I am the moment I recognize the heat in her eyes.

I release myself and open the door. "Good morning, beautiful." Her tongue darts out to touch her bottom lip. "Do you want to join me?"

She drags her gaze over me slowly, stopping at my jutting erection. Without saying a word, she unties the robe, lets it fall from her shoulders, and peels off her tank top and panties. Then she's in the shower with me, and before I can press her against the wall and kiss her as hard as I intend to, she's dropping to her knees in front of me, her lips parted as she looks up at me from under the spray.

And fuck, I almost come right there, her breath on my cock, her eyes hot and desperate. Her tongue touches her lips before it ever touches me, and anticipation coils up my spine and shoots hot through my blood.

She puts her hands on my hips and runs them over my ass, down the backs of my thighs and back up, scraping her nails over my abs before taking my hands and guiding them into her wet hair.

She wraps her mouth around me, and my hips jerk. I have to concentrate to keep myself from thrusting into her mouth—

because *holy shit*, the heat of her wet mouth and the sight of Ava on her knees in front of me is everything.

"Christ, Ava."

She moans, and the vibration sends another shot of liquid fire through my blood. She wraps her tongue around the bottom of my shaft and sucks. I thread my fingers through her hair and guide her lightly because I know she wants this connection, wants this reassurance that she's giving me what I need. Fuck, how could she doubt it? It's so good. I'm afraid I'm going to lose control and push her to take me deeper than she comfortably can. She's barely gotten started, and I'm ready to come in her mouth.

"It's so good," I murmur, and she sucks me deeper and curls her nails into my hip. I don't want to close my eyes because I love seeing her like this. It's my fantasy come to life. It's better than my fantasy. But the pleasure builds at the base of my spine and refuses to let me do anything but submit. "Ava." I tug lightly on her hair, urging her up, but she stays put, and I release a muffled curse as I come.

When I draw her up to me, she's grinning. "What are you so happy about?"

"You. This." Her eyes meet mine under the spray of the shower. "*Us.*"

AVA

"You have a nice shower?" Shay asks when I step into the kitchen.

My cheeks flare hot. The kitchen is crowded with Jacksons—Brayden, Levi, and Carter are at the table with Lilly, and Ethan and Nic are just outside the kitchen in the living room.

Lilly looks up from the table and smiles. "I had my bath last night."

Jake wraps his arm around my waist and tugs me into his side before he drops a kiss to the top of my head. "Shay's just jealous because she's not had a good shower in a long time."

"Way too freaking long," Shay mutters.

Jake reaches around me and grabs two mugs from the cabinet. "Brayden, it's a Saturday morning. Just put the work away."

Brayden sighs and shakes his head as he looks at his laptop screen. "I'm working on getting Molly enrolled in our health insurance. We need to hire an HR person if we're going to keep growing our staff."

"Wow," Carter says flatly. "Amazing idea. Too bad no one suggested it before."

Jake smirks. "Good plan, Brayden. Glad you thought of it."

Brayden rolls his eyes. "If you want me to say you were right, don't hold your breath. It would have been too soon to do it before. Now that we're hiring regional sales reps, it *might* be worth it. Maybe."

"I forgot Molly was working for you," I say. I take the mug of coffee Jake offers me and wrap my hands around it. "How's that working out?"

Levi chuckles at the table. "Brayden met with her in New York last week, and I think he'd agree it's going *really well*."

"Shut the fuck up," Brayden says, punching his brother in the arm.

"Language!" Lilly says, putting on her best stern face, and everyone laughs.

I smile as I add cream to my coffee. I like the idea of Brayden and Molly. I wonder if there's anything to what Levi's saying.

Brayden squeezes the back of his neck, worry creasing his forehead. "It was nothing." He shakes his head. "Anyway, I'm kind of baffled she didn't even tell me about her kid. Why does she keep him a secret, Ava?"

My mug thunks when I drop it on the counter. "Who?"

He taps his finger to his screen. "Noah? Her little boy? She didn't mention him the whole time I was up there training her. It was like he didn't even exist."

"Molly has a little boy?" I ask. Jake looks to Brayden then back to me, and I shake my head. "I think you're misunderstanding something. Her friend has a kid. Could she be trying to get him onto her health insurance?"

Brayden frowns. "It's right here in the paperwork she filled out for her health insurance. Noah McKinley, son, four years old."

Jake puts his mug down next to mine and walks around the counter to look over Brayden's shoulder.

Carter gets up from the table, but he walks over to me. "Maybe it's a mistake," he says. "Maybe she misunderstood something in the paperwork."

Noah McKinley, son.

It doesn't sound like something that could be confused.

"If you feel strange asking her about it, I can call her," Jake says, squeezing Brayden's shoulder. "I'll make sure the paperwork is filled out correctly."

I slide my cell from my pocket, my thumb hovering over the screen, then slide it back in. I feel like Molly and I really connected when she was in town. The idea that she'd keep something as important as a child from me *hurts.* Do Dad and Jill know? Have they kept this from me too? And why? To protect Molly from my imperfect influence? That doesn't even make sense. None of this does.

I didn't even realize Jake has come back to stand in front of me until he holds my face in his hands. "You okay?" he asks.

I nod, then shake my head. "I don't know."

He pulls me into his chest and wraps his arms around me. "Try not to overthink it until we know something for sure."

With Jake's warmth against my cheek and his arms around my waist, Molly's secrecy from me seems less significant.

JAKE

"This is Molly. Leave a message."

I pace across the bedroom, looking up to make sure the door's still closed. "Hey, Molly, this is Jake. Call me back, okay?" Since she's ignored my calls the three other times I've tried her this morning, I add, "It's about work stuff."

Do not jump to conclusions. But it's not much of a jump, and it would be really fucking easy to do just that. If the information on her healthcare enrollment is true, Molly has a son who was born around nine months after we got drunk and slept together. I don't want to overreact, but given the timing, it seems like something we should at least have a conversation about.

"Jake?" Ava sticks her head in the bedroom door. Her smile falls away when she sees the phone in my hand. "Did you get a hold of Molly?"

I shake my head. This gnawing ache in my gut can simmer the fuck down any minute now. "I'm sorry. She's not answering."

She steps into the room, toying with her ponytail, and for a breath, I forget what I'm worried about. Ava's in a bikini.

This isn't a new thing. I've seen her in a bikini before. Hundreds of times, probably. But this is the first time I've been able to touch her in her bikini, and this one—a strappy black thing with a top that crisscrosses over her chest and bottoms that sit low on her hips—makes my hands itch to touch.

I toss my phone on the bed and cross the room to put my hands on her waist, pulling her against me. "You look lethal in that suit."

She loops her arms behind my neck. "I'm glad you like it."

I nuzzle her neck. Ever since Brayden told us about Molly's possible child this morning, I haven't been able to get close enough to Ava. I keep touching her. Bringing her closer. Taking every opportunity to kiss her. I have to remind myself Ava is real. She's here, and she's mine. The rest is nothing more than an unknown. Trailing kisses up her neck, I slide a hand into her bikini bottoms to cup her ass.

She pushes me away, her hands flat against my chest. "Nope. Don't start that. I'm not going to let your sister give me a hard time about what we're doing in here."

I groan as she steps out of my arms, but I let her walk away. She winks as she backs out of the room and shuts the door behind her, presumably so I can change into my beach clothes too. On the bed, my phone buzzes and I snatch it fast even though it's just a text alert.

> *Molly: Crazy day. Sorry I've missed your calls. We're camping this weekend. Can we talk Tuesday?*

I want to talk to her today. Right now. Hell, *five years ago*.

But maybe Tuesday is better. It might be a good idea to have this conversation without half a dozen prying ears listening in.

> *Me: Sure. What time works best for you?*
> *Molly: Call me in the morning. I'll be around.*
> *Me: Great. Talk then.*

I make myself push Tuesday's problems from my mind and change into my swim trunks.

When I head back out to the kitchen, the cabin is bustling with the chaos of everyone getting ready for a day at the lake. Levi's packing the cooler, Shay's gathering towels, and Lilly is hopping around the house, wild in her excitement to get into the water. It's in the mid-eighties today, nice weather for Memorial Day weekend in Michigan, but the water will still be cold. Most of the adults will spend their day sitting on the beach or cruising along our private lake in the family pontoon.

Days like these are my favorite, but right now I'm completely uninterested in the sunshine and the water. Next to me, Ava's rubbing sunscreen into her skin in slow movements that aren't helping me get this morning's shower out of my mind. She reaches for the middle of her back.

"Here." I take the bottle from her. "Let me get that." I squeeze a dollop into my hand and rub it between her shoulder blades. She shivers—at the cool lotion or at my touch, I'm not sure.

"You guys about ready?" Shay asks.

"We should be in a minute," Ava says.

I shake my head. "No. I forgot something." I point my thumb to the bedroom. "I need to make another call before we go, but why don't you guys head out and we'll meet you down there?"

Nic and Mom beam at us, and Shay smirks. My brothers mind their own damn business for once.

When they're all gone and the house is quiet, Ava turns to me. "What call do you have to make?"

"An important one." I take her wrists in each of my hands and tug her toward me. "A really, really important one."

She frowns. "So hurry and make it so we can join them."

I cup her face in my hands and kiss her hard. This morning in the shower was too fucking good, and the way she's looked at me since is *everything*. But mostly, I just can't escape this horrible, rotting feeling I've had since Brayden said the words *Noah McKinley, son, four years old*.

I need to touch Ava. I feel like if I don't *do* something and hold her close now, she's going to slip away from me before I make sense of Molly's secret, and I refuse to let that happen.

I slide my mouth over hers and flick my tongue across her lips.

"Jake," she whispers.

I slide my fingertips into the front of her bikini. "Yes?"

She gasps. "What are you doing?"

"Are you still wet from thinking about the shower this morning?" I slide my hand down farther and find her slick. I groan, and her fingers curl into my shoulders.

"What are you doing?"

"I'm losing my mind. I can't look at you in this bikini and be expected to keep my hands off you."

She smiles. "You don't have to keep your hands off. I'm your *girlfriend*."

"Yes, but my niece is a little too young to see the ways I want to touch you, so your day in the sun will just have to wait."

Her lips quirk into a smile. "I guess that's okay."

I take her hand and lead her toward the basement. "Do you remember when we were in college and you let me teach you how to play pool?"

"Yeah."

I lock the door behind us at the top of the stairs. She looks at the locked handle, then at me with an arched brow. Chuckling softly, she follows me down to the pool table, where I rack the balls and hand her a pool cue.

She arches a brow. "You kept me here to play eight-ball?"

I move to stand behind her and step close as I take her hips in my hands. "I'd get behind you and help you line up the shot, and I'd be hard as hell," I say against her ear. "Your body felt so good against mine, but I couldn't tell you what I wanted."

She closes her eyes and tilts her head to the side, giving my mouth access to her neck. "What did you want?"

I sweep my lips up and down that perfect soft skin. "Jesus. Everything."

She shakes her head. "No. Tell me."

"How about I show you?" I slide my hand back down into her bikini bottoms. "I could see the edge of your pink panties that day, and I wanted to put my hand in your jeans and rub you through them until they were soaked." Her breath catches, and I kiss my way down her neck. I use two fingers to toy with her clit, loving the way she rubs her ass against my dick when I touch her, *needing* the way my panic dissolves when my hands are on her.

She leans her head back into my shoulder. I nibble and suck at the tender skin beneath her ear. She tucks her hips, leading my hand closer to where she wants it.

"Can I tell you how many times I've fantasized about having your mouth on me in the shower? The reality was so much better than any fantasy."

She releases a breath as she closes her eyes. She reaches a hand behind my neck and threads her fingers into my hair. "You liked it?"

"Fuck yes, Ava." I toy with her clit between my fingers. "You liked my hand in your hair, didn't you? You liked giving me that bit of control."

"Yes," she says.

"Did it make you wet to suck me off? Did you want to put your hand between your legs?"

"Yes." She rocks into my hand, and I can tell by the building tension in her muscles that I could make her come like this.

"I've thought about this too many times." With one smooth motion, I pull my hand from her bikini bottoms and turn her in my arms. I release the clasp of her bikini top and let it fall to the floor before I guide her to sit on the edge of the pool table.

"We can't do this here."

"Do what?" I tug her bikini bottoms from her hips and let them drop down her legs. I part her thighs and sink down so I can look at her—wet, swollen, and exposed for me. "I've wanted to do this to you here since the day I taught you how to line up a shot." I don't even try to take it slow. I flick my tongue over her, and she gasps. Another time, I'll get there slowly. I'll torture her with kisses on her inner thighs and teasing touches near her aching center. But today I need to taste her as desperately as I've ever needed anything.

I run my tongue over her clit and into her. As my hands slide under her ass, I lift her hips off the table and bury my face between her legs. She whimpers, then gives me what I want and rocks against my face, abandoning control and turning her body over to me completely.

"Jake."

Just like in the shower, this is so much better than my fantasy. She's so turned on, and *that* is the fantasy—Ava turned on by my words, my body, my mouth, my lips, and my tongue. I work her over, relentless, and time falls away. Nothing matters but the taste of her and the sounds she makes as I push her closer to that edge. I give myself over to her pleasure until she lifts her hips off the table and screams my name.

As she slowly unravels, she releases her grip on my hair. I stand, greedy in my need to see her face and hold her in my arms.

She slinks off the pool table, but I don't get to hold her because she's bending in front of me, moving her mouth over my stomach and her hands down my back before tugging off my swim trunks. "Come here," she says softly, standing again.

I let her guide me to the couch, sitting when she nudges me down. She straddles my hips, and the feel of her slick heat against my dick is so damn sweet that I have to focus all my energy on not sliding right into her.

Taking her face in my hands, I kiss her. I let her taste herself on my lips.

She meets my eyes as she shifts her hips, positioning me at her entrance. "Jake?"

I never meant for us to get to this so quickly, but her eyes are hazy with pleasure, and when she shifts above me, I lift my hips. In the next moment, she's sliding down my cock—no condom, no hesitation—and I fucking love it. I love knowing there's nothing between us, and am grounded by the feeling that this connects us in a way that can't be unbroken.

Her breath hitches as I fill her. "Oh, God." She grips the back of my neck. "Jake, it's so good. It's better than I . . . *God*."

Emotion knots in my throat as I watch her move over me. Her eyes are at half-mast, and her lips are parted. Fighting the instinct to hold her too tightly, I soften my grip on her hips.

She shakes her head and slides her hands over mine. "Hold me." She leans forward, buries her face into the crook of my neck. "Don't be gentle with me."

The whispered plea breaks something loose inside me, and in one swift motion, I wrap my arms around her and take her to the floor. She draws her knees up, opening her body for me, and gasps as I drive deeper.

"You feel so damn good," I whisper into her ear. Between our bodies, I cup her breast and squeeze gently, loving the arch of her neck and the flush in her cheeks. "So good."

When her body tightens around me and her soft moans turn to desperate pants, I cover her mouth with mine and kiss her with everything I'm feeling. It's too much to keep this inside, and I focus on this moment: Ava naked and falling apart in my arms, her vulnerability making me even more aware of mine. I love her, and losing her would destroy me. I can't. I won't.

"You're mine," I say, and there's an edge to my words that's sharper than my building need. *Mine.*

She softens under me. "Yes. *Yours.*"

I take her words as the promise I need them to be and let myself go, closing my eyes and relishing the feel of skin on skin as I release.

Chapter THIRTY-ONE

JAKE

The bedroom ceiling fan clicks overhead, passing cool air over our sweaty limbs and providing a steady rhythm to our lazy Saturday. We gave up on joining my family down at the lake and retreated to my bedroom instead. I sent Shay a text saying we decided to spend the day alone, and she replied, *Remember to hydrate.*

Ava traces the ink across my left pec, a relaxed and satisfied sigh streaming from her lips. We have no interest in letting each other go, so we're enjoying the empty cabin while we can.

"I love you," she whispers.

I press a kiss to the top of her head. "I love you too."

"I still can't quite believe this is real." She hoists herself up onto one elbow and looks down at me, her dark hair falling in a curtain around her face.

"Why did you pretend you didn't know?" I ask. My voice is rough, my stomach in a knot at the memory of putting myself out there and being pushed away. I wanted to ask her a lot of times, but the truth is, she saved our friendship by pretending the afternoon I first kissed her never happened.

I was always too grateful I didn't lose her to call her on it.

"What do you mean?" She lowers her head back down to the pillow, and I roll to my side so we're face to face, our bodies only inches apart, our fingers intertwined as we hold hands between our chests.

"You act like I never told you how I feel." I study her. "I admitted I was in love with you almost five years ago, and you . . ." I swallow, not wanting to label the obvious rejection.

Her eyes fill with tears, but she blinks them away. "You were just trying to keep me from making a bad decision. You shouldn't have done it, but I understood and let it go. I didn't want to let the fight ruin our friendship."

I frown. "What do you mean?"

"I was angry with you for lying like that. I spent a few days contemplating calling off my wedding because of what you said. Then Harrison told me he confronted you. He said you told him you were only trying to stop me from marrying him. That I was like a sister to you."

The memory falls like a rock into my stomach. Harrison was so pissed when he found out I'd kissed Ava. He didn't want me in her life. And honestly, at first, I didn't think I wanted to be. When I left her apartment after telling her I loved her, I thought that if she wouldn't be mine, I didn't want her in my life at all. It hurt too damn much. But by the time Harrison showed up at my bar, pissed at me for kissing his girl, I'd decided I needed to do whatever was necessary to hold on to my best friend. Including lying to Harrison about my feelings for Ava and pretending my night with Molly never happened.

"I lied to him, Ava." I shake my head. "I told him what he needed to hear so you and I could keep being friends. The day I kissed you in your apartment, I meant every word I said." I pause for a beat and close my eyes as the rest of her words sink in. *She almost called off her wedding? For me?*

"Things could have been so different." A tear slips from her eye and begins its slow path over the bridge of her nose.

I release her hand so I can wipe it away. "Maybe. Or maybe you would have married him anyway."

"I loved him. I didn't want to lose either one of you. I didn't think you saw me that way."

"Even though I kissed you?" I ask, my voice rough.

"After having feelings for you for years, what you told Harrison was easier to believe than what you told me."

"I don't even know how long I've been in love with you," I say. "I don't know that I ever *wasn't*. But I didn't understand what I felt until you started dating Harrison. And when I realized how I felt about you, I was scared. I wasted so much time trying to get over you, and by the time I told you, it was too late."

"Then I married him," she says. "You came to my wedding, *danced* at my wedding, and told me you were happy for me. You went house hunting with me and helped me choose the home where I was supposed to grow old with another man."

"I was prepared to do whatever I needed to keep your friendship, but I've always wanted more, Ava. Always." I roll on top of her and hold her hands in mine over her head.

"You have me now," she says. "For as long as you want me."

I crush my mouth to hers before she can say more. I kiss her deeply before I can remember those words that threaten her promise.

Noah McKinley, son, four years old.

AVA

"You're glowing." Ellie grins as she slides into our booth at Ooh La La! She narrows her eyes and shakes her head slowly. "And it's not just a weekend-in-the-sun glow. This is an I've-had-so-many-orgasms-my-muscles-no-longer-work glow."

I look down into my coffee and try to hide my grin. I can't. A weekend of incredibly satisfying sex and endless declarations of love will do that to you. "That's a pretty specific glow."

"Am I wrong?"

"Not at all." I press my palms to my hot cheeks. It's Tuesday morning, and even though I have a dozen things I should be worried about—with the lack of a job at the top of that list, and the question of a potential secret nephew not far below it—I'm happy and calm. Everything's going to work out. I believe that. "I'm so in love, Ellie."

Ellie squeaks and claps her hands. "I love this. You two are so freaking *good* together." Her phone rings, and she pulls it from her purse and frowns at the display. "Shit. I need to take this. I'll be right back."

I wave her off. "No problem. I have nowhere else to be."

She smiles gratefully and steps out onto the sidewalk to take her call, letting me return to my thoughts of Jake and the perfect weekend.

"Ava, how are you?"

I turn to see Harrison approaching my table. He looks handsome and professional in his gray suit and pinstripe tie this morning, but for once, seeing him only warms me with vague nostalgia instead of stinging me with longing. "Good morning, Harrison."

"Good morning." He looks me over and shakes his head. "You look great. Did you change something?"

"I lost my job and fell in love. The change is probably just stress relief."

He arches a brow. "Most people would be stressed about losing their jobs."

I shrug. "It'll work out."

"So you and Jake are for real, huh?" He takes a sip of his coffee. "Damn. I guess I should have seen that coming miles away."

I can't help but smile. "We got the timing right for once."

He grunts and cuts his gaze to the picture window looking onto the street outside. Ellie's out there talking on her phone and pacing the sidewalk. "I guess I had a reason to be jealous of him after all."

Guilt washes over me at the shadow of hurt that passes over Harrison's face. I don't want to feel guilty. He doesn't deserve my guilt. But that doesn't change that I had feelings for Jake while

I was with Harrison. "Harrison?" I wait until he meets my eyes before speaking again. "There wasn't anything between Jake and me before. I can't deny I had feelings for him, but until recently, we've never been romantically involved. I was honest with you about that."

"Oh well. It's ancient history. I guess I'm just surprised. If *I* would have slept with Molly, you never would have talked to me again."

I frown. "You slept with Molly?" I shake my head. That's not what he said. Not at all. "What are you trying to imply?"

He chuckles, and something too much like joy lifts his features. "Good-boy Jake didn't tell you he hooked up with your stepsister?"

My stomach folds over, and I nearly go with it. "That's a terrible lie."

He shakes his head. "If that's what you need to tell yourself."

"Jake wouldn't hook up with Molly." My voice is too loud, and I wince. "Why would you even say that?"

He shrugs. "Maybe it was just the once. I remember seeing them hot and heavy at the back of Jackson Brews. That might be the only time I've seen Jake touch a woman in public, but man, he was all over her."

Why is he doing this? Does he hate that I'm happy?

But instead of insisting that he's lying or shutting down the conversation, I hear myself ask, "When?"

"Jesus, Ava. It's been forever. I'm not saying he's cheating on you."

"I want to know *when*."

He throws up his free hand and releases an exasperated sigh.

Suddenly, he snaps his fingers. "It was the weekend you and I got engaged. Actually, it was one of the reasons I was able to get past him kissing you. I figured he couldn't be too serious about you if he was going to turn around and be all over Molly like that. Either that, or he's a bigger asshole than I ever realized."

The weekend we got engaged. My stomach folds again. And again.

"I should have told you earlier, but Molly asked me not to."

I narrow my eyes. "Why would you care?"

He grimaces. "She threatened to tell you that I came on to her first." He waves a hand. "Back before you and I dated, but I knew it would upset you, so I agreed to keep her secret."

Once, that would have destroyed me. Harrison was the one piece of evidence I had that Molly wasn't better than me in every way, and it would have killed me to know his story about wanting me and not her was a lie. Today, I don't care about that, but the other part . . . *Jake.* That can't be true, can it?

"I figured you'd find out eventually anyway." Harrison scans my face. "Ava, are you okay?"

"You're sure?" I grip my coffee cup so hard that it tilts, spilling hot brew all over my hand and wrist. "*Shit.*"

Harrison reaches across the table for napkins and helps me clean it up.

"It could have been Levi or Carter," I say, mopping soggy napkins into a pile before meeting Harrison's eyes. "Or, heck, it sounds like she and Brayden hooked up when he went to New York last week. Maybe he was the one you saw with her."

"It was definitely Jake. I can tell the difference between my wife's best friend and his brothers."

"That was almost five years ago." *And Molly has a child who's four years old. A child she's kept a secret from everyone in Jackson Harbor.* My throat is thick and tears prick the back of my eyes. "Why are you saying this? Do you want me to be unhappy?"

"I didn't think it mattered. I wasn't trying to cause trouble." Harrison's expression has changed to one of pity, and I hate it.

"You know it matters, Harrison." It matters more than anything. It would matter even if it was one night without consequences. But throw in the fact that Jake never told me, and Molly's secret child?

Is Noah Jake's baby?

Harrison lowers his voice when he adds, "I'm not lying. And I'm sorry he wasn't honest with you. I thought you two told each other everything."

I can hardly breathe through the awful weight on my chest, but I lift my chin and force myself to shrug and wave away the matter like it's nothing. "We'll figure it out."

"I feel like shit. Is there anything I can do?"

I shake my head. "Go to work. Have a good day. Everything's fine."

Harrison's brow furrows, but he nods. "Have a good day, then." He heads out and holds the door for Ellie when she comes back in.

She's smiling as she takes her spot across from me. "Back to what we were saying. I know you're anxious to start a family, but enjoy each other for a while first. Date, flirt, screw in public places. The family will come later."

The weight of what Harrison said is too much, too heavy, and I'm starting to feel numb, but I blink at her when she says this.

"We didn't use condoms." *And I'm such an idiot.*

Ellie's eyes go wide. "Why not?"

Jake might be a father to Molly's child, and I had a weekend of unprotected sex with him.

"Ava, are you okay?"

"I haven't used any sort of birth control since before I was married." But that doesn't change that it was a conscious decision. I had sex with Jake without protection because we love each other, and in that moment, a pregnancy seemed like a wonderful possibility, not a risk. I slide out of the booth and stand. "I need to go, Ellie."

"I didn't mean to upset you."

"It's not that." I press my hand to my stomach. "I need to talk to Jake."

Chapter Thirty-Two

JAKE

"Jake! I'm so sorry I couldn't talk this weekend. How are you?"

I drag a hand through my hair and pace my apartment, not sure if I can honestly answer that question. On the one hand, I spent the weekend with Ava and have never been better. On the other hand, I'm on the phone with Ava's stepsister so I can ask her if she had my child four years ago. The idea is so insane that I laugh. "I'm good, I think."

"You *think*? You're helping the love of your life get pregnant. You should be *grand*." Molly grunts, obviously unamused by the idea. "So, what's up?"

"Listen..." I clear my throat, unsure where to start. "We were going over your health insurance enrollment and saw that you claimed a dependent."

"What?" I hear the shock in her voice and know immediately

that she understands the reason for my call. "I filled that out on the insurance company's website. I thought that was confidential."

"No. It doesn't work like that." *Fuck.* I pace across my living room and back, letting the silence grow between us and waiting for her to explain. "Molly?"

"Is there a problem with me being a mother? Does this mean I can't work for Jackson Brews?"

I close my eyes and sink into my chair. "You know that's not why I'm calling." Another beat. She's silent. "Ava was there when Brayden asked me about your kid. Even your stepsister didn't know about him. What the hell is going on?"

"You told *Ava*? Jesus, is it unreasonable for me to expect that the information I put on confidential forms remains confidential?" She blows out a hard breath. "What a disaster."

"You could have told me you ended up pregnant. You don't keep that from—"

"It's not your business. This is *private*."

"Isn't it? We were together in August." I shake my head and tug on a fistful of hair. I've been telling myself all weekend that it's ridiculous to assume that a child born four years ago to a woman I slept with *once* is mine, but it was easy to tell myself that when I was sure she'd jump right in to name the father. "His birthday is May second." She is quiet too long. "What am I supposed to do with this information?" I sound as desperate and panicked as I feel.

"Ignore it? Forget it? Never bring it up again?"

"Is he mine?"

She sighs heavily. "He's my child, Jake. Not yours, and not anyone else's."

"How can I believe he's not mine?" *Please give me a fucking reason to believe.*

"Noah is *mine*. I'm his parent, so please don't ask me any more questions and *please* don't talk about it." She's silent for a few beats, sighing as if the fight's gone out of her. When she speaks again, her tone softens. "Can you tell Ava it was a mistake? That I screwed up the form or something?"

"I can't lie to her about this." *I won't.* I've already fucked up enough.

"Why not? You went years without telling her how you feel and then years without mentioning our drunken mistake."

"Things are different now. Ava and I—"

"I don't want to know, Jake. Please. You live your life. You enjoy it, but don't make me listen to details about how special the two of you are together. Just *don't*." Her voice cracks, and I feel it in my chest. I know that ache she's feeling and wish I'd never done anything to make it worse.

"You can't keep a child a secret. The father has a right to know."

"You're full of assumptions, and I'm done with this conversation. I'm asking you as politely as I know how to forget about this. If I need to find another job, I will."

And leave her alone and jobless to raise the child? "I didn't say that. You have to admit that, given the timing, I have a right to ask questions."

There's a scrape in the lock. The door swings open and Ava walks in, her face drawn tight. She was so happy when she left here this morning. *So was I.*

She looks at me and then the phone in my hand.

Molly exhales heavily. "I need to go. I'm not going to talk about this anymore."

I open my mouth to object, but the call ends before I can say a word. I take the phone from my ear and stare at it.

"Who was that?" Ava asks.

The anger in her eyes feels like a punch in the gut. "Molly."

She nods and turns away, chewing on the inside of her cheek. "So have you known all this time about her kid, or was it a surprise to you, too?"

I toss my phone onto the coffee table. That call was supposed to give me answers and make me feel better. It did neither. "I found out when you did."

She rubs her arms. "I should have realized something was going on when I saw how much the news affected you." She laughs. "I thought you just felt sorry for me. Poor Ava has such a screwed-up relationship with her sister that she didn't even know she had a nephew." She tosses her purse on the couch and paces between the front door and the kitchen. "But the joke's on me, because you fucked my sister nine months before she had this secret baby."

Everything inside me feels like it locks up at those words. "Who told you that?"

"Harrison." She stops pacing, her back to me, and releases a sardonic laugh. "God, you'd think I'd get to learn something like that from someone *other* than my ex-husband, but no. What fun would that be?" She turns slowly and meets my eyes. "And you can't deny it, can you?"

I swallow, but the lump in my throat refuses to budge. Standing, I cross to Ava and take her hands in mine. "I was upset that you'd rejected me. I was drinking, and she was there and . . . it was *one night*."

She tugs her hands away. "One night is all it takes. One night was all it took for Harrison to ruin our marriage, and one night was all it took for you to give Molly a baby."

"Don't compare me to him. I was with Molly *after* you shut me down and sent me away. I would *never* cheat on you. I wouldn't betray you like that."

"And yet you've had five years to tell me that you slept with my stepsister, and you've never said a word."

"I'm sorry. I swear I didn't know about Noah. Molly never told me she was pregnant or that she had a kid." I turn up my palms. "I still don't know anything, honestly. She didn't want to talk about it. She said he wasn't mine, but . . ." *But she wasn't very convincing.* "Ava, we'll figure this out together. I promise."

She wraps her arms around herself. "Do you know why I realized I couldn't let you give me a baby?"

My jaw hardens. "I like to think it was because you loved me and wanted more than my sperm."

She shakes her head. "No. That's not why."

"Why?" The word is raw, just like every inch of my heart.

"Because I *know* you, Jake. I know that you do the right thing. If I'd gotten pregnant, you would have been right there by my side, helping, and fathering, whether that was the life you wanted or not. I know you'll do the same now for Molly and Noah."

"She said he's not mine." I'm desperate. Panic and confusion twist inside me like snapping fuses creeping toward an ugly explosion.

"Do you believe her? She's kept this child a secret from

everyone for four years, and you're going to believe he's not yours just because she said so on the phone?" She studies me, and her expression falters. "You don't believe it. I see it in your eyes. You think she was lying to you."

I close my eyes. A few days ago, the only child on the horizon was the one I might make with Ava, and now I'm contemplating the logistics of making Molly do a paternity test on her son. "I don't know what to think."

"I can't see you anymore."

At first, I'm not sure I heard her right, and then once the words register, they hit me like a sledgehammer right to the chest. It's a wonder I'm still standing. "Don't say that."

"I can't work at the bar anymore either. I can't do any of it. You have shit to figure out, and so do I."

"So we'll figure it out *together*."

"We aren't any good for each other." The words vault out of her like rocks thrown at a window. I crack at the impact.

"You're angry and confused right now, but we're going to figure this out."

She nods, her face pale. "I know you will, but not with me. I'm sorry."

I reach for her, and she steps away, dodging my touch. I don't have much of a temper, but the little I do have is brewing like a dark storm in my chest.

I can't lose you.

When she looks up at me, there are tears rolling down her cheeks. "I think you're amazing."

Shit. I shake my head, my desperation and panic morphing into anger. "Are we beginning the *it's not you, it's me* conversation?

Because I'm really not in the mood to hear that bullshit right now."

She holds up a hand. "Let me finish."

I force myself to take a deep breath.

"Thinking about you touching her makes me want to crawl out of my skin." She shakes her head and squeezes her eyes shut. "Maybe I can get over that eventually. I don't know. But I do know that I can't be the second family. I already told you that. I can't, Jake."

I'm not even sure where to start. She just carved out my guts. Am I supposed to be empathetic? I understand how hard her teenage years were on her—living with her asshole father and being made to feel like she was a guest in his home. To nod along while she throws me into a category with the man who cheated on her and confirmed all her insecurities? "Do not compare me to the two worst men in your life." My words snap with anger and desperation. "You've never been second to me, and you never will be."

She shakes her head and presses a hand to her stomach. "I can't be second, and I can't be the reason you don't do what you know is right." She steps around me and grabs her purse, heading for the door.

"I would never hurt you like they did."

"You already did."

Those words hit me center mass and take the fight from me. *I already did.* "Don't go. Don't leave like this."

She stops with her hand on the knob and looks over her shoulder. "I have to."

The door closes with a quiet *thunk*, and I feel like she just buried me alive. What am I supposed to do with all this anger and frustration and *helplessness* clawing at my chest?

I walk to the window and watch the sidewalk until Ava appears and walks away. I prop my hands on my head, as if that might give my lungs the room they need to expand when they're being compressed by all this *shit.*

It doesn't work. I want to run after her and demand that she undo what she just did. I want to drop to my knees and beg her to stay.

But I can't do that until I talk to Molly, and I know now that the conversation we need to have isn't one we can have on the phone.

I need to go to New York and find out if I have a son.

Chapter Thirty-Three

AVA

"More ice cream?" Ellie offers me the tub of chunky monkey peanut butter something-or-other. "Or more vodka?"

I push away the carton and groan, rubbing my stomach. "God, I can't. There's no more room."

I called her when I left Jake's apartment, and she met me at my house. After I tearfully confessed everything leading up to and including my breakup with Jake, we spent the entire day binge-watching old *Grey's Anatomy* episodes and eating comfort food.

Her gaze drops to my hand, and she frowns. "What happens if you're pregnant?"

The word makes my chest twinge, but I shake my head. "I won't be. I tried to get pregnant for two years with Harrison and never managed. It's pretty unlikely that one weekend with Jake is going to leave me knocked up."

"But what if it did?" Ellie asks softly. She's been really good about listening and not sharing her opinion today, so I'm unreasonably irritated that she's pushing this.

"Then I'd have a baby and wouldn't need to pay a fertility clinic." I pull my feet onto the couch and wrap my arms around my legs. "I'll never see a child as a mistake, Ell. No matter what."

Her expression softens. "Of course you wouldn't. I just mean Jake would want to be part of the kid's life too, right?"

I swallow hard and look away. When did my life turn so dramatic? Molly has a baby she didn't tell anyone about that might be Jake's, and I had unprotected sex with Jake and might be carrying his child. "I guess I'll cross that bridge if I get to it."

She leans her head on my shoulder. "Give yourself time to hurt, to be angry, but then talk to him. You can't cut Jake from your life. You love him."

"He broke my heart," I whisper. "The night they slept together, I was trying to decide if I should give Harrison his ring back so I could try being with Jake. I was ready to flip my life on its head, and he was jumping in bed with *Molly*. That makes me feel like a fool."

"But he came to you first, right? He was drunk and upset, and that's the only reason he ended up with her."

I nudge her shoulder and scowl at her. "I'm not ready for you to defend him yet."

She nods. "Right. He's a jackass who did a bad thing. It's true. We don't need to discuss the nuances of his choices for at least a couple more days."

I reach for my water and take a sip. "Thanks."

"Have you called Molly?" Ellie asks. "Maybe you'd feel better if you heard about the kid from her."

I shake my head. "I'm pretty mad at her, too."

"For sleeping with Jake, or for keeping her son a secret from you?"

"Both," I whisper. I thought I was done crying, but hot tears prick the backs of my eyes again. "But mostly, I'm angry because it hurts to know she already has what I might never have. And that might mean she gets Jake, too."

JAKE

When I texted Brayden to see if we could talk, he said he was at Ethan's having coffee with Mom. I find them at the kitchen table and kiss Mom on the forehead before pulling out a chair to join them.

"Where's Ava this morning?" Mom asks. She looks good today. There's color in her cheeks, and a light in her eyes that, a short month ago, I was afraid was being snuffed out.

"She's at home." It's only a half-lie. Ava is likely at home, but I don't know that for a fact, since she still isn't talking to me. I don't want to worry Mom with our breakup. Not when I'm still clinging to the hope that I can fix this mess somehow.

Mom nods. "Well, I sure enjoyed having her with us at the cabin again. It was like old times." She pushes out of her chair and grabs her crutches. Brayden and I both stand at once to help, but she waves us away. "I'm going to go read for a bit and let you boys talk business. You're making your father's dreams come true."

We watch her leave, neither of us bothering to sit again once she's disappeared into the apartment behind Ethan's garage.

"I need you guys to cover the bar for me for a couple of days," I say when we're alone. "I need to take a trip."

"No problem. Is everything okay?"

I shake my head. My world is in shambles and he asks me if everything's *okay*. "It will be." I sound more confident than I feel.

Brayden walks over to the coffee pot and refills his cup. "Did you talk to Molly?"

I draw in a breath. "Yeah. I called her this morning." When he looks at me expectantly, I shake my head. "Was Levi serious? Did something happen between you and Molly when you went up there?"

Brayden takes a sip from his mug and seems to ponder this. "I'm usually more professional than that, but we'd had a long day and a few drinks with dinner. One thing led to another. She's stunning, you know. Not just beautiful but . . ." He shakes his head. "I can't believe she didn't tell me about the kid. Is it true?"

Guilt sits heavily on my chest. I hate this. It doesn't bother me that Brayden slept with a woman I had a drunken night with, but I don't think he'll feel the same. "I called her this morning, and Noah is her son. I don't know who the father is, though, and she wouldn't tell me. I'm going to go up there and see if I can get more out of her in person."

He makes a face. "Why do you care who the kid's father is?"

"I need to know."

"But why—" I see the moment it clicks for him, and he blinks at me. "Fucking hell, Jake. You slept with her?"

"It was one night." I wait a beat, then force myself to say the rest. "One night in August five years ago." I can practically see him doing the math in his head, and he closes his eyes. His mug clangs as he slams it on the counter.

"I'm sorry. The kid came as a shock to me too, and—"

"Stop talking."

"I don't even know if he's my—"

His fist connects with my jaw. The right side of my face explodes with pain, and I grab it.

"Go be a fucking man and take care of your kid." He storms out of the house, and I let him. There's nothing else to say.

When he's gone, I grab a bag of peas from Ethan's freezer, press it against my jaw, and pull out my phone to book my flight.

The sun is setting when I knock on the door to Molly's Brooklyn apartment. I close my eyes. Every step that got me here has felt like autopilot, and my brain hasn't stopped spinning. When Molly asked me not to tell Ava about our night together, I thought it was because she didn't want to hurt her relationship with her stepsister. Now, I see her request for secrecy in an entirely different light. Why didn't she tell me she was pregnant? Even if she was sleeping with someone else at the time, there's a chance the kid could be mine. Why didn't she tell me she might have had my fucking baby?

Her reasons don't matter. Ava's right. At the end of the day, if

I have a kid out there, I'm going to be part of his life. So here I am. Because I might have a child. Because this is the right thing to do.

Molly opens the door, and her brow wrinkles in confusion as she looks at me. "What are you doing here?"

"We need to talk."

She lifts onto her tiptoes and looks over my shoulder. "Where's Ava?"

"She's at home. She broke up with me and won't answer my calls, so bringing her along would've been tricky." I sound pissed, like all this is Molly's fault, when it's not. Some of it is, sure. But if this kid is mine, I have to own up to the part I played in that. *What a mess.*

"Broke up with you? Does that mean you two finally got together?"

"Yeah. Briefly. Until she found out about my night with you and your son within a couple of days of each other."

"Mommy?"

My chest clutches so hard and tight at the little boy's voice. I brace myself on the doorframe. I'm not sure I believed he existed. *Don't think too much. Just do the next right thing.*

Molly looks over her shoulder and calls into the apartment, "Noah, honey, Mommy will be back in a minute. I need to speak with someone in the hall. You can watch cartoons."

"Even *Pider-Man*?" he calls back.

"Even *Spider-Man*," Molly says.

I feel like the floor has disappeared from beneath my feet.

Molly steps out of her apartment, and I move out of the way so she can shut her door. She tilts her head to the side and studies my face. "You didn't need to come. I'm sorry about you and Ava, but like I told you on the phone, this has nothing to do with you."

I stare at the apartment door, thinking of the little voice from inside. "You didn't give me much reason to believe you."

When I look back at Molly, her eyes are wide. "*Reason*? You need a *reason*? He's not your kid. Be happy. You're off the hook. You and Ava can live happily ever after."

"Then whose is he?"

"He's *mine*." It's gotta be pushing ninety out here in the corridor, but her words have the bite of the winter wind.

"Who is *the father*, Molly?"

She meets my gaze with fiery eyes. "I don't owe you this. I don't owe you anything."

"Do a DNA test, then. Prove to me he's not mine. I can't walk away until I know."

She throws up her arms. "You want to waste your money like that, then why not? Must be nice to have cash to throw down the drain." She waits a beat, then says, "You seriously don't remember?"

"Remember what?"

"Jake, the night we were together, we didn't even have sex. We were both drunk, but *you* were toasted out of your mind. When we went up to your apartment, I thought we were headed for your bed, but instead . . ." Her shoulders sag as she exhales. "We messed around for a while, then you stopped us. You said Ava wouldn't forgive you." She holds my gaze as she says this. "Noah can't be yours because you and I never slept together."

There's a special place in hell for assholes like me, because I'm swamped with nothing but relief. *I don't have a kid with Molly. Her little boy isn't mine.*

Straight Up LOVE

Please let this be true.

Her eyes are pleading. "Now would you please forget you know anything about this?"

"I don't understand. If you weren't keeping this baby a secret to protect me, then who . . ."

She laughs, but her eyes fill with tears. "You really think I'd have been hiding in New York if I'd had a *Jackson's* baby?" She clutches her stomach, and I can't decide if she's trying to hold in a belly laugh or if she thinks she might be sick. Tears spill onto her cheeks, and she wipes them away. "Will you please leave?"

"Whose is he? I'm not walking away until you tell me." *Ava won't believe me until I have an answer to that question.*

"I can't." Her voice is hard, brittle at the edges, her words faltering. "It doesn't matter."

The door opens, and a little boy steps into the corridor. My breath leaves me in a rush when I see his wild, dark hair and smiling brown eyes. He doesn't look a thing like his blond-haired, blue-eyed mother.

"Hi," Noah says, waving to me.

"Noah," Molly says, pointing into the apartment, "I need you to stay inside."

"It's a *girl* cartoon." He pouts. "I wanted *Pider-Man*. I don't like *My Wittle Ponies*."

"Then play with your trains until I get in there." Her voice is stern, and she spares a panicked glance in my direction before pointing into the apartment again. "Please, Noah. I only need another minute."

"Bye," Noah says before scurrying into the apartment and shutting the door behind him.

"He's a McKinley." No wonder she didn't want me to see him.

Holy shit. It's so clear.

"Of course he is. He's my son."

I shake my head. That's not what I mean, and she knows it. Molly is only a McKinley because Ava's father adopted her. Noah is a McKinley by birth. It's all over his face.

"It's none of your business, Jake. Please stay out of it. Go home to Ava. Tell her you're madly in love with her and make beautiful babies together. Don't worry about me and Noah."

"You're sure you don't want his father to know?"

"Noah *doesn't have* a father," she says firmly. "Just a mommy, and he and his mommy are doing just fine." She takes my hand, and vulnerability creeps into her eyes for the first time when she says, "Please don't do anything that might change that."

It's the desperation in her eyes that makes me understand her secret. *Holy shit.* "The secret is yours to keep or tell," I promise. "You don't have to worry about me, but soon enough, word is going to spread that you have a child."

"Let it spread." She shrugs, but I see the worry on her face. "Don't do that. Don't look at me like you feel sorry for me. I don't want your pity."

She has it whether she wants it or not. "Let me help you."

"You already helped when you gave me a job."

"But surely you need more than that. Let me get you caught up on rent, or—"

She shakes her head as she laughs. "Ava's right. You are a fixer, aren't you?"

"I'm not offering anything she wouldn't."

She sighs heavily. "Not every problem is yours, Jake. This one is mine, and mine alone. I made my choices, and I'll deal with them."

Chapter THIRTY-FOUR

AVA

"Florida's nice," Colton says. "Actually, Ellie and I looked at relocating there."

"Really? When?"

"After Dad brought up the possibility of you moving. Ell hates the winters here, and it would be nice to be closer to Mom."

"It would." Two days ago, I walked out of Jake's apartment, and yesterday, I scheduled my face-to-face interview with Seaside Community Schools. Even though I keep telling myself it's the right move to make, it's hard for me to wrap my mind around the idea of leaving Jackson Harbor. This has been my home forever, and I've passed up any chance I've had to leave before because . . . *because I was marrying Harrison, and we wanted to raise our family here.*

What would I be losing if I left now?

Jake.

I clutch my stomach where the gnawing ache has been hovering all day. I've already lost Jake. I lost him the moment he touched Molly, and I think he knew that. That's why he never told me that it happened.

When my brother came over this afternoon, I decided I didn't want to tell him any more about what was going on between me and Jake than Ellie already had. Ellie told Colton that Jake and I had decided to step back and slow down. Colton was totally on board with that. I think the rest can wait—for Jake's protection, because Colton would go after him with fists flying, and for Colton's, because the last thing he needs is another offense on his record.

Maybe Molly was being honest with Jake, and the baby's not his. While I don't want to be the woman who can't get over her jealousy, I know Molly and Jake's night together will never be easy to swallow. But worse, I've realized I'd resigned myself to a life without teaching drama classes or helping kids find themselves through theater. I'd subconsciously begun making plans to pick up more hours at Jackson Brews so I wouldn't have to leave Jake.

When I realized that, I called Penelope and told her I wanted to schedule an interview for what appears to be my dream job. She was thrilled, but before we got off the phone, I blurted, "I might be pregnant."

Once the words were out there, I couldn't take them back. There was a long moment of silence, and my stomach was lodged in my throat while I waited for her to respond. Did I want her to rescind her offer? Or did I want her permission to have my cake and eat it too?

"Well, congratulations," Penelope finally said. To her credit, she didn't ask about the father. "We have a fantastic benefits package, and you'd have twelve weeks of maternity leave. Normally, you'd have to be with us twelve months for that benefit to apply, but perhaps that's something we could negotiate with your contract."

"It wouldn't interfere with my ability to launch the summer theater program for next season," I said, hearing the question in her voice.

"That's wonderful to hear. We can talk more about some flextime perks when you come down, but please don't think that we value working mothers less than any other employees."

And just like that, all my excuses for pushing my plans to the side fizzled away.

"Let me know what you decide," Colton says now. "If you move down there, maybe Ellie and I can do it at the same time and make it easier on all of us."

"Colton, that's crazy. You can't just up and leave your team so I don't have to move alone."

He chuckles and refills his coffee. "It's cute that you think I'd be doing it for you. The only reason I ever moved back here was because Dad would only pay my tuition if he could keep tabs on me. Then when I started training with Levi, it didn't make sense to leave." He shrugs. "I'm ready to go back to Florida. It's cold as balls here in the winter, and I'm so over it."

"It might not be Florida," I admit. "I'm applying for jobs all over. I'm applying for anything that's mostly drama and theater."

"Good for you, sis." He nods. "I'm really proud of you."

"Thanks." I look down at the list of supplies I've been making for summer theater and shake my head. Everything seems so hard right now, but I remember how debilitated I felt after Harrison left me. If I just take it one day at a time, I'll be okay.

Ellie's heels click in the hall at the front of the house. "Anybody home?"

"We're in the kitchen," I call.

She comes around the corner and grins when she sees Colt. "Hey, you."

He looks her over slowly—from the roots of her dark hair down to her three-inch black heels—and grins. "Damn, girl."

She practically glows under his appraisal, but she waves him off and turns to me. "You hear from Jake yet?"

I nod. "He's called a couple of times. Texted a couple more." I grab my phone off the counter and hand it to her, so she can read the messages for herself. Not that there's much to read. I could probably recite our profound exchanges if I needed to.

> *Jake: You home?*
> *Me: No.*
> *Jake: When can we talk?*
> *Me: Give me space.*

"He's sure about this?" Ellie asks, eyebrow raised. "Like, totally positive?"

I frown at her. "Sure about what?"

She turns the phone so I can see it, and I see that I've missed the latest text.

> *Jake: Noah isn't mine. I went to NYC to find out for myself. Please call me.*

"Who's Noah?" Colton asks.

"Don't read people's private messages over their shoulders," Ellie says.

My chest is a tangled mixture of relief and heartache.

The child isn't his.

He went to New York.

What did he do while he was in New York? Did he and Molly hang out? Did they reconnect? Did she explain to him why she's kept this secret? Does she even care that she's widened this fissure between us? Did he feel anything for her while he was there?

The child isn't his.

"Who's Noah?" Colton snaps.

Ellie flashes me an apologetic wince. "Noah is Molly's son. No one knew about him."

He stares at Ellie like she just sprouted a couple more heads. "Molly?"

"Molly *McKinley*? Your stepsister?"

Colton scowls. "Molly doesn't have a son."

Ellie rolls her eyes. "Did you miss the part where I said no one knew about him? The kid's four years old, and Jake thought he might be the father."

"The fuck?" Colton's jaw goes tight, and his eyes blaze with anger. "I'm pretty sure Jackson wants me to bloody his face."

"Don't," I say. "It was years ago."

"And the kid isn't his," Ellie says, pointing to the screen. She shifts her worried eyes to meet mine. "Does that make this all better?"

I shake my head. "I don't think so." It's not that simple. "Even if Noah isn't his—and forgive me if I'm skeptical—Jake still hurt me."

Colton shakes his head. "Leave it to Molly to keep a kid secret from the whole damn world."

Ellie turns to me. "Okay. Now we know that she's sticking to her story. What's next?"

I shrug. "Next, I need to find a job in case moving to Florida doesn't pan out."

She nods and heads to where my laptop is sitting on the table. "Let's get to it."

JAKE

I have a key to Ava's, so although I'm not breaking any laws when I let myself in on Friday night, I'm definitely in ethically shady territory. She won't return my calls, and her responses to my text messages are monosyllabic more often than not. Then tonight, Lilly came home from play practice, chattering on as she always is, and said Miss Ava is spending her weekend in Florida. *"Isn't she lucky?"*

Florida. Seaside Community Schools and the job I'd pushed from my mind as the least of my worries. Suddenly, it's jumped to the top of that list.

She's on her couch with her computer on her lap and her headphones over her ears. She jumps when I come into the living room. Her eyes widen, and she yanks the headphones off. "What are you doing here?"

"I'm making you talk to me."

She shrugs and puts her computer on the end table. "Okay. Talk."

Hope is a bubble in my throat, and now that she's in front of me, it all feels so fragile. Now that I'm here, I'm afraid my words will be met with the anger still so clear in her eyes.

I'm not sure where to start. "Noah isn't mine."

"That's what you said in your text."

"Molly said we never slept together that night."

A flicker of something—hope? understanding?—brightens her expression, but I see the moment she snuffs it out. "She *said* you didn't, or you didn't?"

I wince. "I don't remember, but I believe her." I sink to my knees in front of her, taking her hands in mine. "I was so screwed up, Ava. I'd finally worked up the courage to tell you how I felt, and you shot me down. You told me I didn't know my own feelings, and then you told me to leave."

She looks down at our joined hands as if she's trying to figure out what she's seeing. "I can't blame you for what you did with Molly."

"Why not? I do. It was reckless and stupid."

She nods and pulls her hands from mine. "Rationally, I know you weren't betraying me when you took her home." She presses her hand against her chest. "But this feeling in here isn't about rational. In fact, it's the opposite of rational thought, and when it comes to how I feel about you—about *us*—it matters just as much."

I take the hand from her chest and press it to mine. "What about this feeling in here? What about this heart that beats for you?" Averting her eyes, she gently pulls away, and I let her. "We'll get through this."

"I can't . . . I'm not ready."

"When will you be ready?"

She shrugs. "I don't know if I ever will, but I need you to give me space while I figure out my life."

"Your life in *Florida*? I'm supposed to sit back and watch you put together a life for yourself a thousand miles away?" I shake my head. "No. I'm sorry, but I can't do that. I've slept without you in my arms for three nights. That's three nights more than I needed to know you belong there. I love you." I put my hands on her knees and squeeze. "Look at me. Tell me what it's going to take to make this right."

"I love you too." The words should feel so good to hear, but they don't. Not in this context when they're more like a reluctant admission than a gift. As if her love is a difficult fact she has to deal with instead of something that's lifting her up. "And I loved Harrison."

I grimace at the mention of his name. It kills me that I've done anything that makes Ava put me in the same category as him. "I'm not Harrison."

"You're not. He found someone prettier and younger, a woman who could give him children. I know you well enough to know you wouldn't leave me like he did. You wouldn't push me aside for someone else."

"Of course I wouldn't."

She closes her eyes. "But maybe that's exactly why I should move, Jake. What's here for me? All I have in Jackson Harbor is a father who disapproves of most of my life choices, and an ex-husband whose new wife is having the baby I wanted to have so badly."

"The *Jacksons* are here." I stand. I'm too frustrated to be still while she feeds me this bullshit. "Don't you dare act like you don't have a real family. We've been your family your whole life. My mom loves you like her own, and my brothers and Shay love you like you're their sister." I thump my chest with my fist. "And I can't let you go."

"I need you to," she whispers. She pushes off the couch, and for the first time since I walked in the door, she touches me. It's brief, her fingertips across the stubble of my week-old beard, but I feel it with every cell in my body. "I believe you when you say you'll do anything for me. You've proven that over and over again. That's why I think me leaving might be for the best."

"Leave if you need to. Leave if that is what will make you happy. But don't you dare tell yourself it's what's best for me."

"Even if it's true?" she whispers. She slowly turns and walks to the front door, opening it before turning back to me. "I can't be with you right now."

Chapter Thirty-Five

AVA

"Do you want me to go up with you?" Ellie asks as I look up at Molly's apartment building in Brooklyn.

"No. I need to do this by myself."

Two weeks ago, I was in Florida interviewing for what is, on the surface, my dream job. I hadn't been down there for twelve hours before I knew I couldn't take the position. Seaside is lovely, but it's not home. I don't want to leave Jackson Harbor for the position, because no job is perfect if it takes me from the town I love. I did the interview and spent time with Mom, and when I left, it was knowing I'd truly considered it but that the move wasn't right for me.

Today, I'm in New York because Jake insisted I still take the trip to see *Hamilton*. Even if I did it without him. When I found the plane tickets and hotel reservations in my mailbox, I missed him so acutely that I could hardly breathe. When I sat through the production last night, I could hardly see through my tears. We were supposed to take this trip together. He was supposed to be by my side as I checked off the incredible bucket-list item of seeing *Hamilton* on Broadway.

He's been giving me space, just like I asked, and I've hated it. I miss my nights at Jackson Brews and surprise visits from Jake during theater rehearsals. I miss our shared laughter and the heat of his eyes on me. If I could rewind to before I knew about Noah and Molly, I'd relive the weekend at the cabin on repeat.

My hand goes to my stomach and I swallow hard, wondering for the hundredth time today if there's a chance I might be pregnant.

Ellie squeezes my hand. "I saw a coffee shop around the corner. Come find me when you're ready."

I nod and let her go, taking a deep breath before going into the building and climbing the stairs. I hesitate at her door, mustering all my courage to knock.

The little boy who opens the door steals my breath. "Hello?"

"Noah!" Molly races up behind him. "Baby, you know you're not supposed to answer the door without me."

She doesn't register it's me for a few moments, and the seconds stretch between us, full of silence because I'm still staring at Noah. *My nephew.* He's beautiful, and my heart feels too big for my chest as I try to take him in, to memorize his perfect face.

He's not a Jackson. I didn't realize I still doubted it.

I sink down to my haunches and offer him my hand. "Hey there. I'm Ava."

"I Noah," he says with a toothy grin.

"*I'm* Noah," Molly corrects him.

Noah giggles. "No, you *Mommy.*"

Shaking her head, Molly sighs and holds the door open wide. "You might as well come on in, Ava."

"Thanks." I follow her into the little apartment. It's small but nice—clean and tidy, with the modern industrial flair of exposed brick and piping overhead. Noah stops in the living room, a space with a couch and a chair, and a toy train track on the rug in the middle.

Molly leads me to a round table with four chairs in the kitchen. "Coffee?"

I nod, then think better of it. I've been cutting down on caffeine . . . just in case. "Decaf?"

She makes a face. "That's against my religion. Water?"

I laugh. "Yeah, water's fine."

She fills a glass from the tap for me and fills a mug with coffee for herself, bringing both to the table. "Now you know my secret."

"You only have one?" I take a sip of my water and do my best to act like meeting Noah isn't a big deal when, in truth, it's everything.

"Only one that matters," she says.

"Molly, why didn't you tell anyone?" I look over my shoulder to where Noah is leading his trains delicately around the track. I feel like I might already know the answer, but I want to give her a chance to explain.

She rubs her temples. "I already had this conversation with Jake, as I'm sure you know. I'm not interested in rehashing it with you. Noah is my son, and his father's not in the picture. That's not a big deal here. It would have been at home."

I open my mouth to protest, then close it again. The single mom part of Molly-and-Noah isn't what would have been a big deal. "Okay," I say. "I'm not here to fight."

She stares down into her coffee. "I know it seems crazy, but it was what I had to do at the time. And then a couple of years passed, and I had this big secret." She shrugs without looking up at me.

"Does Jill know about him?"

Her eyes fill with tears, and she nods. "Yeah. But Dad doesn't. Mom was reluctant but understood why I couldn't tell him . . ." She winces and rubs her thumb against her first two fingers to signify money. "Grad school."

"Wow." I can't imagine Jill keeping that secret, but I have no doubt Dad would have refused to pay for Molly's expensive graduate program if he'd known she was pregnant.

Molly turns her face toward the living room, and the tenderness in her expression tugs at my heart. "I thought about giving him up for adoption, but when I heard his heartbeat at my first ultrasound, I knew I couldn't do it."

"He's beautiful." I shake my head. I could just stare at the kid all day.

She exhales heavily. "He was born not long after your wedding, which is the real reason I didn't come home for it, and I'm sorry about that. I didn't want everyone to see me and find out about the pregnancy. It would have changed everything."

I have to wonder at my own stupidity. I thought I had Molly figured out—that I knew who she was and what she was about. But "Mother Teresa" would never have kept a pregnancy from Dad. She never would have gotten pregnant to begin with, let alone had a secret child and refused to talk about his father. I'm floored by the complexity of this woman and by my own failure to see it before. I've always assumed she had such an easy life because she made it look easy, but that's a bit like thinking an egg is indestructible because the shell is solid.

She swallows hard. "I don't regret my decisions. Only that from the outside it might look like I'm ashamed of him, when the truth is that he's the most beautiful thing I've ever made."

"And his father?"

Laughing, she scans my face as if searching for hints that I might understand. I give her my best poker face, and she shakes her head. "I'd just found out I was pregnant the night I hooked up with Jake."

I blink at her. "You did? I thought you were both drunk."

She winces. "Not my proudest moment, Ava. I didn't know what I was going to do, but I was considering . . ." She shakes her head, as if she won't even allow herself to speak of what she was considering when she first found out about the pregnancy. "The drinks I had that night were the only ones I had the entire nine months."

"You knew you were pregnant, and you hooked up with Jake? That's ballsy."

"Somewhere in my panic, I thought it might work out great. I knew what he'd do if he found out I was pregnant. If I could just pretend I was having Jake Jackson's baby, I wouldn't have anything to worry about."

"Molly, you can't lie about something like that!" The idea alone makes my stomach clench in panic. If Molly had done that, Jake and I would never have gotten together.

"And I didn't." She shakes her head. "I was panicked, but I knew I couldn't do it. He loved you so much. If I'd let him believe the child was his, he might've stepped up and been with me, but he never would have gotten over you. He was such a sad sap about your engagement."

"He was?"

She laughs. "Oh my God, lady. That's the whole reason he was getting shitfaced in the first place. He was *broken* about you. I totally took advantage of him."

"He was an adult who made his own decisions."

Her eyes crinkle in the corners as she studies me. "Sure, but he'd just taken a giant leap of faith and fallen on his face. I think if there's ever a time a guy can get a pass for making some bad decisions, it's then."

My phone buzzes in my purse, and I grab it just to make sure it's not Ellie having some problem alone in the big city. When I see Jake's name on the display, my heart skips a beat.

> *Jake: I hope you're having a great time and that the musical was incredible. I just wanted to let you know we got two pieces of good news today. Veronica had her baby—a little boy she named Jackson—seven pounds, and cute as a button. And Mom's cancer is in remission. The Jacksons have a lot to celebrate tonight. Thought you'd want to know about both.*

I reread the text several times and take in big gulps of air in relief.

"What is it?" Molly asks.

"Mrs. Jackson is in remission."

She throws her hand over her mouth. "That's wonderful. When Brayden was here, he told me how hopeful they were."

I nod, my elation at the good news tempered by this *off* feeling. I should be there celebrating with him. With the whole family.

"So, you and Brayden . . . ?"

Molly rolls her eyes. "My superpower is getting drunk and believing I'm good enough to land a Jackson brother." She shakes her head. "Brayden's my boss. That's it."

"But you two shared something when he was in town?"

She smirks. "I'm easy, remember? It's not a big deal to me."

"I don't believe either of those things," I say softly, but I'm not going to push her about Brayden. Not today, at least. I return my phone to my purse and trace the flower on the tablecloth with my fingertip. "I miss Jake."

"You belong with him," she says, and when I meet her eyes, she adds, "I mean it. I'm not denying that I would've liked to have Jake for myself, but the fact of the matter is he's mad about *you*. Always has been."

"It's just that I . . ." I trace the flower again. "Jake has been there for me longer than anyone. Every time I needed someone, he was there—when Dad left, when my first boyfriend dumped me, when Harrison left."

She laughs. "God, Ava. For a girl as smart as you are, I'm impressed you're stubborn enough not to see the pattern."

I meet her dancing blue eyes, and I can't help it. I laugh too. "Sometimes it seems like my relationship with Jake is so one-sided. He gives and gives, and I don't have any idea how to balance the scales."

"I suppose now's not the time to suggest sexual favors."

I laugh and roll my eyes. "That's not the kind of balance I was thinking."

"I bet you can figure something out." She tilts her head to the side, studying me. "Do you know what he said to me that night? After he took me up to his apartment?"

My stomach turns. "I'm not sure I want to know."

"It's true we messed around, but we never had sex. I wanted to, but he pushed me away. When I reminded him you were marrying Harrison, he looked me in the eye and said, 'I'd wait forever for Ava.' I knew he meant it." She shrugs. "I know you're supposed to be the older and wiser one here, but I have to tell you I think you're an absolute fool if you're going to walk away from that kind of love."

I swallow hard. "I might be pregnant."

She opens her mouth, then closes it. "Does Jake know? Have you taken a test?"

"No, and no. I took so many stupid pregnancy tests during my marriage that I think I developed a phobia. Nothing but disappointment comes from those stupid sticks."

"But your period is late?"

I laugh at that. "I don't exactly have a regular schedule. *Late* is relative. And probably meaningless."

"I'm kind of jealous, you know." Her voice is thick with emotion. "I wanted to be happy when I found out I was pregnant, but I was only terrified—terrified what everyone would think and how it was going to affect my future. I've always been so jealous of your ability to take what you want from life. You're so brave, Ava."

"I don't feel very brave."

She gives me a soft smile. "Figure out what you want with Jake before you take a test. Don't wait to make your decision based on what's going on in your uterus."

I nod, having already decided this for myself earlier this week. "I think I already know."

"Of course you do." She grins. "You might be stubborn, but you're not stupid."

"I love him so much it hurts. I think maybe that scares me."

"It only hurts because you've pushed him away. I've seen you two together. Your love doesn't hurt. It's like your favorite blanket. You always find each other for comfort."

I stare at my beautiful little sister. "Thanks, Molly."

"For what?"

"For letting me in and talking to me." I swallow hard. "For being so wise."

We stand and head into the living room, where I sink to my haunches and open my arms to Noah. "May I have a hug, handsome?"

He looks at his mom, who nods once, then he crashes into me with the enthusiasm only a kid can put into a hug.

"I'm so glad to meet you, little man," I say, mussing his hair. "I'll come again sometime, okay?"

He nods and grins at me. "You're pretty."

I laugh. "Thanks. You're handsome."

"I know," he says, wandering back to his trains, and Molly and I head to the door, laughing.

"I'm glad you came," she says as we step into the hall.

"Me too." I hug her. "I meant it when I said I'd come back. I want to get to know my nephew."

"You're welcome any time," she says, releasing me.

"Molly . . ." I hesitate a beat, looking over her shoulder into the apartment where Noah is playing. "I'll give you three months to figure out a way to tell Colton you had his baby. Any longer than that, and I'll be forced to tell him myself."

"Ava, Colton isn't . . ."

I shake my head. "Don't do that. Don't pretend I can't see the McKinley in him just because you don't want me to. I saw the way Colton looked at you when we were teenagers. I always suspected he moved with Mom to Florida because he was afraid you'd see him as a brother if he moved in with Dad." I draw in a long breath, bracing myself to defend my brother. "Colton might be a little wild, but he deserves to know. And it would be better for everyone if the truth came out before he puts a ring on his girlfriend's finger."

"The truth?" She tilts her head to the side, studying me for a beat before she looks away. "Well, I guess you're right about one thing. It's time for me to figure this out."

Chapter THIRTY-SIX

AVA

*I*f hope alone were enough to make a baby, I'd have several dozen by now. I've peed on so many sticks in my life, and every single time I did it, the action carried so much desperate hope. I've come to loathe these stupid sticks. To me, they represent the bad news they've always delivered.

I can say with utter certainty that this is the first time in my life I've needed to pee on a stick and been totally unsure how I feel about it. How do I feel about a possible positive result?

I still want a baby. That is part of who I am, and it will never change. But now? Now I know I want Jake too, and I'm not sure how a baby will complicate our reunion. I want him back, and I know he'll be a good dad, but what if he's not ready for a child?

I pee on the tester and set it on the counter like I've done dozens of times before. And as I learned to do a year into my marriage, I set a timer on my phone and walk out of the room, determined not to look at it until the alarm goes off.

There are no three minutes longer than the three minutes you're waiting for a pregnancy test to process. Except this time, they go too fast, and my phone is beeping at me and it's time to go look at the results. Instead of hope turning my feet as fast as possible toward the bathroom, I'm scared.

I'm scared of the disappointment I know I'll feel if it's a negative again. And I'm scared of how my relationship with Jake will change if it's positive.

I'm staring at the bathroom door, my arms wrapped around myself. "Is everything okay?"

I jump. I didn't even hear Ellie come in. I exhale slowly. "I'm taking a pregnancy test."

Her shoulders sag. "Finally. Oh my God, the wait's been killing me."

I shake my head and look away. "I want a baby, but it's complicated now, you know?"

"I get it. But Jake *adores* you. Whatever you want out of this, wherever you want to go from here, he'll make it happen for you. I know that without a doubt."

I wrap my arms around my best friend and squeeze her tight. Ever since I left Molly's house, I've been carrying this guilt about knowing a secret I can't share and bracing myself for it to rock her world. "I'm so grateful for you."

She rubs my back and whispers, "I'm grateful for you, too. Are you going to go look at that test now?"

I pull back and shake my head. "It's not going to be positive. I'm jumping the gun with this. My periods are so all over the place that it's hard to know when to test and when to wait."

"So go look."

I nod, but I stand still and stare at her.

She smiles. "You want me to do it for you?"

"Yeah. I do."

She doesn't skip a beat. She rushes into the bathroom and straight to the counter. She looks down at the test and freezes, staring at it.

"What?"

She turns to me, disappointment written across her face, and I'm not sure what that means.

I put my hand on my stomach. "What?"

"I'm sorry, Ava. It's negative."

I squeeze my eyes shut. "Of course it is. It was stupid to think . . ." My stomach cramps. *So stupid.* All the fear and uncertainty from minutes ago is washed away by a rush of disappointment. It's too much, too heavy. Before I lived it, I never understood you could grieve for a child that never was.

I put my other hand on my belly over the first, close my eyes, and imagine what might have been. I imagine telling Jake about a baby. The joy in his eyes. He'd be an amazing father.

When I open my eyes, Ellie's come closer. "Are you all right?"

"Yeah." I swallow and look up at the ceiling. It would be really ridiculous to cry about this. "No. I'm not okay."

"Oh, honey." She wraps me in a hug, and even though I feel foolish for being sad about this, I love her so much for *getting it.* "I'm so sorry."

"Me too," I whisper.

"Call Jake. Don't hurt alone."

"I don't know how to start."

"Tell him what you're feeling. He knows you, Ava. He loves you."

I nod. "I will. I love him too, and I'm done waiting."

"Good." When she pulls back, her eyes are full of tears. "Is there any chance you have another test?"

I wave her off. "There's no need. I'm sure the first one was right."

She bites her bottom lip. "I meant for me."

JAKE

"Where is she?" I left Cindy and the idiot new kid to cover the bar and rushed to my childhood home after Ava sent me a text. *The old hideout is smaller than I remember. And it's pretty lonely without you.*

Brayden points his thumb toward the backyard. "Tree fort," he says. He laughs. "She actually knocked on the door and said she wanted to sit up there for a while. She asked if I'd mind. You two used to hang out there when you were kids, didn't you?"

I nod, but I'm not interested in giving Brayden a history lesson right now. *Ava's here. In* our *place.*

That's where she always went when she was upset and needed me.

I run into the backyard and climb the rope ladder, making a mental note to thank Ethan for replacing it last summer. It's been thirty minutes since I got her text, and I'm afraid I've missed her. I pull myself into the fort.

She's here.

Thank God.

She's sitting in the corner in jean shorts and a Jackson Brews T-shirt, her hair in a ponytail, and her knees tucked into her chest.

"Are you okay?" I gulp in air. I think I've been holding my breath since I got here.

"I got the job in Florida," she says.

I nod slowly. *Fuck.* This isn't what I was hoping for.

I sit next to her—close enough that I could reach her hand if she let me, but not too close. "Congratulations."

She exhales slowly. "Yeah, but I don't want it. I don't actually want to leave Jackson Harbor."

Relief makes me limp, and I lean my head back against the plywood wall. "I don't want you to leave either, but I do want you to be happy. I'm just a little selfish and want you with me."

She rolls her head to the side and scans my face. "Why?" The word is so heavy with emotion that it cracks. "Why do you want me?"

I might laugh if she didn't look so damn vulnerable. "Because I love you, Ava."

"Is that enough?"

I cup her face in my hand, half expecting her to pull away. She doesn't. "It's enough for me."

"I blamed Harrison for my failed marriage, but the truth is, I was just as at fault. I *wanted* him to leave me because that was easier than facing the fact that I couldn't give him children. If he left me, I wouldn't have to confront my own failure every day. I pushed him away, and he cheated on me with a woman who could give him the family he planned for."

I don't want to talk about her ex-husband right now, but I understand why she thinks it's relevant. "Harrison was a fool, but dammit, Ava, I'm glad he left." I roll to my knees so I'm in front of her, holding her face in both hands. "I'm glad you aren't his anymore, because if you were, you couldn't ever be mine. Not the way I need you."

She swallows and searches my face. "When I thought Molly might have had *your* baby, I saw it all in a flash. A future where I was trying to give you a child and failing. A future where I pushed you away because I was so miserable about my body's failure."

I shake my head. She's ripping out my heart, and she doesn't even know it. After all this time and all my screw-ups, she still believes she's not enough for me. "I'm not in any rush for the future. Tomorrow can wait, as long as I get to have today with you."

She closes her eyes and tips her face down. "I'm not pregnant."

"What?"

"I took a test today. I was silly to think I might have been, but I kind of hoped . . . Maybe I'm foolish to think I might ever be."

I can't take it anymore, so I tilt her chin up so she's looking at me and then lower my mouth to hers. She slides a hand into my hair and kisses me in return, but I pull away when I feel her shaking. I hold her gaze while I speak. "You're the woman I love, and I want to be with you whether we can have kids or not." I run my hands down her arms until I'm lacing our fingers together. "I'm in love with you. That didn't change when I thought Noah might be my child, and that doesn't change if you aren't pregnant now or ever."

"I know you're not Harrison," she says, searching my face. "I *know* that because you give everything, Jake. I want to be able to give something to you in return."

I brush my lips across hers again and again. "This is all I want," I whisper. "You. Just you."

"Can I have my job back?"

I laugh against her mouth. "Is that what this is about? A job?"

"I miss it. I miss hanging out with you, and hearing you geek out about beer." She pulls back and looks into my eyes. "Colton says I'm afraid of change, but that's because I like my life. I especially like the parts when I'm with you."

"You can work at Jackson Brews anytime you want, but that doesn't get you off the hook for pursuing a job you *love*."

She nods. "Oh, I know. That's why I talked to the board about expanding the Jackson Harbor Children's Theater program into a year-round community-outreach program. I'll have drama clubs for all ages in the afternoons, and plays year-round."

I gape at her. "Yes. Ava, that's perfect."

"I think so too. The pay won't be much, but I have grant money coming in and am eligible for more now that we're offering afterschool programs." She drags her bottom lip between her teeth and studies me.

I press her hand to my chest, afraid she might disappear if I let go. "What can I do to help?"

"Well, the building I'm leasing needs some work, so I might hire you for some underpaid manual labor if you're up for it."

"You don't have to ask twice. Anything."

She arches a brow. "Even if I make you do the work shirtless?"

I pull her onto the floor with me so we're both lying on our sides. "You could talk me into anything right now. Just say that you're mine."

"I'm yours."

"Damn right you are." Grinning, I pull her body against mine.

"Ellie is pregnant," she says before I can kiss her, and I'm surprised enough that I pull back.

"Colton's?" I ask, knowing the answer. Levi might be in love with his best friend's girl, but he wouldn't act on it.

"I assume so. She didn't say otherwise."

"Does he know?"

"Not yet." She drags in a ragged breath. "I felt bad enough before, but now that she's pregnant it's going to be a bigger mess when Molly finally tells Colt about Noah."

I frown. "What do you mean?"

She props herself up on one elbow and studies me. "Did you see him when you went up there? The kid is obviously a McKinley."

I open my mouth and then close it again. "Yeah, the family resemblance is really clear." But is that because Colton is the father? That's a lot less disturbing than what I thought before leaving Molly's, but I won't upset Ava by speculating out loud. This is Molly's secret. She's the only one with the answers.

"I told Molly I'd give her three months to figure out how she's going to tell Colton. I can't keep this secret from my brother." She shakes her head. "What a mess. I don't want Ellie to be hurt."

"She'll be okay. She has you." I roll over her, resting my weight on my elbows and look down into her dark eyes. "And so do I."

"I suppose you do." She grins. "I think you always did."

I lower my mouth to hers and decide it's the perfect time to show her just how long I've wanted her and how many things I've imagined doing to her right in this very tree fort.

Epilogue

AVA
Two months later...

Lilly is officially the cutest Fern who's ever graced the stage of *Charlotte's Web*, and this production is possibly the best I've ever directed.

"What do you think?" Sydney asks me backstage after the cast is gone and the audience has cleared out. Tonight was the last performance of the summer, and Sydney and Lance have been by my side through the whole thing, helping kids learn their lines and overcome their fears of performing in front of an audience. I'm not sure what's better—watching the young kids perform or the older ones teach them. Either way, this is the best job in the world.

"I think it's perfect," I say, smiling. "I couldn't ask for more."

"Will we get to help next year?" she asks. "And meet at your new building for drama club?"

I grin. "Absolutely."

"I can't wait," Sydney says, and next to her, Lance gives an uncharacteristically excited fist pump.

"Excuse me," Jake says, making all three of us turn away from the stage. "I'd like to congratulate the director." He holds out a bouquet of roses. "For my girl."

I shake my head. "You didn't have to do that, Jake."

He puts the roses on a table between a couple of prop boxes and pulls me into his arms. "I'm trying to get on your good side so you'll come home with me tonight."

Between the production and gearing up for my new program, my summer has been busier than ever, but most nights I'm at Jake's or he's at my house. Sleep has definitely taken a back seat to other priorities the last two months, and I couldn't be happier. "You might be able to talk me into that."

He lowers his mouth to mine, and the teenagers behind him snicker.

"We'll give you some privacy, Miss McKinley," Lance says.

I wave to them and smack Jake's hands away when they drift from my waist to my ass. "Behave," I whisper.

"I'd rather not." His next kiss is longer, lingering, and I get swept under the spell of his hands sliding up and down my sides.

"We'll lock the door behind us," Sydney calls.

Jake pulls away. "Thanks, Sydney! I always liked you." Mischief is all over his face. He stills until the click of the back door echoes across the stage, then he pushes me against the wall and snakes his hand up my shirt.

I arch into his touch. "What do you think you're doing?"

"Getting distracted. I'm back here for a reason, but I've got you alone and want to touch." His mouth trails slowly up my neck, then his breath is hot against my ear. "I have to make up for all those years I couldn't."

I flatten my palm to his chest and push. "Don't be distracted."

His nostrils flare as his gaze slips up and down my body again. "Maybe I'm trying to calm my nerves."

"Nerves?"

He swallows hard and backs up a step. "I wanted to wait until the papers were signed and everything was in place for your new theater program. I wanted to let you get that part of your life in order first."

A chill races up my skin. "First? Like *before* you did something else?"

"Yeah." He nods and lowers himself to one knee.

"Jake . . . Are you . . . Is this?"

Apparently, my stumbling puts him at ease, because he grins and reaches into his pocket. "You said you wanted to give me something." He rubs his thumb over the velvet box, and I want to scream for him to open it, but I bite my lip instead. "You said I give you more than you give me. I know that's not true, because I get to wake up with you next to me every morning. I know I'm the one getting the winning end of this deal every time you laugh with me or prove how deep your love goes."

"You give me everything," I whisper. "Everything that matters."

"Then give me your forever." He slowly opens the box to reveal a sparkling diamond solitaire inside. "If you want to give me more, give me your tomorrows. I want your laughter and tears. I want your good days and the bad." He takes the ring from the box and reaches for my hand. "Because there's nothing else I want, Ava."

I feel the tears on my cheeks as I nod. "Yes. Of course, yes, Jake." He slides the ring onto my finger, and I can only stare at it in wonder. Jake's been my everything even when he didn't have to be. He was my always even when I pushed him away. "I love you."

"I love you too." He stands and presses me against the wall again as he lowers his smiling mouth to mine. His hand tugs at the hem of my dress.

"What are you doing now?" I ask against his mouth.

"I'm fucking my bride-to-be backstage."

A shiver of pleasure races up my spine and down my arms. "Oh."

He slides his hand between my legs. "I love you, Ava."

I gasp as he tugs my panties to the side. "Love you too," I say, breathless. "But I actually need to talk to you about something."

He tugs my panties down until they fall at my feet. "I saw the trash in the bathroom," he says. "Don't you dare apologize about it." He sucks at my neck and rubs between my legs, and I struggle to form words. "We aren't in any hurry, and if I have to fuck you every day for the rest of our lives to try to give you a baby, that's just my cross to bear."

"The test was positive."

He freezes. His hand, his mouth, maybe even his heart. Slowly, he pulls away. "Seriously?"

Swallowing hard, I nod. "Seriously." He searches my face, and my heart is so damn full. "I'm pregnant."

"Are you happy?"

I nod, tears spilling onto my cheeks. "So happy."

"I didn't . . ." He swallows and shakes his head. "I didn't think I could be any happier. I was wrong."

"I never expected it would happen so fast. I'm sorry if—"

He crushes his mouth down on mine. "No apologies. This is amazing." His lips quirk as he pulls back. "You're going to need to plan that wedding pretty fast. You up for that? You have to marry me before our baby's born."

"It's not a *have* to. I *get* to marry Jake Jackson."

"And have his baby," he says, his voice gruff.

I nod. "Exactly. I'm the luckiest girl I know."

The End

Thank you for reading *Straight Up Love,* book two in The Boys of Jackson Harbor series. If you'd like to receive an email when I release a new book, please sign up for my newsletter on my website.

I hope you enjoyed this book and will consider leaving a review. Thank you for reading. It's an honor!

Contact
I love hearing from readers. Find me on my Facebook page at www.facebook.com/lexiryanauthor, follow me on Twitter and Instagram @writerlexiryan, shoot me an email at writerlexiryan@gmail.com, or find me on my website: www.lexiryan.com

Acknowledgments

First, a big thanks to my family. Brian, thank you for believing in me and my stories and for understanding how much time this career takes. I love having you by my side for this journey. To my kids, Jack and Mary, you are the very best thing I've ever made. I totally get why Ava wants kids so badly because you two are amazing. To my mom, dad, brothers, sisters, in-laws, aunts, uncles, various cousins and cousins-in-law, thank you for cheering me on—each in your own way.

I'm lucky enough to have a life full of amazing friends. Thanks also to my workout friends and the entire CrossFit Terre Haute crew, especially Robin, who checks up on me when I disappear too long into the writing cave and likes to remind me that taking care of myself is important too, and my coaches, Matt and Chaz. A huge thanks to Mira Lyn Kelly, who gets me like no other. I've gotten a lot of amazing things from this career, but her friendship tops the list.

To everyone who provided me feedback on this story along the way—especially Heather Carver, Samantha Leighton, Tina Allen, Lisa Kuhne, Dina Littner, and Janice Owen—you're all awesome. Rhonda Edits and Lauren Clarke, thank you for the insightful line and content edits. You both push me to be a better writer and make my stories the best they can be. Thanks to Arran McNicol at Editing720 for proofreading. Clearly, it takes a village.

Thank you to the team that helped me package this book and promote it. Sarah Eirew took the gorgeous cover photo and did the design. A shout-out to my assistant Lisa Kuhne for trying to keep me in line and for putting in extra hours when I need to write. Thank you to Nina and Social Butterfly PR for organizing the release. I've loved working with you and your awesome assistants! To all of the bloggers, bookstagrammers, readers, and reviewers who help spread the word about my books, I am humbled by the time you take out of your busy lives for my stories. My thank you isn't enough, but it is sincere. You're the best.

To my agent, Dan Mandel, for believing in me and staying by my side. Thanks to you and Stefanie Diaz for getting my books into the hands of readers all over the world. Thank you for being part of my team.

Finally, a big thank-you to my fans. My biggest dream was to make a career with my writing, and I still can't believe I'm living that dream. I couldn't do it without you. You're the coolest, smartest, best readers in the world. I appreciate each and every one of you!

XOXO,
Lexi

Printed in Great Britain
by Amazon